A LABOUR OF LOVE

ELLE BLOOM

.

To following your dreams…

To be clear, my dream was to become an author and write.
It just so happens that in fulfilling my dream,
I've written about the stuff of our fantasies.

CHAPTER 1

Lucy awoke, torn from her dreamless, almost comatose, slumber by the harsh timbre of her alarm signalling the early start of another day. She was sprawled on her front in the centre of a decadent king size bed that she had shared, until some months prior, with Mark, her boyfriend of the preceding three years. The room was shrouded in the dawn darkness with a glimmer of light from beneath the utilitarian blinds in her newly rented, sterile apartment casting shadows across the non-descript floor and plain white walls. She was temporarily disorientated – the bed was familiar but the surroundings were jarringly unexpected save for the ornate mirror that too seemed wholly out of place in the room. She had anticipated opening her eyes to the fawn-coloured velvet curtains of her London home and the lovingly chosen wall colour, the aptly named 'nude glow' by Dulux. Whilst really just a warm white, at the time it had felt like a portentous choice, enveloping their bedroom in a seductive hue in anticipation of the paint's name reflecting what was to happen beneath their crisp white sheets.

She remembered how excited she had been to move in together in the run-up to Christmas that year and the delight she'd felt at receiving Mark's gift to her. Although since he hadn't been there when she'd unwrapped it, her faithful best friend, Rachel, had hovered at her side for the grand reveal. Lucy cast her mind back, picturing the scene.

With nervous anticipation and Rachel watching on, she expectantly removed the festive-coloured ribbon that encircled the cream cardboard box. Lucy opened the lid and carefully folded back the tissue paper, hoping to find beautiful lace lingerie or perhaps a delicate negligee nestled therein. Rachel craned forward, sharing the anticipation.

"Oh, they're sheets." And, recovering herself and imbuing her tone with what she considered a more appropriate level of excitement, "How lovely. Silly of me really. I had visions of Mark traipsing around a lingerie shop searching for an exquisite one piece or sensual bra and knickers set. The box was so beautifully presented too." Aware it sounded like she was over-compensating, she continued, "I guess I imagined that sort of retailer would offer a gift wrap service at this time of year. Given we're moving in together soon, though,

sheets are a far more sensible decision and romantic in their own way."

The indignant retort of her best friend, Rachel, reverberated around her head.

"I'm sorry, lovely, but I have to disagree. A gift should be something precious, a treat, something you wouldn't necessarily be able to justify buying for yourself. Had he bought you scandalous lingerie, you'd know he'd have thought about you because he'd have been obliged to take the time to surreptitiously trawl your existing underwear to check your size. Then, he'd have had to overcome any discomfort he might feel at entering such an overtly feminine shop. I can almost picture him weaving his way amongst the displays of sexy garments, fending off the enthusiastic shop assistants as they encouraged him to speak effusively of his girlfriend or wife, her curves, her desires, her sensuality and hence the style of underwear you'd both derive pleasure from him purchasing. Instead, he's just bought some sheets."

"I know it's not as romantic as lingerie but sheets are still thoughtful," Lucy responded, ever keen to defend Mark. *"It will be nice to have crisp new sheets on our bed when we move in together."*

Undeterred, Rachel was characteristically vocal in expressing her opinion on the subject. "Sheets are a necessity. I know you'll argue underwear is too and that, if great quality underwear is special, nice sheets should be viewed the same way. I don't agree though." Blunt as ever, she continued, "To successfully buy appropriate sheets, Mark just needed to manage to purchase ones to fit the size of your mattress. Lingerie is a far more individual purchase, one that necessitates you as the recipient thereof being at the forefront of Mark's mind. Besides, it's misleading and anti-climactic to simply put bed linen into such a beautiful box commandeered for the purpose and to save on the effort of wrapping the gift properly."

Although somewhat deflated, Lucy couldn't challenge her friend's logic. Moreover, Rachel's frank honesty and forthrightness were two key attributes that had endeared her to Lucy in the first place. She could always trust Rachel to deliver her genuine opinion and Lucy recognised that the ferocity of Rachel's indignation was ultimately an indirect demonstration of her loyalty to Lucy. This was something else Lucy appreciated given Rachel was faithfully at her side and Mark was elsewhere.

Apparently perceiving Lucy's shoulders slump in disappointment, Rachel attempted to soften her message announcing, "It's pants!" She giggled her distinctive husky laugh as she pointed at the contents of the box and then continued, *"Actually, it's not pants, which is precisely why it's pants."*

Despite herself, Lucy guffawed too. In addition to always being able to trust each other to be honest, their shared enthusiasm for lame jokes and poor puns helped solidify the bedrock of their friendship. Buoyed by Rachel's feeble attempt to boost her morale, Lucy found herself giggling along with Rachel's individual and infectious, almost sultry, laughter.

"Whilst it's undeniable that you're exceptionally witty," Lucy uttered with a hint of amused sarcasm in her voice, mouth and cheeks aching from laughter. "Maybe Egyptian cotton sheets are his way of showing his desire to make a home together. Maybe we're on the same page," she countered, sounding more serious albeit with the conviction in her voice fading as she regarded Rachel's frown.

Lucy continued, "Aw, you know we're both of the view that you can never truly understand a relationship from outside it regardless of how close you are to the couple in question... and you're the closest of friends to me," Lucy added as a sweetener.

Rachel's expression seemed to soften although Lucy inferred this to be more as a result of her statement around the strength of their friendship than because she was successfully challenging Rachel's perception of Mark. On that front, she imagined her friend could not be swayed. In fact, Mark seemed to be a subject that they always needed to agree to disagree on. Regardless, Lucy inwardly drew a whispering reassurance from her personal adage on the difficulty of understanding others' relationships.

Willing her alarm to have sounded out of turn, she still wanted to believe the cool pressed bed linen she now lay wrapped in had been Mark's understated way of conveying his own carnal aspirations for their future. In hindsight, though, she had been naïve. They had both embarked on their liaison hastily and it had developed so quickly thereafter. At the time, she had foolishly thought their pairing would be perpetuated throughout their lives. For him, however, it had only been lust that had at least temporarily governed their progression to a relationship.

When they had first met, his fervour for her had been palpable. Beyond destiny, she didn't believe in a greater being or awareness, but recalled how mistakenly smug she in turn had felt in her belief that she might have found her 'one' and that the inescapable fire that burnt within him would rage indefinitely. Back then, she had never even been able to contemplate that this inferno might reduce to glowing embers. In fact, lying in what had been their bed, she had to mentally concede that now - when considering their relationship as analogous to a fire - the early smouldering passion had in time disintegrated to ashes. For her, the transition had been imperceptible. Worse yet, she hadn't even been aware of the metamorphosis in his sentiment or, now the rose-tinted glasses had been removed, whether Mark had ever actually been that into her. Perhaps he had instead simply enjoyed the predictable convenience of being in a relationship as that ensured his basest needs, food and sex, were tended to and left him free to pursue whatever or whoever else he desired the rest of the time.

During that initial honeymoon period, though, his carnal desires had seemed insatiable.

She in turn had obediently kept the sheets on a near constant rotation. Their smooth sensuality had served as another enticing coital stimulant encouraging her to acquiesce to his advances. For her, when freshly laid on the sumptuous mattress, the linen had added to the alluring draw of their ornate four poster. In the painful moments of honest clarity she had since afforded herself, she acknowledged she had had a habit of romanticising their relationship, viewing it like the plot from one of her favourite romance novels. At the time, she had consequently felt that they were both finding themselves catapulted under the covers at the smallest provocation.

In the months since his departure, it had gradually dawned on her that it had been more orchestrated on his part than she had discerned. It hadn't been a mutually spontaneous compulsion but a convenient way for him to access his daily sexual and egotistical fix on demand. He'd had a willing and submissive servant at home whom he had readily and consistently manipulated to his own ends. In her defence, he had been her first proper love and everyone had always said that love was blind. A childhood of simplified love stories and fairy tales had conditioned her to believe this. She'd been completely overawed by him, the attention, his charisma, his expensive clothing and organised appearance. This had, in turn, further fuelled his testosterone-induced pursuit of sexual gratification with her. Somewhere along the lines, this fast-paced affair had progressed into – presumably – a more stable, long-term arrangement for him and a deeply meaningful relationship for her.

With a languorous movement, she shifted and rolled onto her back, surveying the room through sleep-filled eyes. In the half light, she could just about discern her solitary supine form in the reflection of the imposing gilded mirror mounted on the wall opposite. *Why on earth did I bring you from London?* she idly wondered. *You're just another gaudy reminder of everything I want to leave behind.*

Willing that fleeting transition between sleep and wakefulness to remain with her so she could for a few moments longer inhabit that hazy dream world where the distinction between fantasy and reality could be blurred, her thoughts betrayed her. Her subconscious still seemed to forget their relationship hadn't been as genuine as she had thought. Despite herself, she often reminisced on the countless mornings she had awoken over the preceding years to see their intertwined limbs reposed amongst strewn sheets and discarded underwear. Where Lucy had perceived those snapshots romantically and preserved them in her mind's eye accordingly, Rachel would have no doubt argued Mark would instead have just been admiring himself therein. To Rachel's acute annoyance and credit, she had always felt Mark's impression of himself was inflated and couldn't understand why Lucy had failed to see this.

Now, some years down the line since receiving Mark's questionable gift, she readily agreed with Rachel that she would have preferred a form-hugging, lacy underwear set from Agent Provocateur or similar. In fact, she'd have chosen something, anything, to make her feel sexy and sultry over the sheets she now lay amongst. *It's a pretty damning reflection on Mark that he could fail to notice I'm into lingerie. Perhaps it's always been more for my own benefit than those around me but he should have known I like and have always liked matching underwear.* She had tried so hard to hold his interest, contriving to ensure the underwear she wore flattered her physique by revealing just enough in its bold colours to complement her pale, toned appearance.

When clothed, the garments she wore belied her nubile body. Beneath her outfits, the beautiful knickers and lacy bras sculpted and accentuated her shape. However, having never felt she possessed much natural style, she took her external inspiration from Rachel. Rachel was forthright, empowered and gave the impression of being a maneater. Lucy toned this down somewhat with her own look, working hard to project a subtle sophistication that downplayed her femininity in order to more readily cultivate the aspiring businesswoman image she wished to convey. She erred more towards secretary than sexpert whilst the persona her beloved Rachel chose to present sat at the other end of the spectrum.

She cast her mind back to the first day of the first assignment she and Rachel had worked on together. Her lips curled into a smile at the recollection.

Lucy arrived at work that morning to be met by Rachel. Rachel was taller than Lucy's diminutive 5 foot 3 but was equally pale skinned albeit freckled and with flame-red hair. That first day, Lucy's initial impression was that Rachel looked like a power-dressing dominatrix. In stilettoed lace-up black leather boots, Rachel seemed to tower over Lucy. Rachel wore these below a dress that appeared to be moulded to her curves, like she'd sewn herself into it sometime between waking up and embarking on her commute. Lucy was struck by the sensuality of the beautiful woman, her perfectly manicured hand outstretched in greeting. Rachel projected confidence, her head held high and shoulders back. Her defiance in eschewing the conventional work attire suggested she likely also had the fiery personality often associated with such red hair.

As they stepped into the ladies' toilet on their tour of the office, Rachel said, "I'm delighted to have another female here." Signalling her body, she continued, "You seemed, by the way, to do a double take at my outfit. I like to dress for myself rather than conform. I'm aiming for a sultry business chic and, as an added bonus, my clothes seem to deter our male colleagues. Well, at least I hope it's my clothes that scare them off and not my personality." She giggled out a laugh that Lucy was sure she would in time find infectious. "Either way, it's a good thing given I've never yet met anyone who compared to my ex from uni. I wouldn't want my outfit to give you the wrong impression, though. I'm genuinely excited that we're going to be working together. Technically, you'll be reporting to me. Yay!" she said, somehow managing an understated clap of her hands to convey her enthusiasm whilst maintaining an aura of elegance that Lucy could never hope to aspire to.

That first evening after work, they headed to a local and pretentious city wine bar. Lucy already hoped they would become friends as she watched Rachel weave between the suit-clad men murmuring about the body to their wine, the effect of it on their palettes and more. Sidestepping them all and ignoring their salacious looks, she sauntered up to the bar and loudly and unabashedly asked for, "A pink grapefruit gin and tonic for me please and one for my friend." Her live for the moment, no fucks given attitude, immediately endeared her to Lucy, who realised she felt a sense of pride at being labelled this head-turning, fiery haired woman's friend.

Once they'd settled in with their drinks, Rachel piped up, "So, you've survived your first day. Congratulations and, rest assured, you did great! I hope you found everyone to be reasonably nice too. I mean, every workplace has a 'Wheelbarrow' and a 'Blister' but, for the most part, everyone's pretty decent."

"Sorry, a wheelbarrow and a blister?" Lucy queried, baffled by the apparently incongruous terms.

"Ha," said Rachel. "A private joke I haven't yet shared. I like giving people one-word nicknames, although I often keep those names to myself.

Our work environment can be stressful and involved. Having private monikers for people reminds me not to take things too seriously. The guy in the cubicle nearest the window, for example, I think of him as 'Wheelbarrow' because he only works when he's pushed. And then 'Blister', at least in theory, sits opposite him, although I'm not sure he was at his desk when I was showing you around. That just confirms my nickname for him is apt." She giggled huskily. "He's 'Blister' because he only ever appears when the work is done."

Lucy, catching on, began to laugh too and soon they both had tears streaming down their faces.

"Now we're out of the office, perhaps you could reveal something more personal about yourself," Rachel uttered, appearing to recover first and seizing the opportunity to segue into a new topic. "Let's call it an ice breaker," she beamed, looking mischievous.

Lucy had skipped lunch because she'd been too nervous to enquire as to when, where and for how long people break for food. As a result, her first few sips of gin and tonic had made her instantly tipsy. Before she managed to stop herself, she heard her own giggly response, like some out of body experience, utter, "My nickname is Juicy Lucy."

Rachel erupted into more, genuine laughter.

"Eek, I'm so sorry. I've overshared," Lucy hastily added, conscious her cheeks must be turning crimson as she felt the heat flush her face. "It's not what it seems. I like fruit and juice. That you ordered something with grapefruit in it feels like a positive omen."

Little did she know at the time that their friendship had been sealed there and then in that upmarket wine bar. Lucy had also given her new friend ammunition on which to base her feeble jesting for years to come. In return, Rachel had brought Lucy into her circle of trust and shared all her amusing one-word monikers for their mutual colleagues. Although they helped brighten the work environment, Lucy considered Rachel's use of the nicknames to be more representative of her frankness and surety of her convictions. For Mark, she had unflatteringly chosen 'Dick' and had resolutely and steadfastly referred to him as such whenever he was out of earshot and possibly sometimes within it too.

Nonetheless, when Lucy and Mark had originally met through work, Rachel's protestations and critical nickname had fallen on deaf ears. Technically, Rachel had met him first as she had been the one to pitch the services of the consultancy business she and Lucy worked for to the firm at which Mark was an executive director. She had then handed the reins to Lucy who had been chosen for the role because she'd been billed as highly intelligent, academically accomplished but self-deprecating.

Lucy had been engaged through the Project Change Consortium by an independently owned firm of financial advisors. In leveraging Mark's firm's accumulated experience, reputation and infrastructure, they'd hoped to provide an investment management service to their more affluent clients.

Admittedly, at one time, she had found the incessant pitches and strategy meetings to secure access to his firm's asset management expertise and platforms interminably protracted and tedious. In her role, she hadn't had any meaningful influence over the content of the discussions nor had she been able to shape the negotiations. Instead, she had organised the meetings, assessed how to implement whatever Mark and the other executives had agreed on and then created the business strategy to pursue their vision.

Those early reunions had felt like a form of commercial purgatory.

To Lucy's great delight and acute surprise though, Mark had apparently immediately sensed that - if he were ever to witness her disrobed - he would find what was concealed beneath her clothes more desirable than her understated attempt at sartorial elegance implied. He had cornered her on a spontaneous night out after a late-finishing meeting and revealed that, "Although the clothes you wear hint at a straight body, I fantasise that they shroud small but perfectly formed pert breasts."

His evocative words were seared into her mind. Conspiratorially, he'd conceded, "Whenever I'm in your presence, I can't help but allow myself to indulge in such sexually provocative musings. I can enliven any dull boardroom meeting by envisaging the trim of your blouse shifting to reveal your silken cleavage or by picturing your herringbone grey pencil skirt riding up your thighs under the firm masculine touch of my accomplished fingers."

Looking back, and in the context of what had since happened, his behaviour had been forward, inappropriate, and imperceptibly predatory. It was also cringeworthy that he'd referred to himself as having accomplished fingers. At the time, she had however revelled in the words he'd used and their resemblance to the text she'd expect to see dancing across the page of one of her favourite romance novels.

Whilst inaudible to their peers, who had been casually conversing and shifting around them, his stream of explicit reveries had instantaneously permeated her being, making her blush and glow from the inside out. Looking back, she realised everything he'd said had sounded rehearsed rather than spontaneous.

She now couldn't remember whether his words had more powerfully triggered her emotions or the tingling pleasurable warmth that came with being around someone you had just realised you were attracted to. Amplified by how taboo any form of workplace relationship was considered to be and the tone he'd consequently used, she had immediately become hooked, desiring his attention.

Despite wanting to remain coy and demure, right then, it had dawned on her that if he were to try to initiate a physical relationship between them, she would be cowed and inevitably submit to his advances. So striking was that realisation that she'd known she would be prepared to keep any relationship between them a secret from their peers or indeed accept the consequences of succumbing to him. Haplessly, this must have been obvious to Mark too who'd taken it as his cue to pursue her relentlessly. He had given her his full attention, showering her in compliments, and she had been so flattered that she'd been powerless to resist.

Over the subsequent weeks, even though it had subjugated her sense of professionalism, she had sought ever more trivial justification to participate in the ongoing meetings with his firm. She knew that, as one of the key directors, he would be in attendance and she enjoyed the tantalising torment of his presence. To err in his favour, perhaps he too had at least for a period of time misinterpreted his pent-up desire for her as an indication of their deeper connection. She still willed this to be the case, as to believe otherwise would mean accepting that she was in fact a glaringly poor judge of character and had jeopardised her career for no sound reason.

Mark's hushed and breathy revelation on that first night out had piqued her interest and she recalled the first meeting thereafter at which his demeanour towards her in the office had subtly begun to shift.

Aware of her responsibility for ensuring the meetings' success, as normal, Lucy was first to arrive in the room. She laid out a presentation pack at each seat around the boardroom table. She double checked the sideboard was laden with platters of pastries, fruit and assorted biscuits alongside urns of tea and coffee, a milk jug, stirrers and teaspoons. In her experience, the meetings could last hours and the discussions always appeared to go more smoothly and be more positive if everyone was fed and watered.

Once comfortable that the room was setup appropriately, she adopted her customary seat broadly halfway down the table's length. It was a neutral position, neither head nor bottom of the table and in earshot of everyone, which was useful as she was tasked with taking the minutes.

Given his seniority, no one would challenge Mark's choice if he were to position himself at the head but, to her surprised glee, as the attendees began to file in, he pulled out the black leather-backed chair next to hers and sat down. He sat upright but casually, feet planted wide apart beneath the table. The overtly masculine stance meant his trouser-clad legs persistently brushed against the smooth finish of her tights.

As normal, the minutiae of the respective firms' commercial dealings did little to enthuse her. She was more interested in monitoring Mark's body language and movements, seeking subtle affirmations of the tension between them. She struggled not to zone in and out of the discussion as a result, more focussed on her own physical reaction to his presence than the meeting itself despite her responsibility for documenting its content.

"This will aid us in identifying additional synergies within both entities' client bases, enabling both sides to increase

wallet share," a suited, self-important man further up the table was saying.

Lucy abhorred the arrogance but accepted it was a necessary evil as the various egos jostled for superiority in the newly evolving business' hierarchy. Listening to the largely male attendees' attempts to outdo each other with boardroom vernacular, she longed for a more straight-talking work environment.

Mark spoke up, commanding their attention and interrupting the tedium of the conversation, to announce, "Right, it's mid-morning. Let's put a pin in that and take a comfort break here for fifteen minutes. Tea, coffee and snacks are available as normal. Please help yourselves. And my thanks to Lucy for putting on the spread."

Lucy was stunned that Mark had recognised her involvement in front of the assembled crowd, loudly crediting her efforts as the executives jostled for access to the food-laden sideboard. That's a first! She glowed inside at the attention. Feeling awkward at what felt like everyone's fleeting scrutiny, she hovered. Trying to appear unaffected, she stood impassive but not convinced she wasn't flushed in the face at the flattery. Her every sense was in fact accentuated, trying to track Mark as he worked the room.

When he approached the refreshments, he poured a tea. He appeared to take very deliberate care over it and then turned to her and said, "Here's a tea."

And, under his breath murmured, "Specially for you" as he leant in to place the white utilitarian cup and saucer in her hands.

Although the drink itself was unwanted, her every sense felt amplified as she allowed her fingers to almost imperceptibly caress his when receiving it from him. In understated acknowledgement, he deftly placed a lingering proprietary hand to her lower back to again guide her to her seat.

To others, it had no doubt just been another insignificant pastoral act. For her, every fleeting touch had felt electric. Rachel, in turn, had subsequently seethed over a shared lunch at such interactions between them.

"He seems wholly oblivious to your preference for juice over tea. He's either unfailingly ignorant of your wants and tastes or, worse, he chooses to ignore them."

"But he specifically singles me out to pour me a drink. I think it's his way of privately conveying that I'm significant to him."

Ever keen to give him the benefit of the doubt, Lucy continued, "Besides, maybe he is actually aware I'd prefer juice but gives me tea to disguise that he knows me better than he should. Perhaps he's trying to honour my desire to keep our relationship a secret. This way everyone around us hopefully just sees a fleeting trivial interaction between company director and change manager."

Rachel commented scathingly, "It feels wrong that, despite persistently overlooking or ignoring your preferences, his actions should be interpreted in a positive light. You and I both know he's pouring you a drink you won't enjoy drinking and yet everyone else views this action as him being approachable and inclusive as he tries to demonstrate he values and empowers his subordinates. If anyone else were to pour someone a drink, regardless of their respective seniority, they'd at least have the courtesy to first enquire which drink they'd like. Dick!"

Lucy could kick herself for not having foreseen how things would end nor indeed for having heeded Rachel's view. After all, had Lucy taken pause to consider Mark's motivation more at the time, she would quickly have identified herself as being the only logical one on whom he could acceptably bestow this behaviour. The remaining women in the respective teams were significantly older than she was or married or too dour or simply unapproachable by virtue of their seniority within either firm. In retrospect, he hadn't been seeking an equal – a power coupling with someone of equivalent seniority – but someone who, by virtue of their comparative youth would defer to his dominance and massage his ego accordingly.

As she now semi-dozed in her bed, she recalled how she had at least ultimately been successful in achieving her brief with the productive talks and subsequent merger culminating in a firm-wide reception at a private art gallery in the city centre.

The venue was carefully selected by an Events Organiser Lucy approached. It was intended to be the embodiment of this newly merged business' sophisticated brand and high-end offering. The gallery was minimalist, all angular lines and sterile expanses with polished Carrara marble floors and clinical white walls. The artwork displayed was pretentious and modern; canvasses of bold shapes or spattered flecks of paint interspersed with the occasional abstract sculpture of something unrecognisable to all but their creators.

For the pretentious amongst them, the work was sublime, powerful, emotive and appealed to their subconscious. For the others, it was regarded as something a child could have created and hence they surveyed it with casual indifference, an inconsequential feature adorning the walls of the background setting. Regardless of the extent of their interest in art, the majority simply appeared focussed on becoming inebriated with their peers. Partly in an unconvincing attempt to conceal their intentions from their superiors, the attendees fanned out over the gallery's various levels and mezzanines, which were punctuated by brushed steel guide ropes in place of more conventional rails and banisters. Music radiated inoffensively from the ceiling-recessed speakers and white shirted waiters flitted around the throng of suited professionals serving ingeniously presented hot and cold canapés.

Lucy was acutely aware of Mark's presence, trying to track his gradual progression around the room as he moved between groups of his employees, pausing to greet and congratulate as he went. Despite appearing wholly engaged in his conversations with his colleagues, he sporadically caught her eye in a way that was indiscernible to all others around him. On one such occasion, his commanding gaze signalled for her to move back toward the cavernous entrance foyer.

Flushing at the memory, she recalled having feigned nonchalance as she weaved through her increasingly intoxicated peers to the atrium as bidden.

One wall of the atrium was dominated by the floor to ceiling glass façade of the gallery which looked out onto a dusky square populated with commuters bustling towards the train stations and car parks to begin their early evening journey home. Overshadowed by the glass façade and at one side of the foyer was the now unmanned coat room. She was confused by Mark's intentions until she noticed an unobtrusive doorway on the opposite wall. It was frameless, built flush to the wall and only given away by its discreetly protruding handle.

Mark meanwhile weaved a determined but circuitous route to the foyer, cutting through the crowd to materialise unobserved at her side. Casual but purposeful, he moved beyond her towards the doorway with the barely visible surround silhouetted into the white wall.

With a self-assured movement, he opened the door, noiselessly motioned for her to step through and then followed her into the impersonal space beyond. He confidently pressed the door closed behind them and twisted the thumb-turn lock to preclude any inadvertent interlopers from interrupting them.

She laughed to herself. At the time, this had all felt dangerously spontaneous but, knowing Mark as she now did, in reality he had probably scoped out the venue beforehand in order to orchestrate their rendezvous in this space.

The door opened into an equally sterile marble-floored and white-walled study, the prestigious curator's own office space. Apparently incapable of exercising any further self-restraint, Mark took a step toward her, reducing the distance between them to just inches. He barely paused to seek out her approval with a salacious look and, on seeing what he presumably perceived to be consent in her eyes, leant his body against hers. Surprised at this assertive movement, she found herself tantalisingly pinned with the wall behind her and his muscular form unabashedly erect in front. Her back was pressed hard against the smooth cool surface and she felt paralysed in position by the expectant mood. His sexual dominance overawed her. Suppressing her reservations and motivated by her misplaced desire to please him, she felt emboldened. She threw caution and reason to the wind to demonstrate to him that she was worthy of and merited his primordial attention.

From their clothed encounters up to that point, she already recognised that his physique was better than that of your average desk-based employee although perhaps not as impressive as his ego implied. He was fit, stronger than Lucy but with the definition of his muscle obscured by a fleshy layer that hinted at his sedentary job. Regardless, he easily lifted her off the ground and rested her backside, like some deviant mannequin, on his contoured forearms. He moved his uncalloused hand, more accustomed to typing on a keyboard than any manual labour, down between her legs and pulled her knickers to one side, grazing the skin of her upper thigh in his fervent haste. In the same well-rehearsed movement, a condom materialised in his other hand, he unzipped and dropped his dark tailored suit trousers to just below his buttocks, lifted his crisp designer shirt, rolled the condom down his length and, aligning his hips with hers, thrust himself hard inside her. With one finger looped through her knickers to ensure he had unimpeded access to her interior, the rest of his large hand grasped and clenched at her rear, pulling and clawing her towards him in time with his own momentum. Ardently arching away and then driving himself back into her, he shifted her weight as if she were a mere doll, lowering her sufficiently to ensure his cock was pushed deep inside. Her backside smarted as she involuntarily slapped down on his thighs with his every frenzied thrust. The single-minded focus with which he had pursued her translated into an equally focussed pursuit of his own pleasure, for which she was along for the ride. He made no attempt to make her feel at ease, alluring or desired, beyond demonstrating that he possessed a pressing physical urge that needed to be satiated. He was instead determined that the limited time available to them be dedicated to achieving his release.

With her legs pinned round his waist by his vice-like grip and her arms draped over his shoulders, she tried to steady herself. She was powerless to resist him and, at the time, didn't think she wanted to. Her pelvic muscles throbbed uncomfortably as, groin to groin, he moved them in a mechanical, orchestrated unison to his personal rhythm. He sometimes interrupted their pulsing energy to slowly withdraw and then penetrate her hard and fast again and again. He sought his own pleasure with vigorous determination.

Repositioning her on just one arm, he used the other to tear at her shirt, hastily unbuttoning it to reveal her black lace balconette bra. He yanked downwards on the dainty, embroidered material. Exposing her small breasts, he manhandled them, alternately cupping them in his hand, then being overcome with his hunger to claim every inch of her for himself and so taking them in his mouth between gruff pants. He rolled his tongue around her pert pinkish nipples with his hoarse breath sending cloying eddies of hot humid air across her skin, followed immediately by goosebumps as the thin layer of his saliva and sheen of sweat he left behind evaporated. He pawed at her exposed chest and mauled at her waist with the span of his authoritative hands encompassing her hip. He nipped at her skin with his teeth and yanked at any clothing restricting his access. The preceding weeks of anticipation built to a crescendo inside him, culminating in this brazen, frantic consuming lust to command every inch of her unblemished body. Having him pounding into her over and over and with most of her weight bearing down on his, he dominated her and in that moment, the tone for the rest of their relationship was set.

Now languishing sleepily in bed, she recalled how she had so desperately tried to conjure a tingling sensation radiating from between her legs, had willed her heart to swell at the romance of their encounter rather than merely beat erratically in her chest as she'd snatched muffled gasps of air between his thrusts. She had wanted to find herself exhaling whimpers of masochistic ecstasy. In reality, had the music in the foyer paused, their peers would have discerned a muted but frenzied thudding as he'd pounded into her whilst she, in turn, had writhed and squirmed in her attempts to accommodate and satisfy him. He'd known how he had wanted the encounter to play out and she, submissive and obsequious, had clung on accordingly. Even now, almost four years down the line, she could feel the familiar traitorous warmth spreading from her core unbidden as she thought about that sterile room.

Now though, like then, she knew the heat would dissipate in the same unsatisfying fashion.

Her sleepy thoughts took her back there again.

Already frenzied, his impaling thrusts gained further momentum. Grunting with the primal effort, he pulled and clawed at her rear, tugging her crotch towards his as he heaved and convulsed in gratification. He climaxed hard whilst gripping her yielding frame, muscles jerking and cock twitching deep within her as she consciously clamped around it, chastising herself for being too slow to respond in kind and to reach her own release.

Now, in what had once been their bed, she lay picturing them in that understated windowless room in her mind's eye. Feeling almost like a spying voyeur, it struck her that perhaps his actions should have served as a warning. In hindsight, despite his perceived abandon in the throes of passion, when she had straightened her clothes afterwards, every single amorous bite or claw mark he had imprinted on her had been perfectly shrouded by her clothing. The apparent wanton abandon must, either consciously or unconsciously, have been more contrived than she had realised, as the network of lustful scratches and nibbling imprints halted at an invisible threshold. He had left all manner of little marks as evidence of his conquest but none that would be exposed if anyone had been to casually glance in her direction.

Where she had just inferred he hadn't kissed her because he'd been so consumed by the desire to explore the rest of her body, perhaps there had been more to it than that. She had after all been able to depart the room with the minimal lipstick she wore and makeup still immaculate, as if freshly applied. She had returned to her increasingly rowdy peers as if nothing had happened when in fact she had felt flushed and very aware of the residual rawness between her legs. Reflecting on it in the present day, on the one hand, he'd wanted her to believe he had been caught off guard by this overwhelming desire to have her and that his actions had been entirely instinctive and unplanned. On the other, despite apparently being swept up in the moment, like a seasoned professional, he had produced a condom, rolled it down his length, lowered his clothing and plunged into her in one practised movement. He'd later argued he had been trying to be respectful to her, but now knowing his more cavalier approach to women generally, he'd probably more likely been just protecting himself as fleeting sexual encounters seemed to be his modus operandi.

She recalled how, whilst appearing visually serene to the unsuspecting eye, it had required a far more concerted effort on her part to regain her composure. In moments, however, he had been able to transition from an apparent state of frenzied enrapture with her to adopting an air of cool and collected professionalism. He'd departed the room shortly thereafter, shirt tucked in, suit straightened and with a cursory run of his hands through his hair. His expression an indecipherable mask as he had left her alone in the room, suggesting they stagger their exit.

Everything had changed thereafter. Having consummated their attraction to one another, albeit somewhat unsatisfyingly from her perspective, their clandestine encounters had become more frequent. He'd wooed her incessantly and, since she'd been unable to resist his attention, they'd fallen into a habit of departing soon after each other from work to head to her flat in Bermondsey. Within only ten minutes by taxi of the recently combined business' headquarters at London Bridge, it had become a convenient bolthole.

Initially, Mark would stay only for a short period of time, long enough to charm her into bed and get his physical release but not so long as to encroach upon any other commitments he might have, nor curtail his personal or professional freedom. Without Lucy really noticing, this pattern of behaviour had become routine.

On finishing work, she would head home, shower, and await his arrival; a kept woman grateful to have him in whatever form he chose. He, on the other hand, had retained his autonomy. He'd always been engaging when they were together; very present in the moment – like he was the sun shining only on her – and she'd told herself that that more than compensated for any periods when he was elsewhere.

Like hers, Mark's role could be stressful and, although he would aim to get to the gym a couple of times a week to ease some of that tension, his preferred fix was a sexual one. Now, furnished with the knowledge of how their relationship had ended and the additional context this afforded her, Lucy could reflect that presumably the easiest, most socially acceptable and professionally least disruptive approach for Mark had been to select an attractive, lithe, younger and intelligent but pliable woman and, at least to her, appear to conform to her expectations of a relationship. In doing so, he'd satisfied his physical requirements of enjoying female company and, given Lucy was also committed to her career, she'd failed to notice his shortcomings and the absence of any real depth to their relationship. She had thought they were happy, inferring the apparently mechanical sex was more a reflection on her than him as he'd ultimately climaxed and consequently, she'd assumed, found her attractive.

She had believed they were incrementally progressing as a couple towards a long-term commitment to each other and that her enjoyment of the physical validation of their mutual affection would improve as they became emotionally closer. Paradoxically, he had been maintaining the status quo, paying lip service to their interlaced future for as long as it had aligned with his own agenda and sexual proclivities.

Moreover, that first frenzied sexual encounter had set the pattern for their future love making.

Mark had never put much emphasis on the romance or passion of it and had approached sex with little emotion. For him, it quenched a physical urge. He would shower her with compliments and attention until her resolve weakened and he had wooed her beneath the sheets only to thrust and pound away at her, positioning her limbs and tugging at her hair to ensure she was always staged optimally to help him reach his climax. At the time, she had unquestioningly accepted his justification that she had turned him on to such an extent that he couldn't control himself. Since then, it had dawned on her that he in fact more likely had had little regard for her and her own sexual satisfaction. Once finished, the few moments where he would linger inside her and that she had perceived as tender, he had actually just been spent, using her body as a convenient resting place whilst he regrouped.

Once ready, he would withdraw, peel off the condom, knot it and throw it away before giving her a peck on the forehead and making his excuses as he slid off the bed and into the shower, either readying himself to leave or to fall asleep. He would sometimes then seek out a repeat performance when his alarm would sound early the next morning in order to set himself up for the day. For the inconvenient few days of each month that her period would come, he would apparently entirely coincidentally have more external commitments than usual. Rather than use it as an opportunity to bring them closer in other ways, he'd just engineered it so as to minimise his time at home with her, dismissing his absence as a series of random circumstances until she would begin to doubt herself.

His actions had subsequently and starkly proven him to be cynical, chauvinistic and governed by an inherent machismo. One day, completely out of the blue, he'd trivialised the time they had spent together by announcing that, "This isn't working for me anymore. After three years, I'd expect to feel more for you than I do. If we were meant to have a future together, you'd somehow feel more significant to me."

And, with that, he had effectively gathered up his belongings from Lucy's apartment which, pitifully and tellingly, had fitted into an overnight bag and he had left, calling time on their relationship as he'd done so and brokering no further discussion.

She hadn't wanted a painful and protracted post-mortem of where it had gone wrong, if indeed it had ever been right in the first place, but a little sensitivity and consideration as to how she might feel and hence how to couch his explanation would have been a fair expectation after that length of time.

This had set the wheels in motion to alter her career path entirely, whilst leaving Mark to climb to stellar heights within the expanded firm. His ascent had been unsullied by the smear of having initiated a long-standing affair with a subordinate contractor. If anything, when it had all come to light, this had conversely garnered him more kudos amongst the largely male business stakeholders.

On reflection, Lucy acknowledged she had taken it both well and poorly. Despite the utter desolation, which had in time morphed into an anger at herself for not having read him and their relationship correctly, she had rallied, steeled herself and continued. She had remained at the merged company throughout. Outwardly at work, she'd maintained the same ethic, unbiased and objective oversight of the change management process as she had done before and during their relationship. If anything, she had immersed herself in the role even further and, despite some of the whispering she thought she'd perceived amongst the male executives, she had seen her contract through to its successful conclusion. Nonetheless, she had been grinning and bearing it, burying herself in the project with a solemn perseverance. It was with both relief and some trepidation that she had delivered all of the objectives she had been set and extricated herself from the contract. After dedicating almost four years to it, she had returned to the Project Change Consortium to be reallocated to another firm or industry. Throughout this period, she had made a compelling and persistent attempt to cast aside her emotions in deference to her career.

Mercifully, the Consortium had national reach and, when she had been nominated for a role somewhere near Birmingham, she had accepted it with limited further thought. A change of job, scenery, location and hence reality could only be a positive. Decision made, it had taken little effort to let her Bermondsey flat to a couple of City-based flat sharers, find an unfurnished rental apartment near Birmingham town centre and have a removal firm relocate her couple of items of furniture and other belongings. And so, here she was, waking up in what was exclusively now her bed in the Birmingham flat she had rented in her sole name and ready – albeit with a mix of emotions – to begin her first day in her new role.

CHAPTER 2

Turner awoke feeling alert, energised and enthusiastic. He wasn't naturally a morning person. In fact, he had always considered himself to be the opposite if left to his own devices and without the constraints of work and other commitments necessitating he rise early. This morning again, though, he had awoken spontaneously, primed and ready for the day ahead and without even the need for his alarm. Ordinarily, he would still be in a deep slumber when its shrill ringing alerted him to the arrival of morning and it would inevitably be snoozed a handful of times before he would reluctantly depart his lair. He was really enjoying his current contract, though, so much so that he would experience a sensation akin to anticipation in the evening awaiting the following day. Temporarily banished was the disappointment that usually befell him on a Sunday night, knowing the working week was set to begin again promptly the following morning.

Construction was, by and large, a satisfying industry to be in. Even when progress on site was slower than he hoped, there was still always tangible evidence of what had been achieved that day when everyone came to down tools. Whatever the elements, in the cloying heat or freezing cold, every day brought a greater or lesser degree of satisfaction, enabling him to survey and reflect on the team's accomplishments as he closed up site. The next morning, they would literally build from where they had left off the night before. A build would take shape like this, day by day, week by week, until – after living and breathing a project for a number of months – he would be able to admire the turn-key finish and hand the pristine new-build house over to the development company that had engaged him or, preferably, to the delighted new homeowners.

In many respects, this project was no different, but he felt genuinely committed and indubitably integral to it. With no immediate superior to report to, he was, as ever, enjoying the autonomy afforded him. Progress was, in essence, being dictated by his enthusiasm and the quality of workmanship set by his dedication and attention to detail filtering out to his team.

Instrumental to the day to day was his ability to instil this zeal in the tradespeople around him, which in turn, motivated them to take ownership of their individual trade on the project. The combined energy on site was palpable and was reflected in the standard and speed with which the superstructures of the houses were emerging. He felt invested in it and, in the absence of formal corporate oversight and guidance, like it was his brainchild slowly taking shape before his eyes.

As the sole site manager for a small development of four detached four-bedroom family homes to be erected on a redundant section of pub car park, it was his role to manage the build, maintain the pace of progress and supervise the tradespeople. The impersonal faceless corporate development company he had been engaged by had had this site in suburban Birmingham languishing in its land bank for some time. At outset, it had bought the land speculatively. Its corporate consciousness then had proceeded to overlook it for a period of time and, as a result, no one individual had responsibility for pushing through the planning permission or discharging any associated planning conditions. Without that driving force, it had mothballed as the corporate behemoth had turned its attentions to larger projects.

Turner was already referring to the car park site as Oakland Walk as that would become its name once complete and, in his mind's eye, he could picture the finished Oakland

Walk perfectly. He had even put the name forward himself. The section of car park in question had been acquired by Contemporary Homes Ltd from a long-standing family pub. Like many, it had been suffering in the wider economic downturn. Moreover, the local area was undergoing gradual gentrification as Birmingham concentrically expanded out, absorbing smaller villages and enclaves into its conurbation. As transport links improved, this area had become convenient commuter belt for the town centre and, over time, the local population had become younger, worked longer hours and more affluent. A traditional pub could no longer expect to see such footfall as it had previously been accustomed to. Instead, the more recently arrived locals sought chic wine bars serving grazing platters and tapas and bijou independent eateries offering freshly ground coffees, artisanal breads and a novel take on the traditional fry up. They'd expect it to consist only of locally reared and butchered pork and free-range eggs all sourced from producers within ten miles of the venue with a vegan, vegetarian and/or gluten free alternative present on the menu too.

Nonetheless, The Acorn pub persevered, continuing to cater to its ageing, largely male, regulars who would come in for a pint or two at the bar on their way home or to escape the missus for a short while. Turner suspected the pub would eventually fold unless it were to reinvent itself in a new more desirable guise and, as a loose nod to the fact the houses were being built in its car park, he had mooted Oakland Walk in Contemporary Homes' street naming competition. He assumed the objective of enabling involved parties to nominate potential names for the eventual run of new builds was to make them feel their contribution was meaningful. Personally invested in the project, it would make it more emotive to them than just another build. In Turner's case, perhaps this had been successful although the competition had hardly been stiff with everyone on site being far more adept with their hands than their vocabulary or creativity. The language could be colourful and sometimes graphic, but largely when bantering with each other or in fanning an inter-worker amiable rivalry. As such, the name Oakland Walk had been selected unanimously. As a happy by-product, if the pub were in the future to become a long distant memory, at least the houses built within its original boundary would be a gentle reminder to some that the more traditional pub had at one time existed.

When Contemporary Homes' land scouts had approached it, perceiving a financial lifeline, The Acorn had willingly offered up a tranche of its car park. With a decreasing clientele and society also becoming ever more conscientious around the risks of drink driving, it never had more than a handful of cars spaced around the bays delineated by thick white lines. The pub sat at a crossroads with the building itself right in the apex of the corner. Dual aspect, it overlooked the two adjacent roads that met at the junction. The car park could be accessed from either road but there was a high kerb line that cut across its middle, conceived as a barrier to deter people from trying to skip the traffic lights at the crossroads by pulling into one entrance, driving across to the other, exiting there and hence cutting out the corner. The kerb line conveniently demarcated the site to be carved out for development.

To comply with planning and Highways' requirements, The Acorn could reduce the depth of a grass bank along the rear of its retained car park, thereby expanding the tarmacked area it withheld and repaint the white lines to mark out additional spaces. This had satisfied the Council and Planners that the amenity value of having a local pub on the site could be preserved. It would also ensure that there would continue to be sufficient parking so as not to impact local residents by virtue of any pub frequenters parking along the surrounding, already clogged roads. Simultaneously, someone at Contemporary Homes had submitted an application that argued substituting an underused tranche of car park for some tastefully appointed new houses would be a sympathetic infill project on what was otherwise an industrial brown-field site. Now, some years down the line, and with Contemporary Homes involved in some far larger projects, it had engaged Turner to be its eyes and ears on the ground to manage the various subcontractors and tradespeople.

He had prior experience of working with this property developing behemoth and enjoyed the autonomy he was afforded when overseeing its projects. As long as he delivered houses finished to a high standard and within its stipulated timeframes, it saw no reason to commit any unnecessary resource to checking in on him. Moreover, he was given the freedom to select his own preferred subcontractors for the different areas of specialist work. As such, many of the faces on site were familiar not only to him but to each other. Whilst each contracted independently within the Midlands, over time, Turner had amassed a band of skilled, dependable and trustworthy tradespeople. They would often all converge on site together for a build then scatter to their own projects only to reconvene to work under or with Turner and the same crew again on the next build.

Somewhere along the lines, Turner had formed his friendship with Andy. They had first encountered each other some years prior and had welcomed working with each other again on the subsequent couple of builds. As well as his good friend, Andy was tall, inconceivably strong and a skilled multi-trade subbie who could readily tackle bricklaying, plastering and tiling. A valuable man to have on site and, despite outwardly being more brawn than brains, Turner knew he in fact possessed both attributes. Turner valued Andy's dogged enthusiasm and stoic perseverance often in the face of extreme weather, tight deadlines and the inevitable crises that would arise. He admired Andy's ability to happily take the rough with the smooth and to reappear day after day with a positive outlook and an extensive repertoire of banter. Seeing Andy's great frame unfurl itself from his battered red van each day brought a certain reassuring continuity to Turner's time on site and normally the prospect of some, for the most part, good-natured humour too.

In contrast to this predictable familiarity of routine and faces, he had received an unexpected call as he was locking up the previous Friday advising him that the firm would be dispatching one of its representatives to Oakland Walk on Monday. When his phone had rung, he'd been wrestling with a chain and manhandling the site gates to secure them with a weighty padlock. The call had consequently been brief. The irregularity of an unexpected visitor had fleetingly piqued his curiosity before he had set off home for the weekend and cast it out of his mind. This was another benefit of his role; during the day, it was all consuming and he was needed constantly and everywhere for guidance, assistance, direction and more. Once the tradespeople had finished, suppliers had closed, site was secured and he headed home, there was no real ability to take his work home with him too.

Despite the change to routine that an impending visit would bring, the prospect of one of the company's suited office-based employees coming out to site did little to temper his enthusiasm that morning. Perhaps he made a little more effort with his appearance, picking out a newer pair of work trousers and less scuffed steel toe-capped boots. Although the site manager, he was hands on and dressed like the other tradespeople in heavy-duty work trousers with myriad pockets of varying sizes. Into these, he could stash the various tools he needed close to hand, pockets bulging. Knee pads were slotted into the articulated darted seams of his trousers to ensure he had full breadth of movement and could comfortably spend a good proportion of the day kneeling.

Although they were still working out in the open on the footings and superstructure of the buildings, it was spring, so Turner opted for a checked casual but long sleeve shirt with a collar. Over that, he wore a dark blue fleecy inside,

Gore Tex outside zip up jacket. The mandatory hard hat and bright yellow hi-vis vest replete with reflective horizontal strips were permanently left in his van to be pulled on as he arrived at site. Unlike many of the other tradespeople, he was able to keep a smaller gun-metal grey Berlingo to ferry himself from job to job. Materials arrived in bulk on wagons and he spent more time supervising and assisting than on the tools so didn't need the same size vehicle as the likes of Andy. Instead, as the site manager, he was technically based in the site office and indeed had his own designated space therein. This enabled him to legitimately duck in and out of its warm interior to consult the construction issue working drawings, make phone calls, coordinate the delivery of materials and more.

At every project, the first item to arrive – even before any of the plant – was the double stacked, metal twenty-foot-long by eight-foot-wide shipping container style modular office. The deep green corrugated unit contained a toilet, a kitchenette and, in the main space, two metal-legged and melamine-topped tables with fixed plastic seats. The kitchenette was little more than a glorified sink, with a small wall-mounted water heater above the tap and a couple of units beneath housing cleaning products and a collection of mismatched crockery and cutlery. In the main canteen area, positioned in the corner to the left of the door, stood a freestanding white fridge with a toaster, kettle, Kilner jar of tea bags, jar of coffee and bag of sugar on top. There were almost always a caffeine-stained teaspoon and discarded tea bag languishing alongside these, which would inevitably draw one's eye on entering the unit. The constant reminders to the lads to clean up after themselves and leave the welfare unit as they found it seemed to fall on permanently, selectively deaf ears.

The fridge would hold the lads' lunches along with milk for the tea and coffee, which everyone could help themselves to in their mid-morning breaks and lunchtime. Mounted on the walls around the room were the mandatory health and safety signs, the first-aid box, eye wash station and pegs serving as a drying area to air damp clothes whilst the lads were having their breaks. To the right of the entrance door, a low-level electric convection heater was strapped to the wall. With the doors and windows closed, the one radiator was more than sufficient to make the space stifling, particularly with the benefit of a collection of brawny male bodies all sheltering in there at points throughout the day.

There was a metal staircase and balustrade affixed to the exterior with the site office stacked above the welfare container. This was technically Turner's designated space. It was divided into a main room with its own kitchenette along one wall and a partition sectioned off to create a smaller more private office space. In principle, this would be where confidential phone calls could be made. In practice, Turner was the only one who used this level and so he would sit at one of the two desks that faced each other in the main area. He had his own allocated floor, about which his parents seemed enormously proud despite his protestations that this sounded more grandiose than the reality. Nonetheless, he would make a point of interacting with the tradespeople and subcontractors on site as much as possible, ensuring he joined them in the lower-level welfare unit for their breaks, to eat his lunch and for any impromptu site meetings that might spontaneously occur over a hot drink.

He had always struggled to find the right balance between being the various tradespeople's superior and equal, somehow both helped and hindered by Andy being his best friend. Managing a collection of subcontractors was less straightforward than someone outside the industry might assume. Unlike employees, who were all to some extent conditioned to work together and constantly receiving training and professional development that reiterated and reminded them of the importance of teamwork, most subcontractors were individuals running their own businesses. They would agree to be engaged by a contractor either for a fixed period of time or a specific scope of work. Each had their own trade – be that plumbing, carpentry, tiling, bricklaying, plastering, decorating and sought, wherever possible, to undertake their role without interference or hindrance from any other trade on site. Moreover, if Turner were to question their standard of work or be perceived as managing them in a fashion that rankled, the risk was that they would down tools, move to another project and not return. Fortunately, although the local construction sector was thriving, the pool of subcontractors was smaller and more interconnected than it might at first appear. As such, Turner was accustomed to the different personalities, how best to approach each individual to garner optimum results from them and had discerned a hierarchy gradually emerge amongst them. Each time they reappeared at a new project, he would note with a certain amused affection how they seemed unknowingly to slot back into their pecking order.

Nonetheless, he appreciated having a space to which he could withdraw when the persiflage grew tedious. The constant banter, ribbing and even occasional practical joke were an inevitable characteristic of the exchanges on site and, for the most part, he found them harmless and amusing and – on occasion – even participated. He was also conscious, however, as were the others, that he wasn't entirely one of them. Even Andy marginally tempered his behaviour. Away from work, they were comfortably equal. Here, Andy loyally tried to maintain a professional distance. Although Turner appreciated the sentiment, he wasn't convinced Andy was particularly successful at it, given he was unable to resist lowering the tone whenever the opportunity presented itself to do so.

That morning as usual, he exchanged the customary post-weekend greetings and pleasantries with everyone in the early spring sunshine. Those who were tumbling out of their vans with seconds to spare before the 8 a.m. start received a raised eyebrow in acknowledgement. Conversely, with a nod, he subtly applauded those who were ready to up-tools at the appropriate time before retreating to his first-floor office. He turned his attention to giving it a cursory once over, wiping down the surfaces, sweeping the dried mud that he inevitably brought in on the tread of his work boots and inadvertently stomped over the heavy-duty vinyl floor tiles. Whilst his hands were occupied with the mundane tidying and perfunctory cleaning, his mind wandered to the impending site visit. With everything in hand, the build progressing swiftly and on schedule, no tradespeople related issues that he was aware of and the materials for both this and the subsequent build stage tentatively on order, he couldn't fathom a reason as to why a site visit was required.

This thought process was interrupted by the sound of a heavy footfall on the metal staircase. It was rare that anyone would come up to his floor. If he was up here, someone would normally shout up from the ground or across from the plant or scaffold to get his attention. Without the formality of a reception area and unspoken rules around the chain of command that might be adhered to in an office, his presence was generally requested with a gruff bellow of "Gaffer" or "Boss" from someone.

Despite the irregularity of someone coming to the door, Turner knew it was Andy approaching. The rapid reverberations of the tread as the gentle giant took the stairs two at a time gave him away. Andy was the sort of man who would wear shorts throughout the year, come rain or shine. Even in the depths of winter, when every breath curled out of their mouths like smoke wafting on the cold air and their fingers were almost constantly numb unless clamped a hot drink, Andy would wear his shorts.

"I figure it keeps me working quickly, Gaff," he had once explained. "If I don't want my bollocks to freeze, I need to keep warm and, to do that, I have to keep moving."

"Gaff" was the nickname Andy used for him on site, seemingly not wanting to draw attention to their personal relationship by calling him mate, despite almost everyone else referring to each other as mate anyhow.

For a large, heavyset man in clodhopper work boots, he was surprisingly agile. Like many of the lads, Turner included, after years of working off scaffolds, platforms and trestles, Andy was as sure footed as a mountain goat. He simultaneously rapped on the metal door and sprung through it, unfurling his limbs as he came upright after ducking through the opening. Animated, he looked at Turner and announced, whilst glancing over his shoulder "Gaff, a… suit's here to see you."

Andy smiled mischievously and, seemingly pleased with himself, continued, "I guess you're going to be spending a bit more time in the office today then, Gaff." Presumably then catching sight of the individual below, he checked himself. He gave Turner a deliberate but disguised wink and reversed back through the entrance. The stairs couldn't accommodate two individuals heading in opposite directions, least of all when one of those was Andy so Turner watched Andy's bulk recede. Over his reverberating footfall, Andy called, "Visitor book's been signed. I'll send 'em up."

This was followed by some muted utterance and then Turner's peripheral vision detected a slighter but nonetheless hard hat-wearing, high-vis clad silhouette taking shape at the top of the staircase. Authoritatively but also more softly, they knocked on the door.

"Come in," he said as he turned from the sink where he had been drying his hands on a tea towel, scooping up his glass for a swig of water as he rotated.

The outstretched hand proffered to shake his was closer than he had anticipated and, more surprisingly, feminine. She must have taken a meaningful step towards him as she had crossed the threshold from outside. Combined with his own momentum as he turned toward the door from the kitchenette and complicated by the glass of water in his right hand, he fumbled, meeting her manicured warm fingers and confident grasp with an awkward attempt at a handshake. Droplets of cold water from his drink splashed across their hands. Her grip was firm and the up and down movement fluid as, apparently unphased, she upturned her face to make eye contact with him.

Although Turner's mother had permeated his psyche with her pro-women values throughout his childhood and he considered himself their proponent, in his experience, there were very few women in construction. On the rare occasion he shook one of their hands, he often found them to have cultivated a vice-like grip as they pumped his own. He always fleetingly wondered whether this was an overcompensation, attempting to demonstrate their equality, their strength even, in a predominantly masculine industry. Somehow, the woman clutching his hand was successful in striking the balance between firm and feminine. His broad palm and muscular fingers wrapped around her smaller delicate hand but it was her clasp and level gaze that radiated cool professionalism.

"Hi. I hope I'm not interrupting. I'm Lucy. I believe Contemporary Homes informed you I'd be on site from today."

Turner hastily regained his composure, pasting a guarded smile on his face. "Hi, I'm Turner. I'm Oakland Walk's site manager." As he tried to subtly survey the woman before him, he continued, "It's unusual for Contemporary Homes to dispatch visitors to us. To what do we owe the pleasure?"

Lucy was small; the term petite seemed fitting. Her presence in this setting and that she had on a hard hat and luminous yellow high-vis vest seemed incongruous. These also drew the eye and, given all safety wear was large or extra-large as standard, the vest and hat swamped her, precluding him giving her a discreet once over. As if she was aware of his quandary and yet indifferent to it, she moved towards the pegs unaffected and, after shimmying out of the high-vis, reached to hang it up next to his own. It struck him how much more graceful her movements were than the exaggerated shrug the lads would employ to remove their safety wear. Her action was more reminiscent of an understated dance move.

Without the billowing effect of the vest, she halved in size before him. She was the first person he had met on a building site who could, in his view, accurately be described as diminutive. Her hard hat sat jauntily on her head and, as she lifted it, it revealed long brown curly hair precisely combed into a ponytail and hanging mid-way down her back. A couple of wayward brown ringlets tumbled out as she removed the hat, framing her face. She was pale skinned but flushed in the cheeks from the cold crisp morning air and wore no make-up with the exception perhaps of some form of tinted balm on her lips. This gave them a wholesome, voluptuous appearance. A girl next-door.

Undeterred, she filled the pause, "I'm assuming it's alright to remove the health and safety wear indoors. Presumably I just wear it when moving around outside so I'm visible."

Still mentally playing catch up with this turn of events, he muttered an ineloquent, "Erm, yes."

She continued, "To your question, the dubious pleasure bestowed on us both by Contemporary Homes is that I'm to be based here for the next little while."

Turner realised Lucy was scanning the room as she spoke, taking in the two desks before her; facing each other but separated by a couple of metres of hard-wearing mottled grey vinyl floor with blue flecks in it. In its favour, the space was bright, making it feel somewhat larger and more welcoming than might otherwise be the case. When the windows were closed, the interior was pitch black, shrouded in a cloak of utter darkness. Each morning, on his arrival, Turner would hinge wide open the shutters cut into the corrugated metal finish of the containers and secure these to the exterior with flip latches. Light consequently flooded in through the glass windows cut into the container's inner skin.

Unsure what her first impression may be and surprised to find he cared how she perceived it, he stuttered, "I tend to work at this desk." He gesticulated towards the one closest to the kitchenette and, tellingly, covered in large scale plans, notepads, builders' merchants' product guides and a closed laptop. He figured the laptop must look exactly as she would assume an uncouth builder's computer would look. It seemed a bit battered from significant use but nonetheless well-cared for. It was a powerful model, renowned for long battery life and durability. Like their usual tools of the trade, she would be imagining it having been carefully chosen to satisfy his requirements of it but it suffered in meeting those needs with its brushed aluminium effect coating scuffed and scratched. Next to it lay a white dongle with its cable trailing back to where it was plugged into a wall mounted utilitarian white plastic socket. He watched as her eyes followed the leads. The electricity supply within the unit was mounted on the wall in white click close trunking that fanned out towards the kitchenette with the wall-mounted convection heater and the double sockets at each corner of the room. As he followed her gaze, he again wondered what her first impressions of his office space might be and what the reality of her previous place of work might have entailed. *I hope she won't be here for long.*

"Shall we take a seat here then?" Lucy enquired as she indicated the remaining empty table positioned just a couple of paces from the first.

Unlike the downstairs cabin, the seats on this floor were dark blue hard plastic moulded over angled metal legs. In response, Turner moved to sit on one side of the table, chair juddering on the vinyl floor as he manhandled it. He observed with feigned indifference as Lucy settled into the opposite seat in a single fluid motion. She looked out of place sitting primly in the unyielding concavity of the seat base. He was conscious of a disconnect in their body language too. She sat in an upright, almost formal position with her knees together and feet softly planted beneath the spot on the table where her hands rested on her own leather-bound document wallet. He could picture the inside; it would inevitably unzip to reveal a pristine A4 notepad, ballpoint pens slotted into little black leather inserts and, probably, business cards. In an electronic age, he couldn't see the point of issuing cards printed with one's contact details. Moreover, the only ones that would find their way onto site came from suppliers touting for business and these got ruined almost immediately. They were inevitably used as packers to combat any inconvenient wobbling of furniture or, worse, as toothpicks if someone were to have a particularly obstinate morsel of food lingering between their teeth after lunch. Reappraising Lucy, he decided she would definitely have business cards.

Meanwhile, Turner lounged in his own seat, leaning back against it, legs and arms spread. From the relaxed position he feigned, he could see both above and below the desk. Conscious of not wanting to conform to any perceived stereotype she might have of construction workers, their propensity to wolf whistle and cat call, he attempted to respectfully halt his survey at her boots rather than obviously allowing his gaze to trail from there up her legs.

Semi failing, he noticed with amusement that below her black pencil skirt and skin-coloured nylon tights, she wore steel toe cap boots that she had securely laced and tied in a neat double bow. No wonder she appeared so small. With the exception of those within his family, most women he encountered would be in a social setting and generally therefore wearing heels. If Lucy felt self-conscious in her gleaming new work boots, there was nothing in her manner that implied so.

In the momentary silence, he could however imagine what Andy and the other lads would be saying to each other in response to the excitement of Lucy's unexpected arrival. Like him, they would also have given her a once over. He was confident it would have been a far less subtle one in their case. Having clocked her boots, they'd no doubt be betting and bartering their respective undesirable tasks, like clearing up site at close of play, on when she would 'land on her arse' in them.

With Andy's checkered history of failed relationships, he'd no doubt be ruing the effect of a fall on her pretty behind. He'd tell the lads "Not to make her the butt of your jokes" and announce that "My future ex-wife has just arrived on site." This would in turn prompt good-humoured cries from the others that, "It'll be a cold day in hell before she gets with you, you scrubby bastard" or words to that effect.

Turner pictured Andy signalling the idling telehandler's hydraulic breaker with his huge paw of a hand, retorting to a chorus of deep, rapturous laughter that, "She'd choose my pecker over yours any day!" and "Yeah, she'd be impressed if I were to show her my pipe laying skills!"

Turner hoped his amused cringe didn't register on his face. All the lads possessed a full repertoire of tool-related innuendoes that they delighted in reeling off wherever possible. His first impressions of Lucy prompted him to posture she wouldn't appreciate any of them.

Almost as if she could read the content of his thoughts like they were written across his face, Lucy sharply interrupted them, "So, as you know, I'm Lucy. It is the consensus of Contemporary Homes' committee of business strategists and market analysts that a slight correction in the property market can be anticipated in the short to medium term. To secure its investment and, importantly, its desired return here at Oakland Walk" —she met and firmly held his gaze—"it has engaged me to optimise the properties' appeal to the target market identified. I will be a Project Manager if you will, largely based here on site and working with you to achieve the maximum gross development value."

She continued, "Whilst this is my first contract for Contemporary Homes, my background is in project and change management, both roles which, until moving to Birmingham, I pursued in the City." She paused and needlessly clarified, "of London rather than Birmingham town centre."

Frankly, he didn't *will it* but considered it inappropriate to voice this sentiment.

"Having reviewed comparables in the vicinity, both of new builds and existing homes, these houses clearly need to be pitched as family residences. It is my objective to ensure that we exceed the ceiling price in the area with adjustments to the properties' appearance and specification that would be sympathetic to our target buyers' expectations. These tweaks and their associated impact will need to be assessed and calculated using various metrics and undergo rigorous cost benefit analysis. They will then be implemented at my discretion subject to committee imposed budgetary threshold."

She droned on, "I will liaise and coordinate with the relevant stakeholders, where necessary, to arrange updated drawings and file and pursue non-material or minor planning amendments."

Outwardly, Turner was confident he was sporting a suitable expression. In so far as possible, he was aiming for polite and professional but aloof. Internally, he bristled. Lucy's monologue jarred, leaning towards condescending and her language incompatibly corporate in the setting. The lads would find her manner and tone discordant. If the pair of them were to work together, he would inevitably be obliged to bridge that gap, although, with mild indignation, he found himself wondering why he should mediate. Whilst Contemporary Homes was vocally pro-equality and equal opportunities in the workplace, it also needed to know its – or, in this instance, her - audience. Whether Turner liked it or not, her sexuality, small stature and fluent ability to articulate herself would also be counterproductive amongst the exclusively male tradespeople. Uncharitable though it sounded, his role was to manage the site not facilitate hers.

In this vein, he could only assume that she thought he might not recognise that Contemporary Homes was looking to achieve the maximum gross development value by imbuing the houses with an upmarket, executive quality. He placed no less importance on ensuring it progressed on budget and on time too. Overshooting a 'build complete' deadline extended any credit lines or other liabilities and, crucially, might mean a development would be ready for marketing out of prime season. Seething at the perceived slight, he felt as equipped to discern trends in the sector as anyone and was perfectly aware that the property market experienced peaks and troughs. Cyclical on a macro scale, it displayed fluctuations in line with shifting public policy or proportionate to changes in tax legislation and he resented the way her manner appeared to imply she didn't think he would know this.

In fact, he could cite many examples of such scenarios. Since the last recession, successive governments had been trying to reduce debt in the housing market, increase home ownership and temper house price rises as a result of investment purchases and spiralling mortgages. Turner doubted Lucy had also witnessed first-hand the anticipated and indeed unanticipated effect of each of these policy changes on individual property values and the wider construction industry.

Independently of political or economic manipulation, he knew there were intra-annual patterns too and hazarded a guess that he had more knowledge of these than Lucy. Sales figures were often more buoyant in spring and then more muted over the summer when people were keener on holidaying than house hunting. Market activity would then pick up in September as children returned to school but, shortly afterwards, ease off as Christmas approached.

Lucy again pierced his thoughts, "Whilst I am keen to collaborate with you, there is a clear division between our respective responsibilities. Like you, I am mandated to be based here on site for what could be the remaining duration of the build or at least until specification for the builds has been agreed and the show home is nearing completion. As site manager, I understand you are to continue to supervise the tradespeople, manage the physical build, order the requisite materials and coordinate the pertinent trades at the appropriate build stage. I, on the other hand, will be tasked with identifying any opportunities and means by which we can increase the desirability or end values of the four units in an economically viable fashion. I will liaise with, and communicate any, build relevant implications to you as they are approved, supply any required documentation, such as drawings, specifications, supplier information and their lead times, and you will be incumbent on incorporating them into the actual build."

Lucy paused, seemingly only to draw breath rather than to garner his opinion. Turner, conscious of a burgeoning sense of indignation, interjected before she could continue her lecture. He clawed together a collection of suitably complicated words to retort, "I can't see that this is either necessary or justified. Whilst my background isn't in economics, business or finance, it surprises me that Contemporary Homes would decide – on the basis of its own cost benefit analysis – that expenditure on a third-party consultant's remuneration will be more than offset by any fiscally viable up-spec conceived and implemented across a development of *just* four residential units."

Turner hadn't excelled at school and didn't consider himself academic but he was still well educated. His teachers and those who had met him since, would call him an all-rounder as he possessed a practical ability that couldn't easily be taught or learnt and strong powers of logic. He could also find interest in everything and, as such, had a broad general knowledge base. For a reason he was unable to fathom in that moment, he wanted to subversively demonstrate to Lucy that he too could in fact employ large words and understand finance.

Perhaps childishly, Turner had also emphasised the *just* in his previous sentence. His ego smarted as the underlying message of Lucy's soliloquy appeared to be the belittlement of the project at Oakland Walk and, by association, his role. With his intonation, he wanted to insinuate to her that any such reflection on him would have a similarly tarnishing effect on her too, given they were both to be at the helm of an apparently trivial project.

Lucy's eyes flashed but, in a measured voice, she objectively clarified the situation, "It is immaterial whether you or I consider this to be the leadership's most judicious course of action, be that for monetary or other reasons. We are, however, both contracted to Contemporary Homes for the duration of this scheme and both have a vested interest in achieving the business' objectives for this project. This will be far more readily accomplished by working together to deliver Oakland Walk on budget, on time and with a view to securing the highest possible sales values."

Formulating his retort, Turner inhaled but Lucy more demurely cut him off, "So, would you like to give me the tour of our site?"

Turner bristled at the suggestion that Lucy could consider it *our* site despite having only arrived minutes prior.

Frustrated and momentarily disenchanted, Turner silently acquiesced by unfurling himself from his chair and getting to his feet. Lucy stood too. Even if she were to draw herself up to her full height, he realised with some satisfaction that the top of her head would barely reach his shoulders. Whilst somewhat juvenile, he felt mildly pleased that, even if she could make herself and her role sound important, she would be obliged to literally look up to him to convey that message. This of course conflicted with the values his beloved mother had gone to great lengths to instil in him; the stalwart matriarch of the farming family she had married into. Reasonably small in stature herself but surrounded by a towering husband and sons, she had ensured he understood the importance of being respectful to women.

Checking himself, Turner pulled his luminous vest and hard hat on in a smooth – but he hoped profoundly masculine – motion. He simultaneously opened the door and, in silence, observed as Lucy stretched up to lift hers from the peg and shrug it over her shoulders. The hard hat appeared precarious, sitting at an odd angle as her ponytail of curly hair left it perched on the crown of her head. She looked entirely out of place, a suited, formal corporate type shrouded in luminous yellow polyester and nylon material that swamped her. Nonetheless, if he were feeling charitable, he conceded to himself that he had to admire her poise. Beneath the unflustered shell, she must be feeling out of her depth. He banished the benevolent thought as he casually wondered how long she would manage in the role. "Ladies first."

CHAPTER 3

Lucy breathed a sigh of relief as she stepped over the threshold and back out onto the metal stairs. She grasped the rail as she found her footing and very deliberately descended the steps, desperate not to stumble under the inquisitive scrutiny of those on site. Rapidly replaying their first encounter in her mind's eye, she supposed Turner had given her the cool reception she should have anticipated. The briefing she had received about the role had given her the impression that Turner was accustomed to running his sites in isolation. Everyone on site reported to him and he, in turn, seemed to be under no obligation to report to anyone until the eventual handover of the completed scheme. For a corporate to take such a laissez-faire stance, surely meant he must consistently deliver positive results. Just as she reached the bottom step and resolved to remain open-minded about Turner, not to judge him detrimentally purely because of her previous error with Mark, she stumbled in her chunky boots.

From somewhere off to her side, the same tradesman who had shown her to the cabin quipped, "Watch your step... You wouldn't want to start off on the wrong foot."

Lucy was sure she heard a stifled snort escape Turner's pursed lips in response to the deadpan delivery. Lucy flushed crimson as she turned to meet the man's gaze with a scowl and eyes blazing.

Before she could stutter out a response, he followed up with a smirk and said, "I'm Andy." He laughed. "Oh dear, have I put my foot in it?"

Lucy thought she caught sight of Turner casting a reproachful glower in Andy's direction but he made no comment.

Apparently impervious to her anger and on reaching the bottom rung, Turner went to brush his hands against her shoulders in a belated and seemingly mocking attempt to steady her. Unable to quieten the hint of challenge in her voice she retorted, voice pitched somewhere between indignant and amused, "I see your team has mastered sarcasm... Well, I can muster a play on words too so..." She paused for effect. "Let me bring you to heel. I too can think on my feet and one way or another, I'm pretty sure my presence here will keep you all on your toes."

In response, Andy said nothing but cast a self-satisfied, knowing smile in Turner's direction as if commenting on her assertion that she'd keep them on their toes. She couldn't tell whether the look that passed between them meant Andy thought Turner would appreciate or dislike her apparent feistiness or indeed whether Andy considered her to be a personal or professional challenge for Turner. For his part, Turner simply turned away as if Andy's body language and silent message had gone unnoticed.

Regardless, Lucy exhaled a small smug breath at having been able to verbally recover herself with a quick-witted response. Andy's gaze continued to seem to move between the pair of them. The knowing expression remained plastered to his face, although, still none the wiser, Lucy had no idea what he thought he knew. Uncomfortable, she reeled at having temporarily entertained the prospect of lowering her guard a little. *Not a chance!* She was desperate to make this work and perhaps should have expected this male-dominated environment to be no more welcoming than the one she had left. On the plus side and based on her first impressions of Turner, at least here there was no way she'd get involved with the boss!

Unconsciously passing her hand over her right hip, she thought of the tiny, personal tattoo indelibly and permanently positioned there reminding her to be strong. Lucy reassured herself that, with Rachel's support and vocal encouragement, she had seized the opportunity to up sticks to this new city, thereby escaping the vestiges of an unhealthy personal relationship and the resulting hostile work environment.

As Lucy tried to regroup and spun on her heels ready to do the tour of site, she could picture her devoted friend giggling at her. Snippets of their long telephone conversation and pep talk the night before replayed in her mind. Together, they had resolved that she would make being far from London, from a poisonous workplace and an inconsiderate and callous ex-boyfriend into a positive fresh start. Her doting friend's reassuring words echoed in her ears.

"Juicy, life doesn't always give us second chances, but sometimes it presents an opportunity for a fresh start."

Lucy smiled at Rachel's use of her childhood nickname.

I'm going to make this a resounding success, she thought to herself. *I'm going to focus on carving out my own path.* She winced at the turn of phrase, picturing Turner and Andy guffawing at her terminology given their infuriating enthusiasm for feet-related puns. Drawing instead on her friend's overt optimism, she reassured herself that her new work environment was certainly different.

Unnerved, she realised she was also acutely aware of Turner's masculinity. The prospect of working so closely with him triggered an element of apprehension and perhaps a twinge of something else. She couldn't immediately identify what though. His presence had certainly filled the office as he'd self-assuredly draped himself across his seat with legs spread wide, thick work trouser-clad crotch casting an open V-shape in her direction. Whilst the manager of the site, he displayed none of the stereotypical physical attributes of the sedentary managerial office worker she was accustomed to. Conversely, what little she could discern of his physique from his work attire suggested he was fit, toned and virile.

She had little time to contemplate this as she followed Turner across the site's uneven terrain. As he approached them, the lads' behaviour seemed to shift. In so far as a gang of burly men could, they projected an air of deference. At roughly six foot tall, he towered over her but was physically no larger than the other men. If anything, Andy was the bulkiest, a mountain of a man.

Despite being amongst all that masculinity, in Turner's presence, she sensed his own undercurrent of testosterone most palpably. She hastily made a mental note to banish any such thoughts or sensations as, from excruciating experience, that way danger lay.

Unlike her ungainly descent of the stairs, Turner had bounded down the steps behind her, creating a deep rumbling reverberation through the shipping containers with each assertive tread. Even now on level ground, she faltered in his wake, feeling out of her depth and conspicuous in this new and unfamiliar scene. With a furtive but sweeping glance, it was painfully obvious that her appearance seemed at odds with the setting. In hindsight, the black pencil skirt and matching fitted suit jacket were an incongruous and impractical choice. The standard issue high-visibility vest was clearly not conceived with someone of her stature in mind and billowed around her like a sail in the wind whilst her hard hat wobbled in time with her gait.

Having had the importance of wearing appropriate personal, protective equipment drummed into her at induction, she was also now wearing the chunky steel-toe-capped boots that had caused her to lose her footing moments before. Appropriate footwear had to be worn on site at all times; ironic, she thought, that the safety boots should be the very thing that caused her to trip and risk injuring herself. *If only I could kick them into touch* she thought wryly.

She cringed as she envisaged the tradespeople internalising their own less than witty observations. Unlike Andy, at least they might extend her the courtesy of choosing not to voice them. She had no idea what form their thoughts might take but extrapolated at 'what a plank' or 'she looks like a tool'. She immediately checked herself with a personal warning not to lower herself to the level of Turner and his team in order to endear herself to anyone. Her impromptu repartee of building related puns would be unlikely to inspire respect or confidence. Not renowned for her wit, she imagined their comments would contain more expletives.

With long and purposeful strides, Turner rapidly moved away and Lucy, feigning confidence, trotted after him.

"As you can see," he began, gesturing with his hands, "the groundwork is largely complete, the drainage runs have been created and the trenches for the utility connections have been excavated and loosely backfilled while we await the infrastructure providers' installation dates."

Lucy cast her eyes down at the crisscross of scrapings and scarring in the old tarmac of the pub car park. These – as Turner indicated – presumably denoted trenches housing cables, drainage, foul runs, utility supplies and more.

"Even after all this time in construction, it always strikes me that so much work is undertaken before a building comes out of the ground," Turner continued.

"At this end of the run, the courses of red engineering bricks below damp on the external skin have already been laid. The concrete block inner skin is also to damp proof course and the block and beam floor is in and will be screeded in the next few days to ensure it's a solid base for the internal footprint of the properties. This will be the show home so will be our priority.

"You will know from the plans that the houses are all two storeys. The front door sits centrally in the front elevation. We are standing outside plot four. You will cross the threshold at the front, into an entrance hall. The houses are mirror images of each other. In this one, however, to the right of the hall is the kitchen and opposite the kitchen entrance, across the hall, is the dining room."

Although she hoped not, Lucy was sure she already looked completely confused as she and Turner stepped onto the block and beam floor via an imaginary front door and, to all intents and purposes, were stood on a rectangular concrete pad with a barely ankle high wall around its perimeter.

Perhaps Turner could sense her bewilderment as she struggled to orientate herself. Conciliatorily, he positioned himself alongside her and, standing shoulder to shoulder, explained, "So, you come through the front door and into the hall. The first door on your right is the kitchen and the first door on the left is the dining room. Beyond that, there's a downstairs toilet that sits beneath and to the side of the staircase. The building is approximately ten metres wide and the entire rear is designated as being an open-plan living space. On the rear wall, there's to be a window bringing natural light into one half of the room and basic patio doors giving light to the other half. These will also give access to the rear garden."

He slowly revolved through 360 degrees with Lucy following his movement, their sides brushing briefly as they rotated. Taking a deep breath overwhelmed her senses with his scent. If confidence were to have a smell, Turner's would be the definition thereof; a combination of an earthy sandalwood, a masculine spice she couldn't place, and the outdoors.

He was alternating between looking at Lucy and then surveying the concrete pad. Even just from his side profile, Lucy could see that he was conjuring a three-dimensional life-size model of the house. In his mind's eye, he was walking around a tangible building. She on the other hand could invoke no such imagery as she stared at a muddy building site punctuated with concrete pads.

"Upstairs, there will be four bedrooms; three doubles and a single with a large family bathroom to share between them. The void at the top of the stairs will be fashioned into an airing cupboard just off the landing. The stairs of course take up quite a large amount of space and, as such, the two bedrooms on the right of the house as you look at it from the road, will be larger than the two left-hand bedrooms. The front right bedroom is a bit larger than the rear right one. It would potentially therefore be the master although it overlooks the driveway and road beyond rather than the rear garden."

He paused and expectantly swivelled back toward Lucy, his emerald, green gaze moving over her face to look directly into her eyes. His thick dark hair framed his face and accentuated their colour, complemented further by the dark stubble over his chiselled jawline. She hoped he didn't just see bewilderment reflected back at him. From experience, she knew it was best to be non-committal at this stage. Rather than voice her initial impressions which, could in time prove incorrect, critical or ill-informed, she needed to refrain from articulating her embryonic thoughts. That wouldn't be hard. Her overriding sentiment at that moment was one of pure panic and that she was clueless as to what to think or say under his scrutiny.

One thing that did strike her was that Turner was very attractive and she felt the intensity of his focus directed at her. His presence seemed to induce a slight fog in her mind.

Beyond that initial mental hurdle, the second but arguably more significant thought was that perhaps a history of project management coupled with renovating her London flat was insufficient foundation knowledge for this role. Whilst her head was erring towards disliking Turner's character, he was clearly exceptionally knowledgeable, confident and in his element in this environment. Whilst not essential to impress him, she desperately wanted to demonstrate the value she could bring to the project and bringing him on side would undoubtedly be the first step. That her property related experience was incidental to her career rather than pivotal to it, she was sure he would look on unfavourably.

"And what about the external appearance please, Turner?"

He threw a glance in the direction of a small housing development diagonally across the road. "They will look much like the other new builds locally. Red bricks, grey tiled roofs and white uPVC windows and doors. All of the drawings are in the cabin if you need to further familiarise yourself with the plans."

With that, Turner hopped off the block and beam, and set off towards the bricklayers working to bring the remaining three houses up to damp too. Lucy hung back for a moment, continuing to try to get her bearings. Conveniently also, this would give her the opportunity to observe.

There was an obvious but loose hierarchy amongst the tradespeople although they were all interacting freely, clearly at ease with each other. Two young lads, who were tall, gangly and still needed to fill out and, seemingly, grow into their limbs, appeared at first glance to be the labourers or perhaps apprentices. Both seemed to be tasked with keeping the bricklayers working at full speed. Shouting in their general direction, Andy, apparently a bricklayer, called, "Chop, chop, lads. My spots aren't going to cover themselves with mortar and there's more loading out to do."

One of the youngsters set to shovelling grey slurry from the quarter cube tubs of ready-mixed mortar into a battered, concrete-splattered barrow. He wheeled this over to the brickies and dropped a couple of shovels of wet grey mortar onto what appeared to be square wooden boards after first nudging them closer to Andy with a few thrusts of his foot. She inferred the 'spot' must be the board the mortar was being shovelled onto.

"Kev," Andy called to the other, "load out, mate, please."

Kev looked up, seemingly startled.

"Yes, you, Shit Nut," he reiterated pointing at Kev. "I was using your proper name because we're in the presence of a lady!"

Lucy balked at the thought that someone could appear shocked to be referred to by their own name rather than such an inappropriate moniker. Moreover, this implied Shit Nut was the name by which he was accustomed to being addressed. Without an ounce of indignation discernible at his dubious title, the smaller of the labourers, who still looked like he should be at school, scuttled off towards the packs of bricks and blocks stacked neatly along the front of the site.

The telehandler Lucy had spotted idling in the corner when she had arrived must have evenly distributed the palleted packs along the length of the site to minimise time expended ferrying the materials to each plot. Kev was then stacking smaller piles of ten or so blocks around the immediate perimeter of the house, starting with the section closest to Andy. As she watched, she realised Andy and his fellow bricklayers barely needed to move or even stretch from where they stood to grab a block or dip their trowel into the mortar. The two labourers, continually scuttling backwards and forwards, tended to four bricklayers between them. To a passing pedestrian, the setup may look a bit haphazard but, in reality, the mismatched group were working in efficient unison.

Encouraging them, Turner called out with overt enthusiasm, "Looking good, gang!" He hadn't displayed either emotion in her presence with the exception of in relation to the build progress.

Nonetheless, bemused, she thought she could see the well-wrapped-up men react by standing a little taller and speeding up their pace with the barrows and bricks or their laying. Whilst she may not yet be convinced by Turner, he had clearly earned the admiration of this manly crew of broad-shouldered bricklayers and lanky labourers.

Lucy took a deep breath, steeled herself and walked over too. Whilst Turner's sudden departure was more likely him signalling he had fulfilled her request of him to give her the tour and that the walk round was over, she ignored this insinuation. With some trepidation, she realised this would be as good a time as any to introduce herself. Turner made no attempt to facilitate it so she decided to dispense with the stereotypical formalities of a more conventional corporate workplace and announced, "Hi, everyone. Sorry to interrupt. I'm Lucy."

Everyone looked up briefly and, to her great relief, smiled genuinely and openly.

They introduced themselves with a chorus of names as they signalled themselves.

"Andy," Andy said, bringing his paw of a hand up to point to his chest. "We've met," he added, beaming.

"Josh," said the other bricklayer.

"Kev."

"Stu."

With no outstretched hands for her to shake and their monosyllabic introductions called out, each cast his eyes back to the task in hand. Lucy hovered, thinking Turner might elaborate about her role but he instead stood impassive.

"I'm sure we'll make our introductions properly over the next few days" she continued, internally wincing at the artificial joviality in her tone. "In the meantime, I'm going to be based here in the first-floor office for the foreseeable future. Please know my door is, metaphorically speaking, always open."

Some smiles, a "Yes" and an "Okay" were all she received in acknowledgement. She was baffled that nobody had asked what her role would be. She hesitated but, given Turner's continued silence, turned on her heels and forged an unsteady but upright route with head held high back to the cabin. As soon as her back turned, the silence lifted and the yellow De Walt battery powered radio perched on the wall under construction was turned on. By the time she'd reached the cabin stairs, deep and tuneless singing could be heard interspersed with guttural laughter and the scrape of a trowel along the blocks and bricks.

She paused, thinking she detected the tenor of someone's voice uttering something about, "Seeming proper", "Meeting the parents" and "Seeing her boobs". Some of the words didn't carry to her on the cabin stairs but it sounded like someone was delivering a coarse joke at her expense.

Turner's stern retort did however reach her. "I'm going to stop you there. I'm sure you're right that she's proper so, let's be honest, there's almost certainly no chance of you getting to meet her parents and even less of seeing her breasts. Put the idea to bed now."

Another low, rumbling and unintelligible reply followed before Turner again cut in to clarify with a hint of amused exasperation in his tone, "No, I said the idea to bed not the woman to bed."

Another voice piped up before he replied, "No, there will be absolutely no nailing! Also, no backward elephants! No one wants to witness one of those, least of all a lady. You've had your jokes. That's the end of it. Now let's be respectful please."

As Lucy turned and continued to the sanctuary of the first-floor office, she couldn't conceive what a backward elephant might be. Suspecting she'd probably prefer not to know, she made a mental note to perhaps ask Turner should they ever become sufficiently acquainted for her to feel able to broach the subject. He had however risen somewhat in her opinion because, at least indirectly, he had defended her. With some admiration for him, she inferred the lads had heeded his admonishment as they obediently swapped back to accompanying the radio with a deep, toneless baritone.

Lucy closed out the cold spring air and the alien environment. The internal space felt no more familiar. Unlike the sophisticated, tastefully decorated, pretentious city offices she had worked in before, the cabin was modest, spartan and utilitarian. She had read widely before taking on this project, from home décor and lifestyle magazines to trade specific publications and even architectural tomes. The cabin reminded her of the post-1930s' modernist architects' motto that 'form follows function', the premise being that the function of a building should determine its form. Certainly, there were none of the decorative elements or 'ornament' that they would have considered superfluous in modern building.

On the plus side, the first-floor office space would be conducive to work as there would be no distraction from the role, with the exception perhaps of Turner's presence. Whilst she was accustomed to open-plan offices punctuated by waist-height partitions that divided entire floors into quasi cubicles, the unsettling tension she'd earlier felt at the prospect of being in such close proximity to Turner returned unbidden.

She removed her PPE, hung it neatly on a hook, filled and boiled the kettle and pulled her Tupperware of sliced lemon from her bag. Conditioned to consume a hot drink in the workplace, she had come to accept sliced lemon in boiling water as a passable compromise between her preference for juice and the ever ubiquitous tea. Amongst the mismatched crockery, she found herself a large mug and whilst having her first couple of scalding sips of lemony hot water, began to align and organise the printed plans. She was simultaneously arranging her scattered thoughts.

She cleared her mind to the extent possible despite the very subtle waft of men's aftershave lingering in the air. She consciously resisted the temptation to inhale deeply as she had inadvertently done outdoors during the tour. She must avoid sucking in the hint of raw testosterone and male pheromones that hung there. Instead, she pored over the drawings showing the floorplans for the slab of the house she had just walked around.

Surely the most important factor influencing potential sales prices would be the desirability of the houses. Contemplating the needs of a family, she inspected the plans further, tracing her finger around the layout as she tried to picture imaginary parents and their two imaginary children moving around their house. Creating as versatile a space as possible would be of most appeal. A blank canvas. The objective must be to cater to the ideal of modern open-plan family living. Where the drawings showed a kitchen and separate dining room, very few families would regularly use a formal dining room aside from at Christmas. It would surely be more appealing to have a combined kitchen, dining living area across the rear of the properties with a view to the private enclosed garden than have them separated from each other by the entrance hall and overlooking the tarmacked front driveway, block-paved parking spaces and busy road just beyond. Similarly, if a household were to have access to a private self-contained garden, it would make sense to capitalise on that by substituting the patio door and window along that rear elevation for full width bi-fold doors that would bathe the rear living space in natural light.

With some carefully chosen storage solutions and a well-conceived layout for the kitchen, which she envisaged being repositioned on the left side of the open-plan rear room, a breakfast bar could be created to accommodate at least four diners. Additionally, the current drawings showed the ground floor space as four distinct rooms. Lucy felt that if the partition wall that separated what was initially meant to be the dining room from the rear space could be removed, it would become a more inclusive space, maximising its flexibility. A large L-shaped room would be created that could easily be zoned into a living room, dining area and kitchen. If a future homeowner were to prefer to have defined spaces, they could always insert some double doors to carve off a section. Meanwhile, the room marked as the kitchen on the current version of the drawings could become a snug or playroom separate from the open-plan space.

She progressed to envisaging her notional four-member family climbing the stairs. What would each individual be hoping to find? What would she want to see if she were amongst them? It occurred to her that if all the bedroom doors were closed, the stairs would feel dark and uninviting. Simply installing a window in the stairwell would create a sensation of light and space instead. She continued to imagine the interior, gaining confidence as more ideas presented themselves.

The tentative thoughts dispersed though at Turner's rumbling approach up the stairs. As he entered, the space in the cabin seemed to perceptibly shrink, his presence consuming the air therein. Determined not to reveal this to him, Lucy resolutely continued to stare at the plans, willing herself to appear confident, accomplished and with meaningful contributions to make.

Spying some labelled-up elevations, Lucy meanwhile was able to glean a clearer indication as to what the finished houses that Turner had described to her would look like. The mental image she conjured felt a little lacklustre so, trying to eschew her nerves and uncertainty, she retrieved the elevations from the stack. Without seeking Turner's permission or opinion, she opened her pencil case, plucked out her myriad coloured pencils and began to colour in the detail of the elevations using the annotations on the drawings and casting regular glances towards the houses over the road as her inspiration.

The houses opposite were perfectly nice, inoffensive, but hardly possessed the wow factor. Lucy updated the white uPVC windows on the paper spread in front of her by colouring them an anthracite grey. She blended the rear patio doors and window into one large set of bi-fold doors and inserted a window over the stairs. She then created a small porch roof over the front door and protruding from the external wall so any hypothetical future homeowner would be sheltered from the elements whilst fumbling with their keys.

The hours flew by as she honed her designs. She shaded the roof tiles in the same grey tone of the anthracite windows and inserted a blue grey brick sill detail beneath the windows on the front elevation. Her research, prior to moving northward from London, had taught her of the industrial significance of the nearby Black Country. In doing so, she had discovered a local brick called a Staffordshire blue. Incorporating this into the houses' appearance would surely imbue them with gravitas, reflect that those behind the development are sensitive to the region's heritage and sympathetic to its industrial past. Whilst not guaranteed to make the houses more valuable, such details might enhance their appeal and there would be implied value to Contemporary Homes in having the site sold quickly even if not for more money.

Lucy entertained the sensation that she could feel Turner's eyes on her from time to time but couldn't bring herself to lift her gaze to confirm so. Instead, trying to appear unaffected, she dedicated the afternoon to shading and embellishing her drawing to gradually bring it to life. Once comfortable with the design, she dug about in her handbag for the clear nail varnish she was sure she had seen lurking discarded at the bottom somewhere. She applied the clear polish to the windows and her newly created bi-fold door to try to give the effect of glass. More satisfied with her efforts than she had anticipated being at the start of the day, she packed up her belongings as the drawings dried. With Turner presumably overseeing everyone downing tools outside somewhere, she left the drawings on her desk ready to discuss with Turner in the morning.

CHAPTER 4

As Turner clambered out of his van to again begin the daily battle to unlock the site entrance gates, he realised he felt off kilter, discombobulated even, which was uncharacteristic of him. His thoughts kept turning to Lucy. They had been working together in the cabin for a few weeks now and, grappling with the chains and padlock, he contemplated that her personal life remained a complete enigma. He surmised she was unlikely to be married or to have a fiancé as she wore no ring but, beyond that, for all he knew she could as readily be in a committed relationship or indeed single or even celibate. He felt a twinge of surprise at realising he'd consider that to be a shame for mankind.

As he climbed the cabin steps, he pondered how many of the lads at Oakland Walk were already married or in long-term relationships. The reality of their personal lives, or at least what he knew of them seemed alien to him. Andy, for instance, appeared to be embroiled in a permanent dispute with his girlfriend, someone who despite Turner's long-standing friendship with Andy, he had still never met. Whilst Andy protested that he just liked to compartmentalise, Turner was confident that it was more likely that Andy just hadn't yet met the right woman. If he had, he would surely revel in socialising together. He appreciated, however, that Andy's current situation was complicated by virtue of sharing young children with an ex-girlfriend who, as far as Turner understood, had a proclivity to be irresponsible and unreliable.

He admired Andy for persevering with the mother of his children. In saying that, although no one could dispute Andy's work ethic or dedication, Turner was sure he had explained away at least three absences in the months early on, before they had become proper friends, as being due to the death of his grandmother. Either Andy's own upbringing therefore had been more complicated than conventional or his personal life was, despite him being a skilled tradesman, a shambles too. Although he was a gentle giant with a good heart, Turner failed to fathom how Andy's new partner could tolerate his persistent jocularity regardless of the setting, let alone his complicated web of interconnected and interdependent personal relationships. Turner's impression from the snippets Andy had chosen to share on the subject was that he spent at least as much time being kicked out of their shared flat and breaking up as he spent making up. Not a relationship status that Turner aspired to. He instead sought something akin to the loving perennial relationship his ageing parents were fortunate enough to share.

The anecdotal stories of the lads' relationships caused him little concern unless they translated into haphazard attendance at work. Turner was however conscious that many of his own friendship group were beginning to settle down. The mates he had grown up with since primary or secondary school were all gradually entering more committed long-term relationships. There seemed to have been a slow shift amongst those closest to him, from young bachelors to married family men, and he was yet to be entrained into the current.

Pulling himself back to the present and taking stock, Turner acknowledged to himself that the build was progressing smoothly and Lucy's presence was not as offensive as he had first anticipated it would be. She still largely maintained a professional distance, which Turner felt was particularly apparent in her interactions with him. Nonetheless, she had softened to the banter. Having looked shocked and uncomfortable initially, to the lads' obvious delight, she would now sometimes engage with them.

Only the day before, Turner had watched with curiosity as the motley crew appeared to linger around the cabin when they first arrived on site rather than fan out towards their respective posts. It was only when Lucy parked up and walked amongst them, that he realised they'd all vaguely been waiting for her to materialise in order to interact with her. Yet to tire of the foot jokes, Kev had called out, "Looks like you have a spring in your step today, Lucy."

Good-naturedly but in a deadpan voice, she'd replied, "Ah, more foot jokes… Take a hike".

As Kev stood apparently trying to decipher whether she was teasing or meant it, her face had lit up with genuine warmth and amusement before she'd continued, "Did you hear about the foot fight, Kev? It all kicked off."

Turner smiled. Although Lucy now bantered a bit, she couldn't bring herself to use Kev's onsite nickname. Regardless, the lads had all gleefully fallen about, doubled over with raucous laughter that seemed entirely disproportionate to the joke delivered. Before they'd recovered themselves, she'd announced with a deliberate pregnant pause inserted in the middle for dramatic effect, "Ha, I knew my foot puns would…knock your socks off."

More baying laughter had erupted around her.

"Yep, rest assured, you need pussyfoot around me no longer. Do you know why?" she'd asked, teasing as she'd scanned the assembled, delighted faces before her. "I can give as good as I get because..." Another suspenseful pause as she played to her enraptured audience. "I'm always one step ahead!"

Turner had watched with a sense of wellbeing as everyone had happily dispersed in her wake, each still chuckling to himself as they disbanded. Still smiling, Lucy had continued to the cabin but, in the moments it had taken for her to peel off her high vis and resume her post at her desk, the cool professionalism had returned.

As he contemplated this, Lucy appeared at the door.

"Good morning," she said, her mouth curving into a small smile.

"Morning," Turner replied, studying her as she shimmied out of her luminous yellow vest, with her back to him. "Did you have a good evening?" he enquired, hoping she might volunteer some snippet or detail about herself.

"Yes, fine thanks," Lucy responded as she turned round and walked over to her workspace. Busying herself with her papers, it was clear she had no intention of elaborating further and, from the focused expression on her face, nor did she look like she was about to ask Turner how he was.

Attempting to turn his attention back to his own task list for the day, he realised he was instead staring at his desk trying to make sense of his feelings around her presence. Leaving what he hoped was an appropriate amount of time for her to feel settled into the cabin for the day, he was then unable to contain the impulse any longer to try to articulate his thoughts.

Lucy still looked entirely engrossed in the task before her and yet, as he drew in a quiet breath ready to speak, she seemed to sense his intention and simultaneously raised her eyes to his face.

He smiled involuntarily. "Lucy, I don't understand how it is that you can appear wholly focussed on what you're doing and yet, almost before I know I want to say something, you look up at me with this expectant expression."

Lucy's face mirrored his own cautious smile. "I guess I'm getting used to beavering away in close proximity to you. Admittedly, it felt a bit claustrophobic in here initially, like we worked in awkward silence but…" Her voice trailed off as if she felt she was oversharing.

Turner gave a tentative nod of agreement and he continued, "I'd like to think it's now less of an awkward silence and perhaps more a cautious camaraderie. I'm not really sure how to articulate it or whether it's necessary to but, for full disclosure, I feel compelled to confess that initially I thought sharing the confines of my small cabin office with you would be difficult. At outset, I think I was almost tolerating your presence. I want to reassure you, though, that, today in particular, it's struck me that at some point over the last few weeks, I've actually come to enjoy it." He paused and, teasing, clarified, "Well, almost enjoy it."

"Erm, thanks, hardly glowing praise but, given it's the first positive observation you've made, I'll take it as a compliment." Lips curving mischievously, she continued, "For what it's worth, I too feel like we're now verging on comfortably coexisting despite the different perspectives from which we are approaching the build."

Buoyed by Lucy's response, Turner felt more praise bubbling unbidden from within. "I know it's taken a few weeks for me to acknowledge your contribution but it's only fair that you know my initial reservations started to fall away almost immediately."

Lucy inclined her head quizzically.

Encouraged, he elaborated, "I couldn't resist the temptation to look at the drawings you left on your desk at the end of your first day, the ones you had coloured in and embellished. I was expecting to be unmoved but feel now's the time to confess that, even back then, I was impressed and it caught me off-guard. I try to avoid making assumptions about people and, out of principle, am at pains to acknowledge it when I'm wrong. So, this is me acknowledging it," he said, feeling rueful. "I hovered over your designs and, well, you'd brought the buildings to life. I know you'd only made minor tweaks to the houses' appearance but they were…" He paused as he tried to find the right word. "…inspired. It also took me a good few moments to work out how you'd managed to get the glass in the windows and doors to actually look like glazing. What did you do? Get out your nail varnish?"

Lucy nodded hesitantly in response.

"Well, congratulations, it makes you truly one of us. Being on site often requires us to find ingenious ways of repurposing tools and materials to address the task at hand. I've never seen anyone on a building site with nail varnish before, let alone use it in such a resourceful way!" Little displays of initiative such as this over the preceding weeks had prompted him to think that perhaps there was a meaningful place for Lucy's practical femininity after all.

"I'm genuinely intrigued to see the full extent of your suggested modifications albeit possibly a little apprehensive at what they might entail given the potential impact they may have on the rest of us." On the one hand, he couldn't envisage her proffering any significant revelations as the architects had drawn up acceptable plans at outset. Nonetheless, if her sketches were an indication of her potential, he was beginning to find himself rooting for her.

Each day as he'd observed her at work she'd appeared studious. She'd pored over the plans and, as far as he could tell, listened attentively to what he chose to impart to her, both at the initial walk round and over the intervening period. The elevations she had coloured in were not only artistic but represented a genuine improvement to the proposed appearance, design quality and grandeur of the build and street scene.

Admittedly, her attentiveness seemed to be guarded, cloaked by a professional distance that revealed little of the underlying individual. He often found himself wondering what her background story could be.

"Don't tell the lads," he said, "as I have a reputation to uphold and don't want my opinion of any of them to go to their heads, but I have a bit of a soft spot for conscientious, dedicated and hardworking people. Each in their own way, they work hard, exactly as you do and you all deserve to succeed as a result. It denotes an equilibrium between right and wrong; those who work hard should be rewarded accordingly. Of course, I know that sadly isn't borne out in practice for all who work hard but it's uplifting when it does, and, Lucy, you clearly work hard."

"Erm, thanks," Lucy acknowledged, scanning his face with a bemused expression as if she couldn't gauge how it was intended and didn't therefore know how to respond to it.

"There's a genuine compliment in there," Turner clarified.

The issue that tempered his burgeoning positivity about Lucy was simply the aloofness she projected. It made it hard to identify with her as it was difficult to be enthusiastic and passionate about someone who so consciously controlled their emotions. Confoundingly, she seemed more at ease with the lads than with him. Turner considered himself to be emotionally intuitive, in no small part due to his mother's influence and he kept finding his brain invaded by the conundrum as to whether Lucy was devoid of obvious emotion through a desire to retain a professional distance or for some personal reason. At this rate and given she wouldn't be on site indefinitely, he also realised he likely wouldn't be given the opportunity to understand.

"Lucy, if I'm completely honest, perhaps I've been a bit unfair to you. I liked having the freedom to run Oakland Walk as I wanted but I'm conscious that isn't cause for resenting your presence here. Like me, you've been brought in to undertake a role and, if I was in any way obstructive or unhelpful, that's counterproductive and I apologise."

Privately, he also recognised that presenting barriers would only serve to extend the length of her contract as it would take her proportionately longer to draw her own conclusions about the build and present and implement her recommendations. The sooner she could complete her scope of work, the sooner he could return to focussing on his own. His mind yo-yoed. Conversely, perhaps having her on site for longer would be no bad thing. His mouth ran away with him, voicing the thoughts he had intended to keep to himself.

"It's strange having a female presence here and it's altered the dynamic, at least for me anyhow. With every additional day that passes, I find myself gravitating more towards our shared first-floor office than the ground floor canteen I've always previously preferred to inhabit with the other lads." The colour rose in Lucy's cheeks as he spoke.

It was disorientating to find that a space he had previously had to himself, but often chosen to abandon in favour of the company downstairs, could feel welcoming and that the addition of Lucy, instead of being cloying, was comforting. He liked the subtle aroma of her feminine scent that would envelop him as he entered the cabin. He definitely preferred it over the loud, bantering lads and the musty wet dog smell of their steaming clothes drying in their breaks as they sheltered from the elements. Unable to say he liked the scent of her and reluctant to appear too effusive given his previous comment had already made her blush, he settled for a more neutral observation.

"Without the mess of heaped up dirty crockery, discarded teabags and all manner of food containers, crisp packets, chocolate wrappers and high energy drink cans, the cabin feels like a haven of calm."

As he spoke, Turner realised his desire to be one of the boisterous lads was dissipating in recognition of the more formal, detached but somehow still softer ambience she fostered. It was unnerving that, despite its austere furnishings, the cabin suddenly felt more inviting. However he dissected his conflicting thoughts, he inevitably concluded each time that Lucy was the indirect trigger for this dichotomy between his emotions.

Her soft, teasing voice pierced his thoughts, "So, to summarise, it sounds like you're saying everyone likes a bit of strange." Lucy left the words hanging in the air.

Turner struggled to find an appropriately witty response, wondering whether a slight hint of suggestion lingered in the space between them.

Unable to conjure a suitable reply, they fell back into what Turner considered a somewhat awkward silence. The irony of having explained to Lucy that he now found working in companionable silence with her enjoyable instead of uncomfortable was that he seemed to have successfully made it so again. He kicked himself. Ordinarily, he'd seize on such an opening to make a light, suggestive quip that could be interpreted however the recipient so chose. Lucy however tended to show so little emotion, reveal so little of herself to him, that it was difficult to know where to pitch a reply.

In the silence that ensued, Turner surveyed the room. If he were to attempt some Freudian interrogation of what little Lucy displayed of her personal attributes, he might conclude her desk hinted at her persona. It was an organised semi-chaos of books, post-it note thoughts, observations and reminders scrawled in her barely legible, but somehow still patently feminine, handwriting. Whenever he would try to steal glances in her direction, it was apparent that she had a system. Admittedly, whilst not clear to him what it was, she seemed to instantaneously lay her fingers on whatever snippet of paper she wanted at any given moment.

Hoping she wasn't aware that he would often surreptitiously observe her, from doing so, he was sure there was a pattern to the pen colours she used too. She had a collection of gel pens in every shade and there appeared to be a theme or a code associated with which colours she used to somehow facilitate the visual consolidation of her thoughts. There was no unnecessary sifting or rustling of documents, no frustrated sighs as she sought anything. She exuded a quiet confidence in her professional ability and projected an aura of academia. For some reason, however, this self-assurance didn't seem to translate into her interactions with him. Her teasing comment that 'everyone likes a bit of strange' had been a notable exception, like the barrier had momentarily slipped before quickly being lifted back into place.

Lucy represented a convergence of juxtapositions and he found his thoughts spiralling back on themselves as he contemplated her. Refocussing his attention on her professional involvement, her thoughts on the builds would be beneficial. Maybe he was doing her a disservice in having originally hoped they would be creditworthy simply because she warranted success. Having just subjected her to his stream of consciousness, he'd concluded her recommendations would in fact have objective merit in their own right. At the very least, from what he had nonchalantly observed to date, he was confident they would be well reasoned and the culmination of much careful consideration.

He could also accept that the pair of them weren't in competition with each other. He had no need to see her as a rival. Moreover, being witness to her focussed approach encouraged him to redouble his own efforts. Whilst he was comfortable that he was successful, he was becoming aware of an embryonic desire to achieve more and surmised this was again the influence of her presence.

On a personal level, though, Lucy had an uncanny ability to make him feel both uncomfortable and at ease. Unwittingly, she helped focus his mind and, at the same time, cloud it. It had been so long since he had gravitated around a woman. He could count on one hand the number of times anyone of the opposite sex had visited this project, or indeed any previous ones, during the build phase. Beyond his parents' habitual 'pre-construction' and 'build-complete' site visits, as they enjoyed seeing the before and after, he couldn't think of another female having visited aside from prospective buyers as the projects neared completion.

Deep down, he knew the lack of women in his life was not a question of his aesthetics; reasonably good looking, a decent muscular body, relatively affluent and with sufficient scope for career progression to be able to support someone. He was just always so focussed on his work or at least had not yet met anyone who warranted the change of pace. His work also just so happened to be in an environment where he almost never crossed paths with anyone female.

Ironically, the more time that had elapsed, the more selective he'd become. Having decided not to pursue other women previously, he would then talk himself out of chasing the next one who came along too precisely because he had elected not to break his pattern of behaviour for the one before. It was not a question of lack of opportunity. Women were often bold enough to make their advances but he couldn't bring himself to compromise for anyone other than the right one. He had had his fun but predominantly with encounters that were transactional in nature, defined by mutual satisfaction and enjoyment. Largely on his part, polite disengagement then followed so as to ensure no one would develop feelings he wouldn't or couldn't reciprocate. Now, though, he wanted something meaningful or not at all. Of course, he wasn't yet convinced that Lucy was any different from those who had gone before. Nonetheless, her mere continuity in his day-today life and that he, on some level, liked that continuity, was confusing.

Moreover, he was sure they sometimes shared a moment and he was gutted again that he'd not capitalised on her 'bit of strange' comment. Unless he was imagining it, on occasion, a palpable sexual tension seemed to permeate the confines of the cabin. He resolved to contrive to enquire about her relationship status, trying to persuade himself it was because of nothing more than a friendly interest.

Turner brought his gaze back to his own desk and wearily rubbed his eyes. He had slept poorly as all of these thoughts had swirled around inside his head and he wasn't convinced that seeking to articulate them to Lucy had helped. Attempting to heed the advice he had imparted to the lads countless times previously about leaving their personal lives at the site entrance, he wasn't convinced he could achieve this. After all, at some point during his internal toing and froing, the apparent source of his turmoil had made one mildly suggestive remark. Whilst she was now quietly concentrating at her desk just two paces from him, his mind was instead in overdrive.

His eyes focussed back in on Lucy over their desks as she also again happened to look up and meet his gaze. Another hesitant but genuine smile curled the corner of her mouth and radiated from her eyes.

"Turner, have you got a minute please?"

Hoping she might be about to reveal something of herself or expand on his comments, he nodded.

"My ideas for the site are gradually coming together and, before I progress any further with them, I would really appreciate your opinion. You're the expert and, although I think I have some reasonable proposals, I'd value your guidance. Would you mind please?"

Probably for the first time since they had been working together, Turner beamed openly at her. Whilst it wasn't necessarily the subject he'd wanted her to broach, at least she was initiating conversation. "Yes, of course, I'd be happy to. Your desk or mine?" he semi-teased.

In answer, Lucy spread the plans on her own desk, and Turner thought he detected a hint of a blush creeping up her neck and across her pale cheeks as he walked round to her.

"So we're looking at the plans from the same perspective..." he uttered as he pulled his chair up alongside hers. Feeling bold, he positioned it somewhat closer to hers than was necessary. In reality, he was more than capable of reading plans upside down, backwards etc. but, if she found his justification unconvincing, she was either too polite to comment or perhaps, he found himself hoping, not averse to the physical proximity.

"I've been through various iterations of the houses' layout and I'm keen to make some quite significant changes assuming you agree that they would work."

Turner had of course already confessed to sneaking a look at some of these but, not wanting to deter her, made a conscious effort to hold his tongue, to instead listen and encourage her to continue.

"Firstly, I'd like to make the kitchen, which is currently shown at the front of the house, into a snug or playroom and move the kitchen into one side of the rear room to create an open-plan contemporary kitchen and dining living area. To maximise the appeal of this new room, I propose swapping the window and patio doors for bi-folds that stretch the full width of the rear of the building and overlook the enclosed rear garden.

"It's not my area of expertise by any stretch of the imagination," she said with genuine modesty, "however it looks from the working drawings like the intention is to house the boiler in a kitchen unit. This means a kitchen unit is forfeited and that the units would all need to be deeper along the end wall so that they align with the depth of the boiler. Would it therefore be possible to relocate the boiler to a void under the stairs? I realise the ground-floor WC is beneath the stairs so already uses some of this space but I assume the ascending treads of the stairs would mean that the ceiling height reduces on a diagonal in line with the stairs. If the back wall of the WC is positioned where the head clearance reduces, presumably a cupboard could be created on the reverse side of the back wall to make use of the void beneath the lower stair treads."

Turner, kicking himself for not having already conceived of such a beneficial and easy to implement change, nodded. "Absolutely, that's a great idea! Building regulations dictate how steep, or otherwise, staircases in new builds can be. The size the treads are required to be and the depth of those treads means there'd be plenty of space to accommodate the boiler if we're clever about it."

"Yay." Lucy smirked. "If that space could be accessed from the new snug," she continued, as she trailed her finger over the plans, "the boiler could go in there." Indicating the void under the stairs, she elaborated, "We would then reclaim full use of the tall unit in the kitchen, which would otherwise have been sacrificed to the boiler."

As Lucy spoke, she pulled out a pad of graph paper on which she had drawn the proposed new layout.

Turner was struck by her attention to detail as he observed, "It's to scale," with a nod of approval.

A small smile of pleasure curved her mouth as he repositioned himself in his seat, inching yet nearer to Lucy. He was now close enough that he thought he could sense the warmth radiating from her legs and body. He felt alert to her, hairs standing on end and skin electric to the potential touch. The soft floral scents of her hair and perfume permeated his senses. He had to make a conscious effort to avoid flaring his nostrils in an attempt to more deeply inhale her essence.

Lucy became more animated, he surmised buoyed by his enthusiasm. He found it endearing, infectious even, as they both leant in closer.

She continued, "I notice the airing cupboard at the top of the stairs, created by the stair bulkhead, opens onto the upstairs landing. It's a good use of the space but, if we could close off the existing opening and place it on the other side of the cupboard, it would lead into the master bedroom instead. With only a very slight tweak to the layout of the master bedroom, which would just involve stealing a nominal amount of its space, we could then market the house as having a master with walk-in wardrobe. This would also save any future homeowners from trying to finish the room by planning freestanding or built-in wardrobes. They would instead already have use of all that space over the stairs. It would really help create a high-end sophisticated feel.

"Additionally," she continued, without pausing to draw beath and sounding genuinely excited, "I would like to create an ensuite against the external wall of the master bedroom. It only needs to be narrow with a toilet at one end, shower cubicle at the other and a sink opposite the centralised door. Although the space would be small, we could make it feel larger and open it up with a sun tunnel in the roof."

Turner was impressed. He had had his reservations but all of Lucy's proposals would make the houses more desirable and without having too great an impact on the financials or build schedule. He was suddenly acutely aware that she had his complete attention, not just intellectually as she strategized about the build and his brain followed, but that of his body too. He registered his physical proximity to her. His groin tightened at the occasional inadvertent caress of her legs or arms as she gesticulated and fidgeted in her seat with her dynamism.

With his head bowed, his eyes swept from the pad she had drawn on up her delicate hands, along her feminine arms, over her perfect chest and up to her gleaming blue eyes framed by her naturally long lashes. He was enraptured. In trying to read her, he was also vaguely aware that they were mirroring each other with their body language; in the same position as they sat close, heads lowered conspiratorially.

They continued swapping ideas in this manner, bouncing enthusiastically off each other as Lucy outlined her thoughts and they mulled them over together, discussing the pros and cons. He could happily have stayed in this moment for the rest of the day.

Suddenly the cabin door swung open, shattering the intimacy in an instant. Both their heads whirled round to face the door. Turner was sure his was the picture of guilt for being interrupted in this private moment. He felt like a hormonal teenager when his parents had walked into his room while he'd had a girlfriend over. The suited man standing before them was a stranger, silhouetted by the sunlight shining behind him and through the open cabin door. Incredulous, Turner wondered for a split second how Lucy could have bewitched him to such an extent that he hadn't even heard the man's footsteps ascending the stairs.

As he made to stand, he caught sight of Lucy's expression in his peripheral vision. She looked bewildered, her contagious enthusiasm of seconds beforehand evaporated completely, an ashen mask in its place. For a fleeting moment, Turner entertained the pleasurable thought that perhaps she too felt self-conscious that a third party might witness the embryonic intimacy forming between them. But it was more than that. She looked like she had seen a ghost.

In the protective hope of affording her a few seconds to recover herself, Turner outstretched a hand in greeting towards the stranger. Arrogant and obnoxious, the stranger made no attempt to shake it and instead looked right through him at Lucy.

"Hi, baby," he announced a little too loudly and clearly overcompensating. "I heard you'd secured a contract, project managing a build, and had to satisfy my curiosity with my own eyes. And here you are in your luxury first-floor office," he continued, eyes scanning the room and voice dripping with condescension.

"How the mighty have fallen now you're no longer basking in my light. My little Lucy – who had never before even contemplated heading north of Watford – reduced to scrabbling around for work on a building site in Birmingham. Fear not," he bulldozed on, "I've trekked to this parochial backwater to tell you I miss you, it was a mistake to leave, and I'd like you to forget it all happened and return to London with me." These words were delivered with a complete absence of emotion.

He'd spoken them so perfunctorily that Turner almost expected him to tick each point off on his fingers.

Turner bristled. The intruder projected an air of contemptuous arrogance and the withering look that accompanied his tone angered him. *What a dick!* Turner couldn't imagine any woman reacting positively to such a misogynistic, patronising approach, least of all Lucy. He pulled his indignant stare from the new man's face to contemplate hers. He fully expected a calmly delivered put down from her, much as he and the other lads had come to anticipate from her in response to their friendly teasing. Conversely, for someone who had to date displayed very little emotion and seemed quietly confident in her abilities, she appeared frozen in place. Any retaliatory words he'd expected her to utter had dried up on her soft inviting pink lips, with her cowed into silence by this obnoxious individual's presence. It was uncomfortable watching her stricken face as she wrestled to regain her composure.

"Hello, Mark," she stuttered, eyes reluctantly and almost deferentially lifting to meet his.

When she offered nothing further, and Mark continued to effectively tower over her, with her semi-cowering in her seat, Turner felt a pang of possessiveness, a confounding desire to protect her like one would a wounded helpless animal. The confident, self-assured Lucy had dissolved into a fragile being in the presence of this overbearing man. The petite delicate frame he was coming to realise he found so attractive suddenly seemed even smaller and more fragile as a result of the way this Mark seemed to use his size and presence to usurp her.

Turner stepped between them to break Mark's fixated stare. "Mark, I'm Turner. I'm the site manager and we don't encourage unannounced visitors on the premises. It is after all, and as you've clearly noticed, a functioning building site. Perhaps you could make an appointment with Lucy for a more mutually convenient time."

Curtly, Mark retorted, whilst continuing to stare through Turner at where Lucy was sitting, "I don't need an appointment to see my girlfriend. Step aside."

Caught off guard by this assertion, Turner was unsure what to do or say next when a cautious and submissive voice behind him almost inaudibly uttered, "Ex".

The irritation in Mark's voice was apparent, "Damn it, where's your voice, Lucy?" Mark's tone and the volume at which he spoke was unjustified in the small space.

The air in the cabin had gone from cosy to claustrophobic. Torn between this unexpected desire to shield Lucy, and the knowledge that – once she'd recovered her composure – she likely wouldn't thank him for intervening given she usually came across as the sort of independent woman who fought her own battles, Turner hovered. His eyes flitting from Mark to Lucy and back.

Composing herself, Lucy brushed herself down with a sweeping motion across her waist and over her hips. Seemingly finding her strength, she repeated, "Ex-girlfriend." And, hesitantly, "This is neither the time nor the place. However, as far as I recall, you left me, not the other way around. You poisoned our colleagues with your chauvinistic tales and ensured anyone who wanted to cling to even just a shred of dignity would be obliged to move on. I've found a good job, it could be the beginning of a successful career in property and," with the confidence growing in her voice, "I'm no longer going to bend to your will. I won't come to your beck and call. I'm no longer the naïve graduate you overawed and manipulated all that time ago, moulding me into your personal plaything and then discarding me when I had served your purpose. You tired of me because I no longer satiated you or kept you entertained in the same way I'd done when you first pursued me. Once you'd secured the attractive intelligent and green graduate for yourself, to the braying praise of your obsequious cronies, and then relied on me as your subservient little woman keeping home for you for a period of time, you grew bored and went in search of a new conquest."

Lucy paused, casting her eyes down before glancing in Turner's direction, cheeks reddening. He felt for her, being obliged to have this conversation at all let alone with Turner standing awkwardly in earshot.

Turning back to Mark and taking a deep breath, she simply continued, "I can't see that your presence here on site is constructive and think it would be best if you were to please leave."

"Don't be ridiculous, baby, you're overreacting! I've come all this way today for you, to make things good between us. You know it wasn't my fault. You made me leave with your jealousy and insecurity. You brought our break-up on yourself but I can see now that we're perfect for each other. Be reasonable, you'll never find anyone as good as me and yet, here I am, ready to take you back home."

In a firm but quieter voice, Lucy met his stare, "No, Mark, we no longer share a home. I'm making Birmingham my home now. In fact, I have house viewings booked. I'm going to set down roots here, buy my own home and on my own terms. This is a conscious decision and it's one just for me. It's not to get away from you. Instead, it's purely for me. This is where I want to be. I'm sorry, Mark."

Turner was irate to hear her apologise but proud that she had found her voice. From Mark's perplexed expression, it could conceivably be the first time she had stood up to him in this way and he lacked the empathy to be able to process the slight.

"From here on, I'm going to stand on my own two feet!"

Turner's immediate impulse was to want to draw attention to the use of another foot-related expression but he quietly suppressed the temptation. In fact, he considered that, although Mark would be blissfully unaware of the significance of the foot reference, perhaps Lucy's message was in part aimed at Turner too. Hoping he was sufficiently in tune with her meaning, he heeded it as a warning not to step in. Then came the realisation that he felt disproportionately elated to learn that Lucy would be making Birmingham her home. Until a few moments prior, he hadn't even appreciated it wasn't already her home but suddenly, the revelation that she intended to be here long-term, left him feeling imbued with the potential for an ongoing relationship of some form.

The sensation was rapidly followed with one of incandescent rage that this suited punk could invade his domain and make Lucy squirm before him. He felt something else too, an unconstructive and surprising stab of jealousy that this arrogant idiot had ever been Lucy's boyfriend, the object of her affection, intimate with her.

"Mark, I think we've heard enough," he said authoritatively. "We don't condone intimidation of any form on site so, unless Lucy feels otherwise, I echo her sentiment that it's time for you to leave. I can't for a second fathom why she'd want to contact you but I'm sure Lucy knows how to if she were to want to."

Ignoring Turner, Mark aimed his departing words at Lucy. "Lucy, this is the only time I'll come for you. Most women would jump at this opportunity to reconcile. Leave with me now or accept you've missed your chance."

For an awkward drawn-out moment, Turner and Mark studied Lucy's expression. Turner willed her to categorically reject Mark, to put him firmly back in his place. From the expression on Mark's face, he was hoping for the opposite. *Surely he's delusional!*

To Turner's relief, muted but with conviction, Lucy carefully enunciated each word, "Thank you for coming, Mark, but goodbye."

"Whatever, Lucy. You were never really good enough for me anyway." With that childish parting shot, he turned and slammed the cabin door closed, leaving Lucy and Turner in stunned silence.

Unsure how to process the swirling emotions, Turner uttered in as measured a tone as he could muster, "Why did you apologise to that monumental twat? If this is where you want to make your home, it sounds like he's the last person to deserve a say in that. Never feel the need to apologise for what you want."

He met Lucy's gaze and, perceiving bewilderment there and the threat of tears, he made an effort to redirect the rage he had felt towards Mark away from her. He tentatively said, "Lucy, someone who is very special to me and conveniently fond of quotes and motivational vignettes and, incidentally would be appalled by my crass foot jokes, would know what to say here. I have no doubt she would put this far more eloquently and convincingly than I can but would nonetheless tell you not to let a dick like him determine your story. Actually," he corrected himself, swiping the word away with a wave of his hand, "she wouldn't say dick but the sentiment rings true because she would be encouraging you to take centre stage. Be the heroine of your story not a supporting role in the narrative someone else has chosen for you." Turner cast a glance around the room. "In fact, she too used to work out of an office a bit like this one and pinned to the noticeboard next to her computer there was a calligraphy typed card with a mantra credited to Melinda Gates: 'A woman with a voice is, by definition, a strong woman. But the search to find that voice can be remarkably difficult'."

Awkward, he raked his fingers through his dark hair. "Fuck, I'm struggling here, Lucy. This isn't the sort of workplace issue I'm accustomed to navigating. I'm used to someone getting cement in their eye or nail gunning a finger," he said, trying to lighten the mood. "I don't want to make this any more uncomfortable for you than it already is and I could have completely the wrong impression here but I'm going to give you some advice if you'll let me."

Lucy gave a barely perceptible nod in acquiescence so he continued, trying to make his voice sound soft but with conviction, "The best revenge for being unappreciated, cheated on, whatever it is that happened between you two, is simply to live well from here on, in the place of your choosing with the people of your choosing."

Faltering, listless and with no sign that she had even heard him, Lucy finally stood and stepped towards the kitchenette. She paused aimlessly but in easy touching distance. Swift and unthinking, Turner pulled her straight into his arms as if it were the most natural thing in the world, something they had done many times before rather than being their first embrace. He enveloped her, cautiously pulling her small frame and temporarily fragile soul towards his chest. He was shielding her from the unpleasantness both physically and emotionally. She tensed at the contact and he thought she might pull away. With conscious effort, he stilled, keeping his stance steady but loosening the pressure of his grasp, allowing her to choose. To his relief, she yielded, moulding herself to his torso and seeking comfort from him as she rested her head on his chest. There they stood, pressed tightly against each other, her jagged breath softly warming his torso through his clothing and giving him goosebumps. He hoped she found the embrace as comforting as he found it sensual.

Turner tried to focus his attention on Lucy's quivering, gulping breaths as she fought to regain her composure. He was also uncomfortably aware of his arousal, willing himself not to harden further with the intimate proximity and this unplanned, somewhat unexpected and, at least in that moment, inconvenient attraction to her. With her body pressed firmly into his, her hair tickling his chin and the alternating warmth and cooling of her breath spreading across his chest, in that instant, she felt bewitchingly feminine.

As Turner continued to try to keep his breathing regular, willing his erection to subside, softly, almost apologetically, Lucy spoke. "If it's alright with you, I don't want to talk about this now please. Mark is from my past. Admittedly my recent past but that's where I want him to remain. Maybe I need to articulate it, get it all out in the open to get some closure and feel ready to move on, but I'm not sure whether you're the right person to bare my soul to. I'd like, therefore, please to be allowed to view him as a figure fading ever farther into irrelevance when I choose to cast a glance in my life's rear-view mirror."

Whilst curious to hear Lucy's account of her relationship with the complete douchebag he'd just encountered, Turner was relieved. He preferred to focus on the delightful, gentle vibrations her muffled voice had sent through his chest as she spoke whilst leaning into him. Having seen Lucy's emotions laid bare for a few excruciating minutes, he was now acutely aware he wanted to know more of her and had limited desire to hear about his competition – past or present. His impression, however, was that, first and foremost, she needed a friend to trust and lend an ear. If anything, her having Mark for an ex-boyfriend would help him understand and dissect her demeanour a bit better. That Lucy seemed to maintain this barrier, only letting her guard down occasionally and when animated about the build, suddenly felt easier to reconcile. She was fresh from an unhealthy relationship. Silver lining; it might not mean that she wasn't interested in him and instead she was just fearful of falling for the wrong person again. He gave her a little squeeze of acknowledgement with a faint tightening of his arms circling her diminutive frame and then very deliberately instructed himself to release her.

The moment passed, bringing him back to the disorientating reality of standing in the cabin, as Lucy disengaged herself from his embrace. Turner was flooded with relief as she raised her piercing eyes to his – the blue accentuated in the light. The alternative would have been much more uncomfortable. Scanning down over his body would have left her in no doubt as to the physical effect she had on him, the traitorous bulge in his trousers altering his silhouette.

She looked as if she might say something, appeared to then think better of it and instead uttered an artificially jovial and aloof, "I'm going to head off early today. After all, you've now heard most of my ideas for the build and the rest are documented in the drawings and accompanying annotations on my graph paper. From these, please pass your recommendations to the Board as to which of my suggestions should be pursued. Once whatever you and they consider of merit has been approved, I'll set to work securing the relevant approval from the Planners, formal drawings from the architect, designs for the newly created kitchen and master ensuite and so on. In the meantime, although Mark eclipsed me as always and stole my thunder on it, I'm going to see a property this afternoon. It's a project, but one for me to live in and, in time, hopefully call home."

Thrown by the intimacy of the previous few moments being again replaced by the descent of Lucy's professional detached façade, devoid of emotion, Turner mumbled an "Oh, okay, good luck."

Lucy immediately set to collecting her things together then headed for the door. Turner watched her progress, reflecting on the momentary insight into her personal life as he did so. Having witnessed the depth of her emotions and grappling with the sudden realisation that she was of growing significance in his day to day, he was struck by how their first-floor office somehow shrunk as she left it. It felt oppressive, confined and hostile, having been tainted by the encounter with Mark. Turner had however held her as a result, the soft curves of her body shaped delectably to the muscular angles of his own. In that instant, it dawned on him that he wanted, needed and desired to be around her more. For now, though, the cabin was again shrouded in silence. Surreal.

CHAPTER 5

Lucy was conscious she had bolted from the cabin and site, almost tripping over her own feet in her mortified haste to leave. Just as she had been softening towards Turner, Mark had exploded into the room as if he'd had some sixth sense about her flutter of interest in another man, then had undermined and humiliated her. She chastised herself for having been so naïve as to think he wouldn't have popped up when his enthusiasm for whichever other female he was now pursuing had begun to wane.

It was characteristic of Mark and his ego to think he could literally crash back into her life, arrogantly present himself as her bigoted saviour and expect her to emotionally give way at the knees. Typically, he'd assumed that she would drop the new beginnings she was going to great lengths to make a success of and flee back to London with him, her tail between her legs. She still felt rattled and embarrassed. She and Turner had been on the same wavelength with the builds, sharing their work, their visions and perhaps something more. She found herself hoping that connection might return, maybe even develop further, with the benefit of more time together on site. After all, she could do with a friend, particularly given that she was planning to remain in the Midlands and the only people she knew up here were the burly crew on site. Whilst she now enjoyed interacting with them all, she couldn't envisage them becoming long-term friends or inviting them over to her future home but, for some reason, she felt like she perhaps could with Turner.

Maybe she had compromised that too though by seeking solace from him after Mark had left. Feeling traumatised by the intrusion and subsequent exchange, a momentary lapse in judgment meant she had turned to him, the site manager and arguably her superior at her new job, the job she so desperately wanted to make a success of and turn into a career. *Have I learnt nothing from the fiasco with Mark?* The culmination of allowing the boundaries between her personal and professional lives to collide had resulted in the cataclysmic implosion of both with him. Blindly following a similar path with Turner would be foolhardy, not least given that her first glimpses of construction suggested it to be a far more male-dominated industry than the City one she'd left. Somehow it felt less hostile though. Yes, the lads teased mercilessly but there was an open, warm cheeriness about it. Initially, she'd been taken aback but she had soon realised there was no malice to it and no one individual got singled out for teasing. Everyone was fair game for the jibes.

Despite the turmoil, she found her mind wondering who this special woman was that Turner had been referring to. Maybe a girlfriend, past or present. He hadn't mentioned one but why would he blur their professional boundaries by doing so. Yes, he had awkwardly tried to come up with something to say to comfort her but that might just have been out of a sense of courtesy. Perhaps he had been in a relationship with a work colleague before. After all, he had implied this significant individual apparently worked in an environment like the cabin. Maybe they'd met on a previous project, had worked in close proximity to each other like Lucy and Turner were now doing and romance had blossomed. Perhaps they were still together. Lucy hadn't mentioned Mark to Turner before so it was conceivable that Turner had omitted personal details of his own too.

Regardless, for a moment, Lucy had felt safe, secure, protected in Turner's arms and yet now she was scurrying to her car willing the ground to open and swallow her up. Her reliable silver Yaris called to her like an overshadowed beacon amongst the scattered commercial vans parked in spaces or bounced up on kerbs. She fought to dispel the barrage of thoughts clouding her mind. If anything, Mark bursting in had made one thing blatantly clear. Birmingham, working on new builds, the cabin – all of it – in just a short time, had become her territory. She hadn't appreciated that she was coming to value this new place, grow attached to it until Mark had suggested she leave with him. She realised it wasn't just that she didn't want to leave with Mark, she simply didn't want to leave. In fact, this Midlands town (which she uncomfortably acknowledged she would have at one stage considered to be in the north, given its location relative to London), was conversely beginning to feel comfortingly familiar. Like her town, her home...

As she drove, her thoughts dovetailed into the upcoming viewing. If her break from her past were to be complete, she needed to sell the flat they had shared in London. Although Lucy had owned it before Mark had been on the scene, it reminded her of him and all the negative emotions associated with that period and their subsequent break-up. Despite this, she hadn't felt strong enough to sell it until now. She realised she had been keeping it as a safety net so that her Plan B could be to scuttle back to her bolt hole in London if she hadn't been able to make a success of Birmingham. Suddenly, the decision to sell felt easy. With Central London house prices soaring, even her relatively bijoux ex-local authority first-floor flat in South Bermondsey would release her the capital to acquire something with material potential in Birmingham's conurbation.

She had no real friends locally outside work and, at best, Turner as her one friend in work. In the absence of friends and the welcome distraction they might be, she had instead been spending the evenings in her temporary, characterless rented flat, scouring the internet for somewhere to buy. The only two familiar items in this space were the bed and mirror she had moved with, taunting her with reminders of her past. She now couldn't wait to leave them behind in this interim accommodation once she had identified somewhere of her own. As her confidence on site at Oakland Walk grew, so did her conviction that the property she sought would be a project.

Nearing the property she was en route to, she felt increasingly optimistic that it would be perfect. For less than the value of her two-bedroom flat in London, which by happy coincidence was located within sight of the recently finished Shard and had consequently soared in value, she had identified a pair of semi-detached houses for sale that sat on a large plot. Within the boundary of each house's garden, she was optimistic of securing planning permission for the construction of a further detached house. As such, in time, she intended to refurbish and extend the existing two houses, making one her home in the process, and then subsequently turn her attention to securing planning for and then building two new-build properties either side.

Pulling up outside, she instantaneously knew they were exactly what she was looking for. Although located on a busy trunk road, they were set back from it, with the short, shared tarmacked driveway shrouded by rhododendrons and all manner of varied vegetation and flowers. The two houses were non-descript. With veiled delight, she noticed that the trees in the overgrown and neglected front garden were largely native species. Somewhat less joyously, she could see the tarmac of the drive had cracked irregularly as it had settled but this somehow imbued the image with a certain charm.

As she stared at the dated pair of buildings nestled in the centre of the plot on Sunnyside Road, she could see they bore the scars of their 1960s origins. Having already quizzed the agents at length over the telephone, she knew the houses had been neglected by their previous ageing occupants. They had then remained vacant after their owners' deaths whilst their children, preoccupied with their own lives, had left the solicitors to gradually tick through probate. At one time, though, the houses had been loved; mother and father in one and spinster daughter occupying the smaller one next-door. Although now desperately overgrown, this was evident from the thoughtful configuration of the gardens. Despite the plants now choking the site, she pictured how the elderly couple might together have lovingly tended to and restrained them at one time.

Studying the facades, she realised the exterior of the ground floor wasn't made of brick as such but instead was clad in concrete, moulded into shapes to resemble bricks projecting from mortar. Both had a sorry porch over their front doors. The exterior of the first floor was covered in a mildewed white render that had dirtied over time with the effect of rain and grime. The smaller house, which formed the left side of the building when looking at it from her vantage point on the roadside, was a three bedroom with a pitched tile roof. The larger side of the semi was a five bedroom with an unsightly flat roof. Both houses had matching rectangular bay windows projecting from the front elevation and to the side of their respective front doors.

Lucy didn't even need to leave her car let alone step inside either of the houses to know she would love them. From the online listing, she knew the houses were dated, the interiors a neglected retro finish that suggested they had remained unaltered since they were first built some sixty years prior. The key was their potential. With the skills she was honing at Oakland Walk and from beforehand as a result of having done up her London flat, she could see what her new house would look like. The reality before her, nestled amongst the overgrown flora of the front garden, bore little resemblance to the home in her mind's eye. Where she had initially struggled to picture the finished effect at Oakland Walk when she had first arrived on site, she experienced no such difficulty here.

Excited, she re-conjured her mental image of what her home's layout would be. With a cursory greeting to the agent as she hopped out of her car, she trotted up the drive and crossed the threshold, silently praying it would be structurally sound and that the dimensions and its stripped-back shell would accommodate her plans. *Play it cool, Lucy* she thought to herself. *Downplay your interest.* Walking over the scarred carpets from tired room to tired room, she saw through the chipped paint and dated décor to the sturdy house beneath.

The walls were decorated in a retro and dated swirling wallpaper with artex ceilings. This theme continued to the kitchen, where dark varnished wood units were mounted on two sides of the room. The appliances here appeared to have been added more recently than the rest of the house. The tiled floor, however, was scuffed with years of tread, faded and slightly concave along the main thoroughfare from the back door. She came back out into the hall, eyes scanning up the stairs and already mentally installing an understairs WC where a storage cupboard was currently positioned.

Eagerly, she approached the near vertically steep stairs to the first floor with the treads creaking wearily as she scampered up them two at a time in her enthusiasm. Almost subconsciously, she noted that the gradient of the stairs would likely no longer pass building regulations if they were installed like this in a new build. The observation made her realise Turner had permeated more of her professional and personal psyche than she was inclined to acknowledge.

On the first floor of the larger home, there was a bathroom at the top of the stairs with a maroon suite and electric shower over the bath. The walls were adorned with cracked peach-coloured tiles with a wall heater with exposed element and pull cord mounted on one. It reminded her of childhood visits to her grandparents' old home; the heater being of the kind that would smell of burning dust when turned on and make an unexplained but persistent ticking sound as it cooled after use, element slowly fading from a glowing orange back to a tarnished metallic grey.

The landing split into two directions at the top, with two bedrooms off to the right, two bedrooms to the left and a box bedroom back round the landing and over the front porch area. She would sacrifice this box room to create stairs to give access into a loft conversion that would fit beautifully into the space formed by lifting the flat roof and replacing it with a pitched one. It seemed entirely logical to extend into that space to follow the line of the smaller house's roof next-door. Additionally, the small bedroom to the right of the stairs, would be replaced by an ensuite. Given it shared a wall with what would become her master bedroom, in doing so, one entire side of the house would become her master.

The bedroom itself would be at the front of the house, overlooking the drive, road and neighbouring properties beyond. She performed a contented pirouette in the centre of the master bedroom, already picturing the room as it would be rather than allowing her gaze to focus on the tired, dusty surroundings in which she stood. In future, she would pass through a walk-in wardrobe across the width of the room to enter her decadent ensuite with roll top bath as its focal point and a large, tiled shower enclosure to the opposite side.

With relief, she noted the house was comfortingly silent inside despite being in a residential area with a busy road to the front. The surrounding houses ran in ribbons that peeled away to its left and right with further houses nestled just beyond the rear garden boundary fence. From what would be her bedroom window, she felt the nearby properties were close enough for comfort but not so close as to leave her feeling overlooked.

Almost everything she needed to know about the houses and their potential she had gleaned from the online sales brochures and link to the satellite view. Seeing their position had crystallised the decision. This would be her home. Gung-ho though she was, as she toured the houses, opening kitchen units, looking in cupboards, examining the boiler and light switches, standing at the windows and looking up and down the street and over the rear garden, she concluded that neither house would be habitable in their current state.

She would make it work, though, instantaneously resolving in her mind to invest in a caravan, live on site until her house was habitable in some shape or form and then move in. In the meantime, her caravan could serve as her home from home, her site office and welfare unit – like the cabin at Oakland Walk – and, once it had served its purpose, she would sell the caravan on to recoup as much of her outlay as possible. It would be a compromise to spend an extended period living in a caravan, through England's variable weather, but one she would tackle willingly.

Bubbling with barely concealed enthusiasm at the possibilities, she decided to put forward an asking price offer on the houses. Ready to burst with excitement, she was keen to be able to share the news and it dawned on her that, for the first time since she had known Rachel, it wasn't her she wanted to call first. With a conscious effort, she forcefully dismissed the idea, resolving to keep him at arm's length, literally and figuratively, going forward. *Although being enveloped in his arms, our bodies pressed together…feeling his heart beating, his chest rising and falling, his muscular arms circling me… No, I'm not going to make that mistake twice* she told herself.

On returning to her sterile rental, Lucy nervously awaited the estate agents' feedback on her offer, the various possibilities and contingencies running through her head. With every fibre of her being, she willed them to call her back, thereby setting her on a new trajectory towards owning these houses and becoming a developer in her own right. Excitedly she contemplated that fulfilling their potential could, in turn, help her achieve her own.

Unable to focus on anything else as she waited for news, the seconds ticked by excruciatingly slowly. What would the existing owners' decision-making process entail and would they all be in agreement as to how to respond to her offer.

What if they were away, uncontactable and she had to wait indefinitely for their response.

With these thoughts cascading around her brain and her phone still expectantly clutched in her hand, she was interrupted by its shrill ring and simultaneous vibration.

"Great news! Your offer has been accepted," the agent's staccato voice crackled down the line, the significance of her words not quite reflected in the muted tone. Presumably she must make phone calls of this nature all the time without appreciating their potentially life-changing weight for the recipient.

"Thank you so much! That's brilliant!" Her own voice sounded almost manic with delight in comparison. She couldn't wait to get off the phone to get the wheels in motion, appoint solicitors, make plans.

The next few weeks passed in a frenzy of activity. The elation she felt at making a break from her past, embracing the idea of a challenging new project in her own right and independently of anyone else was both exhilarating and daunting. Inspired by the street name, she too would look on the sunnyside.

Joyously, her Bermondsey flat was snapped up almost immediately, its proximity to the City making it a desirable home for an over-worked employee keen to minimise travel time to and from their office-based work. Around her commitments at Oakland Walk, she oversaw the flat's sale, keen to have the transaction completed as quickly as possible to preclude the London lawyer from invading her inbox and voicemail. The unwanted contact was a persistent reminder of the life and downtrodden version of herself she was trying to leave behind. In the evenings, she waded through all of the searches and associated paperwork for the conveyancing for her houses. She drew and redrew the internal layouts she envisaged for the properties, contemplated the materials she would use, the finishes she desired and how best to approach the project.

By day, at Oakland Walk, despite making a conscious effort to personally distance herself from Turner and contriving to maintain an aura of cool professionalism, he had emphatically supported her proposals for the builds with the Board. He had made it clear that the ideas were Lucy's, that she deserved full credit for them and every suggestion had been painstakingly but unanimously approved. To that end, she spent her days focussed at her desk in the cabin liaising with designers, architects, structural engineers, planning consultants, suppliers and more to ensure her modifications could be implemented with the least inconvenience to Turner and his on-site team. For his part, Turner seemed keen to try to engage with her on topics that reached beyond Oakland Walk. Each day, he'd punctuate their conversation about the builds with a subtly probing more personal question.

"Did you get up to much at the weekend?"

"Have you made any new friends up here?"

"Are you out tonight?"

Fortunately, how preoccupied Lucy was with the details for the build provided a ready justification for deflecting the attempts he made to broach any subject beyond their shared work. Although she was outwardly belying her burgeoning feelings for him, her inner resolve was weaker. To combat the fact that her willpower to keep him at a distance was wavering and to indirectly acknowledge the professional support he gave her, she channelled her energy into finalising every aspect of the tweaks she had proposed, in order to make his role as straightforward as possible. *I can't let him see that I'm catching feelings for him. If he has his suspicions, it can only be because of the lengths I've gone to to try to make his role easier, not because of any personal revelation.*

Once the groundworks had been finished and the super structure completed, Lucy marvelled as Oakland Walk took shape rapidly. With Turner expertly overseeing teams of roofers, plumbers, plasterers, tilers, electricians and then decorators, the houses progressed discernibly from one day to the next. The priority was to complete the show home but, economies of scale and having specialist trades on site, meant the other houses evolved rapidly too. Turner appeared to be in constant demand, pulled from one task to the next, required by each subcontractor simultaneously. He was perpetually moving deliveries and materials around site and with his mobile phone ringing throughout. She marvelled at how he still found seemingly quiet moments to try to engage with her. Concurrently and somewhat to her consternation, her admiration for his abilities grew.

On one such morning, Turner seemed uncharacteristically distracted.

"Turner, is everything alright?" she queried softly. Rather than a focussed but calm whirlwind of activity, he was fussing, purposelessly tidying and cleaning the cabin. In such a confined space, Lucy couldn't have failed to notice his behaviour if she were disinterested let alone given the way his presence crowded her senses; the masculine silhouette as he moved around the room dominating the space.

Still fussing and distracted, he said, "Yes... I mean, no." Flustered and pacing, he clarified. "Yes, everything is fine. I have important visitors arriving shortly. Their opinion on progress, build quality, everything, is really important to me."

Suddenly, she shared his angst. "Why haven't you mentioned this? Do I need to have prepared?" Mirroring his nerves for a moment, she raised her gaze to meet Turner's as he shook his head. "Okay, in that case, is there anything I can do to help you get ready?" she volunteered.

Before Turner could answer, a reverberation of footsteps on the cabin's external metal stairs interrupted them. A knock and two greying well-dressed adults, a man and a woman, appeared at the door. Turner embraced the upright but elderly man and then leant in to kiss the smart, matronly woman's cheek. With a sweeping motion indicating their surroundings, he said, "Welcome to Oakland Walk." Turning in Lucy's direction, he said, "Lucy, meet Prudence and Michael."

Somewhat bemused as Turner had provided no context or explanation for these two individuals' presence, her own polite smile was magnified and reflected in the warm beams on their faces.

"Mum, Dad, meet Lucy."

"Lovely to meet you, dear," Prudence responded with her open, friendly smile still in place. "We've heard a lot about you."

Lucy looked to Turner quizzically, surprised but touched that he had spoken of her.

Michael continued, "We always make a point of coming to visit Turner's sites early in the builds, somewhere in the middle and again once they're complete, so we can feel involved, picture him at work and inevitably brim with pride at his achievements."

This version of Turner, standing somewhat awkwardly at his parents' side, was at odds with the commanding and accomplished site manager she had come to know. Willing him to feel at ease despite her presence, she commented, "That's a lovely sentiment. Can I make you both a drink and then I'll make myself scarce so Turner can give you the grand tour?"

"Aw, no dear, I understand from our son that you're working together on this one and he's been very impressed by all of your input."

Lucy stared at his mum, a little surprised. She couldn't reconcile this high regard that Prudence had declared Turner held her in, with the demeanour Turner himself normally adopted around her.

Unphased, Prudence continued, "Turner has explained that you haven't been here long and that you've embraced the steep learning curve. From the way he speaks of you, it's clear you're making a valuable contribution and that you've earned his respect along the way."

In her peripheral vision, she thought Turner looked embarrassed.

Busying herself, Prudence turned towards the kitchenette. "Let's make that tea." As the kettle boiled and Turner and Michael started their own separate conversation, Prudence, in a more conspiratorial fashion said, "Eleanor Roosevelt, a woman after my own heart, once said that 'Women are like teabags. We don't know our true strength until we are in hot water'."

Lucy smiled politely. Unsure how else to react, she regarded Prudence's countenance and realised there was no prejudice, criticism or condescension in those words. Her expression instead seemed homely, open and genuine.

"I'm not sure that applies to me. In all honesty, I'm more of a juice woman." Lucy smiled. "No, in all seriousness I'm doing my best, Prudence, but would never be capable of doing what your son can. He seems so in control, so unflustered in the face of what sometimes appears to be utter chaos. He controls and oversees everything that happens on site and yet manages to be both a peer and also the boss of all these big burly lads. Each has their own views and their own role and somehow he manages to coax the best results from them and successfully ensures they all work together and around each other without incident. Although I like to think I could make a success of most things I put my mind to, I could never hope to learn those skills."

Prudence spoke through her indulgent smile. "Ah I don't know, I think you're probably stronger than you think if you're working with these lads day in day out and still here. Besides, just because they're large, practical lads, they can still respect the contrasting strength you bring."

Unwittingly opening up to the kindly older woman and revealing more of herself than she intended, Lucy shook her head. "I don't feel strong. Almost by coincidence, I've run from London, found myself here and I'm just trying to make a go of it. It's a steep learning curve; it feels very much uphill."

She thought of the mortifying exchange Turner had witnessed between her and Mark and the negative impression of her he must surely have received from that. Before she had had a chance to conclude whether Prudence was aware of that sorry incident and what Turner might have relayed to her about it, Prudence continued, "I can't take credit for this one either. I believe an anonymous but, in my view, wise, individual once said 'a strong woman knows she has strength enough for the journey, but a woman of strength knows it is in the journey where she will become strong.'"

Drawing comfort, Lucy wondered whether Prudence was referring just to the build or to Lucy's circumstances more generally. Perhaps Turner was more perceptive than she'd given him credit for, reading between the lines and gleaning more from her decision to move from London and the interaction he'd witnessed with Mark, than she'd realised.

Without leaving Lucy much opportunity to dwell and reflect, Prudence lightened the mood. "I understand you're in the process of buying a site of your own up here? A project to make your home?"

Brightening, she gushed, "Yes, I'm anxious but so excited at the prospect. The houses are wonderful. Well, actually… they're awful but they will be wonderful. In fact, it's a big day! I'm not sure how I'm managing to keep a lid on it. My purchase should be completing today. We've exchanged already so completion is pretty much a formality but I'm on tenterhooks waiting for the news."

"Congratulations!" Prudence interjected, her voice radiating warmth. "How wonderful! Turner, did you hear that?" she enquired, turning towards her son and interrupting the separate conversation between him and Michael. "Lucy's purchase should complete today!"

"Great news, congratulations!" Turner replied, catching Lucy's eye, genuine warmth and encouragement reflected on his face.

"Thank you." She smiled, before turning back towards Prudence. "I'm such a bundle of emotions. I'm anxious, elated, daunted, excited all rolled into one."

"I'm not surprised. That's entirely understandable," the older woman said softly. "Incidentally, I'm sure Turner would be glad to help you work on it."

"Oh, I'm not sure. I can't imagine he'd be that keen to help me renovate somewhere. I love their potential but the houses are in fact so awful in their current form, that I'm going to buy a caravan and get it setup in the garden so that I can live and work from there until at least part of the larger house is ready for me to move into."

Prudence turned towards Turner, again interrupting his exchange with his father, "Turner, you'd help Lucy renovate her new home wouldn't you?" Clearly, the question posed of her son was a rhetorical one and without waiting for a reply she continued, "And are you aware that Lucy is planning to live on site in a caravan, presumably alone?"

A number of emotions flitted across Turner's face. To Lucy's surprise, he almost looked enthusiastic for a moment at the prospect of helping her but his expression quickly turned incredulous as he looked aghast from his mother to Lucy and back again. Before either had a chance to comment further, Prudence turned towards the door, steaming mug of tea in hand, announcing, "Let's have the grand tour then."

Lucy remained behind in the cabin, revisiting the conversation in her head. Had Turner genuinely been keen to assist her or had he feigned so because it would be difficult to suggest otherwise in the face of his devoted mother's unwavering faith in her son's chivalry and construction-related ability. Why then had he looked so aghast; was that purely in relation to her intention of living in a caravan or was he uncomfortable at the prospect of challenging his mother's perception of him?

Regardless, Turner was then occupied showing his parents around the site and, thereafter, disappeared with them for lunch. When he returned, he was needed by everyone everywhere simultaneously and she had no further opportunity that day to broach the subject with him. On the plus side, though, a whispering voice in her head reassured her that the woman he held in such high regard and whose quotes he had used to buoy her, was in fact his mother. Prudence radiated such refreshing, unabashed friendliness. Perhaps, just maybe, there might not be a girlfriend on the scene after all.

CHAPTER 6

Turner wanted to leave site early so went to seek out Andy, whose rumbling laughter made him easy to pinpoint. As he approached, Turner heard the apprentice, Kev, tasked with shadowing Andy that day, ask, "What do you need?"

Andy guffawed. "I need a screw, Shit Nut. No worries, though," he continued as Kev turned to rifle through the plastic boxes of miscellaneous screws, nuts and bolts. "Just tell your mum I'll be over later," he boomed.

Turner smiled at his juvenile friend's guttural, infectious chuckling. The good-natured tone made it impossible to be offended and even Kev released a snort-cum-giggle in response, despite being the butt of yet another crass ribbing.

Attempting to give as good as he got, Kev retorted, "You sure it's a screw and not a nail you need?"

"I can work with either," Andy replied deadpan. Continuing, "I'll give her a good nailing too if you like. Besides, it's not about the screw or the nail, it's about the hammer you knock it in with."

"Ugh," Kev cried in mock disgust. "You're not a hammer, you're a wrecking ball!"

Inadvertently giving Andy more ammunition, the gentle giant interjected with, "Well, I've never heard your mum complain."

Turner hovered to give them an opportunity to recover themselves. "Lads, surely the mum jokes are starting to get old now.

"Andy, can I give you the keys to site please? I have some errands to run so am going to head off." As he handed the keys to Andy, mercifully his friend merely raised what appeared to be a knowing eyebrow, accepting the task rather than probing and redirecting his teasing at the boss.

As Turner strode away, his thoughts returned to the source of his desire to leave site early.   His parents had clearly liked her when they came to visit and he considered both to be a good judge of character. More significant than that, though, was the realisation that it felt particularly important to him that they like her. Technically, he and Lucy were just work colleagues and yet he had very much wanted his parents' seal of approval. Unsurprisingly, the qualities he had failed to notice at outset were apparent to his mother from the moment she'd laid eyes on Lucy.

He had relished the relative calm of a long lunch away from site with them but his elation at his parents' reactions to progress at Oakland Walk felt less significant than when his mother had commented, "Son, you're infatuated with Lucy. Either you're stubbornly ignoring that reality or just not yet ready to confide in your mother. Either way, it's obvious to me."

The thought had remained with him over the couple of days since. If he were honest with himself, what had shocked him the most was the rush of emotion he had felt at the thought of her living alone in a caravan. Lucy seemed a little apprehensive but nonetheless excited at the prospect. Turner however had been blindsided by an overwhelming concern for her safety and, with that sensation, came a powerful desire to protect her. Of course, although he tried to ignore his strength of feeling for Lucy, his mother would have known that mentioning the prospect of her living alone in a caravan would have obliged his subconscious to acknowledge that she meant more to him than a simple colleague. *Conniving woman,* he thought affectionately.

Ever supportive, Prudence never forced him to air his thoughts but would insinuate her way into them to bring them into focus for him. She wouldn't countenance a lie from him either. They both knew he made a terrible liar. The only time he had ever gotten away with lying to her was when she had taken pity on him for attempting to do so and had let it pass unchallenged, both acutely aware of the untruth but she choosing to humour him. Since then, Turner had always accepted he would have to sink or swim in the truth with his mother and she, in turn, had impressed upon him the need for absolute honesty with all women.

Obliged to face the reality of his deepening feelings for Lucy, he resolved to pay a visit to her new home. *It feels like one minute she places an offer on the houses and, the next, she's taking some leave from site to move. Fuck, I sound like the founding member of the Lucy fan club!* Nonetheless, he had to concede that, although they aimed for twenty-eight days to exchange when selling the new builds, the transactions almost always overshot this. Credit where credit's due, Lucy had achieved it and, technically, on three properties, her flat in London and the two semis.

Much as he was reluctant to admit it, he had also felt her absence from the cabin acutely over the past few days. Knowing she would be attempting to get settled at the new house, he could visit her and casually explain away the desire to do so as being a curiosity about her new project rather than an urge to see Lucy herself.

Turner already knew broadly where Lucy's new property was located, given she had shown him the listing when her endearing, childlike enthusiasm for her plans had temporarily outweighed her guardedness. He hoped the road name proved apt and representative.

Heart thumping as he drove to the address, he pondered how much he enjoyed his work as a developer. The thought however of making Lucy's designs and visions for her home into reality, rather than creating a blank canvas for a house purchaser on behalf of a largely faceless corporate entity, genuinely excited him. He had built houses, property, buildings to live in but never a home. If he could persuade her to allow him to assist, it would be both a privilege and an opportunity to gradually peel away at her layers. He couldn't tolerate the niggling concern that, if he were too slow to demonstrate how keen he was to be involved, she might appoint a different contractor, thereby giving someone else the opportunity to refurbish her home, help her set down roots and maybe even win her affection in the process.

Numbers 79 and 81 Sunnyside Road were easy to identify from the street and, as he pulled to a stop and studied them from his van, he silently praised her for having recognised their potential. To many, the crumbling exterior and neglected appearance would be off putting. Lucy, however, had only spoken of the site's potential and how amazing it would be. He admired her overt optimism.

Nonetheless, and somewhat to his surprise, he found himself imagining what it would be like at night-time. In his mind's eye, the untamed plants cast shadows across the overgrown garden with the bushes offering hiding places for anyone sinister or curious enough to be out at night. He could also picture it as people returned from work, their lights coming on inside, the comfort and warmth of being able to observe brief vignettes of their lives through their lit windows colliding with the contrasting reality of living in a cold cramped caravan. The darkness and the moving shadows, with menacing silhouettes slipping amongst them, were at the forefront of his mind.

In a bid to banish such thoughts and disguise his nervous excitement, he climbed out of the grey van and, feigning confidence, walked towards the front door of the larger semi. Finding it ajar, he did a cursory knock and called out, "Hellooo, Lucy. It's Turner."

Her silky voice was discernible from inside, "Ooh, my first visitor. Welcome! Come on in."

Although Turner suspected that Lucy would have spent the last couple of days moving items from the rented Birmingham flat into her new home and hadn't got many personal contacts in the Midlands area even if she'd had the time to welcome them, he was relieved to find himself to be the first guest. Before he could engage brain, he clumsily uttered, "To be your first; I'm honoured."

She smiled coyly as she came into view in the hallway. Despite the dusty and dated surroundings, Lucy looked beautiful with a girl next-door appearance. She was wearing no make-up and had her hair pulled back which, even in the relative darkness of the hallway, accentuated her features. He appreciated her fresh-faced countenance far more so than the more obviously done up women he would meet on his rare nights out. He realised he was gripped by this diminutive, inexperienced figure standing before him and that she was taking on such a project. He had to again acknowledge his first impressions of her, back when she'd initially arrived at Oakland Walk, had been incorrect. With surprise, he realised it both felt like yesterday that she had come into his life unbidden and unwelcome and, simultaneously, like he had known her far longer.

"Nice of you to come over; thank you. I'm touched. Welcome to my humble abode! I'm just working my way around the house removing any window coverings I can find. We don't need damaged blinds or discoloured net curtains covering them all. I'm keen to get some natural light into the rooms and banish all this stale air."

She paused and turned to hold his gaze for a moment. With a teasing tone, she said, "Speaking of my first, the layout on the ground floor will remain largely as is so shall I start the tour in what will be my master bedroom upstairs?"

With this, Lucy sashayed past him and indicated that he follow her. She seemed at ease in this environment, less guarded. Turner was accustomed to being on sites where everyone dressed in what he regarded as standard workwear, trousers with large pockets and handy keeps for hooking tools to. Here, at her own project, Lucy was instead wearing a pair of skin-tight yoga leggings. As she scampered up the stairs in front of him, his eyes were drawn to her pert and shapely behind.

Once on the landing, she glanced back at him and, with an amused expression that left him questioning whether she had noticed the trajectory of his gaze, she seamlessly continued, "So, this is my bedroom; it's where the magic will happen."

Was she flirting with him? He couldn't be sure whether she was purposefully continuing the double meaning he had initiated with his comment on being her first or entirely unaware of the suggestion behind her choice of words. In the half-light seeping through the shrouded windows, she proceeded to animatedly share her visions for the room. She explained it in such detail that Turner almost felt as if they were standing in her finished low-lit boudoir rather than amongst sorry textured wallpaper walls and the sort of design and colours on a carpet you would expect to only these days see in a traditional pub.

Lucy described, "A bright airy room by day, albeit with muted neutral tone. I want it to have a more intimate and romantic feel by night. The bed is going to be positioned on the windowless section of wall opposite the door."

Turner nodded, following her description "So, as you enter the room from the door, you'll look diagonally to the right and see the bed. Is that correct?" he queried, purely to demonstrate he was interested and listening.

She smiled in response. "Yes, and then the walls will be painted in a luxurious smoky grey. I'm planning to create a recess into the plaster of the ceiling to accommodate a low-profile rail for the curtains. I've no idea how I'll achieve that or who'll be able to do it, but the shallow profile should make the decadent silken taupe fabric appear to hang in a gentle wave directly from the ceiling. When pulled closed, the light should be unable to penetrate around the perimeter of the curtains."

"And for the wall where the headboard will rest?" Turner enquired.

"This will be wallpapered in a complementary tone with a slight glimmer or sheen to it so it reflects the natural light during the day and casts a romantic hue at night. I'm envisaging an understated bed albeit with a feature headboard. The linen will be a natural white with two pillows on each side and, in front of these, smaller textured cushions in greys and toffees with a large faux fur throw spread over the lower half of the bed, pulling together the spectrum of warm greys and browns. Either side of the bed there'll be oversized chests of drawers with large feature lamps with crystal bases centrally atop them. Behind these, I'll hang circular mirrors to reflect the rays from the lamps and from the sunlight entering through the large window."

"Wow, you've thought of it all," Turner interjected. "I'm no expert in soft furnishings but you paint a clear picture."

Lucy beamed at him. "Can you see the refracted shafts of light from the lamps' crystal bases dancing around the room?" she asked with a delighted, whimsical expression on her face as she studied his.

Turner was sure his imagination failed to do justice to her vision for it. Nonetheless, he slowly rotated in the centre of the room attempting to envisage the master bedroom in its future glory. Try as he may, his mind focussed far more readily on creating a tantalising fantasy of Lucy reclined on the bed than the detail of the bed itself and its surroundings. He could feel his body's physical reaction to the mental image of her sprawled supine across it. His gaze darted in her direction but he noticed with relief that she was no longer looking at him, seemingly focussed on conjuring her own mental image of her room. His pang of arousal had appeared to go unnoticed.

Lucy's excitement was contagious as she practically skipped to the front window, grabbing a hop-up en route that had been leant up against the wall. She stepped up onto its battered metal platform, arms outstretched to lift the curtain pole and sun-bleached curtains away from the window opening. Turner was caught in the moment observing her lithe form, the curve of her bum, the perceptible definition of her core muscles beneath her top and the toned shoulders. With a small jump, she nudged the curtain pole from the metal support that hung awkwardly from the wall. The bulbed end of the pole dropped towards the floor as the disturbance pulled the middle frame support from the wall.

Clearly caught off-guard, Lucy wobbled to keep her balance. Turner sprung towards her, gripping either side of her waist to stop her falling.

Struck by his proximity to her perfectly shaped bottom, which was held in position almost at his eye level, and the feel of the curve of her hip beneath his spread fingers, he tried to downplay the effect this had had on him. "Steady Eddie. How was your trip?" He cringed at hearing himself utter such a ridiculous question. He hadn't used the 'how was your trip?' joke since he'd been a schoolboy.

Giggling, Lucy rotated beneath his grip to face him, leaving his hands in position to glide over her stomach and lower back as she turned. Looking slightly down at him from her height on the hop-up, with a sparkle in her eyes and cheeks slightly flushed, she said, "Good thanks, I enjoyed the view."

Is she playing along with the double entendres? Aware that his hands still lingered unmoving at her waist, he wondered whether she was coquettishly teasing him or simply being friendly. *Perhaps she's making reference to the sight from the window she's just revealed by stripping the curtain. I've got no idea.* Unsure, he simply tightened his grip on her midriff and lifted her down from the hop-up, carefully setting her back on her feet whilst avoiding eye contact and muttering that curtain poles were his nemesis too.

"Eeee!" she exclaimed. "My master bedroom already looks so much better with those mottled monstrosities down."

The sun spilled into the room, flooding where Lucy now stood with light, making her dark hair appear to glow and shimmer. She stilled and met Turner's gaze with an almost sombre intensity. "Turner, I'm nervous. I'm not sure whether I can do this. You've just had to step in like my knight in shining armour to help me half remove a curtain pole. You're like a mountain goat on site and I'm really not. If I can't remove a curtain pole alone, how am I going to manage to refurb two existing houses and orchestrate the construction of two more? And I'm apprehensive about the caravan too. It sounded so refreshingly exciting but with the reality that tonight will be my first stay in the caravan alone, does it sound lame to say I'm feeling some anxiety about it?"

"Lucy," Turner reassured her, "firstly, although I can build houses no problem, curtain poles are honestly my nemesis so don't judge yourself harshly there. Secondly, you don't need to do this alone. I'm in awe of you for taking on such a project. You're intriguing. I've only been here a few minutes and am already being drawn in by this infectious and unabashed refreshing enthusiasm you possess."

Lucy wrinkled her nose in response, so he quickly continued, "And yet you're feminine too but neither fragile nor helpless. Although I concede there's a certain vulnerability in acknowledging your concerns, that's okay. There's also courage in doing so.

"My mother, who having only met you once and who now appears to be one of your biggest fans, would have a useful titbit to say here. She's not a woman it's easy to speak for but, nonetheless, I'm pretty sure I heard her tell you something along these lines in the cabin, that it takes a certain strength to recognise you need help and to be brave enough to ask for it."

With watery eyes, Lucy gazed back at him. "So, you are in fact here to be my knight in shining armour?"

Not wanting to spoil the moment but equally keen to make light of it, Turner stood back to look round the room. "I'm just a builder and, fortunately for both of us, not my mother. For a start, she wouldn't have been able to catch you just now." He chuckled.

Lucy giggled too and then her expression changed as she studied his face. "Wait a second, did she make you come here?"

"No," Turner guffawed. "I'm here because *I* wanted to come. In terms of advice, though, I can consequently only impart one of the first things I learnt when I was apprenticing on site. I was told you can build it fast, build it good or build it cheap, and that, on any project, only two could apply. So, what's your plan?"

Considering his question, Lucy replied, "Well, I have a limited budget and can't therefore afford for the cost to run away with me. I guess that consequently counts out having it fast so my plan will be to have it cost as little as I can manage without compromising on the quality of the finish. Erm, so cheap and good?" She shrugged.

"Great! See, we have an embryonic plan forming already!"

Lucy paused, breaking his gaze and then, still sounding unconvinced, said, "Yes, I guess so although it's a sobering reminder that I'll be in the caravan for some time. I suppose we focus on my master bedroom and linked ensuite and walk-in wardrobe first so that I can move into at least a portion of the house as soon as possible."

"Okay, well, I have nothing on tonight so why don't we make a start? We can save the rest of the tour for another time and, for now, just begin to strip the wallpaper from the walls, pull up the carpet and give ourselves a blank canvas to work from?"

"Turner, you don't need to do this. I appreciate you offering to help a damsel in distress but you must have better things to do with your time."

"Actually, no, I don't. I can't think of anywhere I'd rather be this evening than helping a friend."

Lucy blushed but, eyes twinkling, quipped, "Does that mean you'll accept mates' rates as apparently, I'm looking for someone cheap and good?"

Laughing and enjoying the banter, Turner couldn't resist saying, "Well, at least for tonight, I'm all yours."

With genuine excitement, he dashed out of the room to his van, pulled it onto the sorry cracked driveway and hauled out some basic tools from its rear. On returning to the bedroom, he noted with pride that, in the few minutes he had been gone, Lucy had regrouped and set up her wallpaper stripper. With steam now swirling around her and to the background noise of the steamer's boiling water hissing and bubbling, she was determinedly scraping at the walls.

They both worked in companionable silence alongside each other as the daylight gradually faded outside and dusk set in. Whilst perfectly comfortable not speaking in favour of toiling away together, Turner felt very aware of Lucy's every stretch and bend as she scraped vigorously at the dated textured paper.

Suddenly breaking from the monotony of the repetitive scraping, Lucy pivoted to Turner with a coy smile. "Does mates' rates extend to accepting a home-made, well… caravan-made dinner as payment?"

Turner looked up to see Lucy illuminated by the artificial glow of the exposed bulb overhead, suspended by a white cable from a ceiling mounted pendant. "Wow, it's dark outside. So, yeah, sure, now you mention it, I'm pretty hungry," Turner responded, trying to imbue his voice with an off-hand casual air whilst attempting to disguise his body's involuntary shiver of anticipation at accepting the invite.

"Great! I can't really make you dinner in the house's kitchen. It's pretty grotty but it overlooks a beautiful wizened apple tree. I can't wait to be able to admire it from the window of the spectacular kitchen I'll eventually be fortunate enough to have."

"No worries, you go ahead. I'll clean up here and then take a look at the kitchen on my way out to join you."

As Lucy reached out her warm dainty hand to press the house key into his, he realised her going ahead whilst he stayed back to finish the tour unaccompanied and then lock up, would give him the few moments he needed to compose himself.

His eyes guiltily followed Lucy's receding form as she bounced out of the room and down the stairs. He then set to turning off the wallpaper steamers, bagging up the strips and scraps of soggy wallpaper that had accumulated on the floor and then switched out the lights. Once downstairs, he took a detour via the kitchen, which contained standard albeit antiquated appliances and dark wood unit doors with a traditional understairs pantry to one side. Beyond it, there was a dilapidated sun room which stood as a soulless threshold between the kitchen and the rear garden. Little more than a glorified lean-to, it had limp lace curtains hanging along a plastic cord. No wonder Lucy had suggested eating in the caravan instead. Rather than the kitchen being the heart of this home, he envisaged it being the place that the soul would come to die. Lucy was taking on a gargantuan task. He admired her for it. Instead of wallowing in the kitchen's current sorry state, she directed her focus on its sole positive, a good view from its window. He too admired the tree and, with yet more respect for her, he turned off the lights downstairs, pulled the warped front door to, heaved up the handle and turned the key.

Although there were only a few paces to the caravan, he pictured Lucy walking these as he strode the short distance. In that context, imagining her covering this path morning and night, the walk appeared further and more sinister than he would like. He rapped on the caravan's outside panel. In response, Lucy pushed open its flimsy door. He felt concerned for her safety, the enormity of the project she was so enthusiastically taking on and, underlying that, a little nervous like he was attending the caravan for a date rather than just to talk through her plans for the houses over food.

Accompanied by an over-the-top flurry of her arms, Lucy announced, "Welcome to my humble abode... Actually, it's a 2015 six berth Elddis Crusader Tempest so don't worry, it's quite spacious for a caravan. We won't be on top of each other."

"Er, thanks," he uttered as her last words prompted him to conjure a mental picture of the pair of them that demanded his attention and couldn't easily be ignored.

"Please take a seat," she encouraged. In the narrow aisle of the caravan, Turner carefully pirouetted round Lucy to reach the table and seat she was indicating he sit at. At the front of the caravan and on either side of a fixed chest of drawers, stood in-built symmetrical sofas. In the middle section of the caravan, on the side furthest from the door, and where he now sat was a 'dinette'; a small removable laminated worktop that served as a table when erect with seating either side of it. When seated at the table, one would either be looking toward the front or rear of the caravan. Adjacent to this, along the left side and next to the narrow external door, stood the integrated kitchen. The entire caravan was decked out in a pale wood effect.

From his seat at the dinette, Turner rotated 90 degrees to face the kitchen, which was almost three units wide. The latches appeared to be plastic, brushed chrome effect push buttons. There was also an integrated chrome gas oven with a three-gas-ring hob above. This was set into another pale laminated worktop that matched the dining table surface and next some cupboards with metal sink over and a low-level black heater with cutlery drawer above. He noted with fleeting interest that it was compact but functional; a good use of a comparatively small space. Both the hob and sink could be covered by shatter and heatproof textured glass that hinged from the worktop like the lid on a toilet seat. Behind the sink and hob was a large window that filled the void between the base and wall units.

Whilst the builder in him observed the various different creative space-saving solutions with passing curiosity, it was the figure standing between him and the kitchen units that drew his eye. Still in her fitted yoga leggings, Lucy's upper leg muscles and curvaceous glutes flexed mesmerizingly as she shifted her weight from foot to foot whilst prepping their food. His eyes savoured the close-up view of her behind whilst his nose inhaled the wafting aroma of the hearty dinner she was preparing. It appeared to be a seared chicken breast accompanied by a lentil, leek, chilli and cream side.

Time must have stood still as he appreciatively observed her because, in what felt like a matter of moments, Lucy was bending to retrieve plates and cutlery. Her movements were efficient and yet graceful too. Rotating on her heels, steaming dishes in hand, she served the food.

"Voila! Dinner. I'm all about tasty ten-minute meals."

As Lucy slid into the seat opposite him, Turner realised that in the confined space, their feet and lower legs would brush together under the table as they shifted in their seats. Realising Lucy's warm calf was resting very gently against his own, he resolved to remain still so as to prolong that understated but pleasurable touch.

Lucy laughed as Turner sat, fork poised above his plate. "So, mummy's boy," she teased, "if your mother were here and assuming a picture can say a thousand words, I think she'd be observing that the way to a man's heart is through his stomach."

She giggled. "You look awestruck. I'm really not that much of a chef. I just figured that if I'm paying you with dinner, I need to present you with something other than beans on toast."

"Yeah, this looks and smells amazing, thank you," he uttered whilst uncomfortably aware that Lucy had read his expression correctly but misinterpreted the look on his face as being one of appreciation for the food when in fact it was for the understatedly beautiful woman serving it.

Temporarily drained after spending the previous few hours scraping at the tired walls on top of a busy day's work on site, he assumed Lucy must also feel exhausted as they ate much of the meal in relative and amiable silence. Turner appreciated the camaraderie of it, the absence of any awkwardness prompting either to feel the need to fill the void. Lucy kept stretching and contorting in her seat, unwittingly but provocatively arching her chest towards him. Clearly aching from her efforts wallpaper stripping, she did so to offer her fatigued muscles some respite. Turner found each feline movement a turn-on.

She sought out a couple of ibuprofen and, after taking them, muttered, "So I'm not too stiff in the morning."

It necessitated all of Turner's willpower to refrain from stating, 'That makes one of us'. He kept his lips forcibly sealed.

With the benefit of food, he could feel his energy returning. Similarly, Lucy began to talk animatedly about her plans for the house and garden. Turner continued to marvel at how infectious her enthusiasm was and found himself riveted. The meal was delicious and yet it seemed almost bland in comparison to the enjoyment he derived from Lucy herself.

Although they both ate with gusto, he lost track of time as they sat in their relatively cramped surroundings and it wasn't until Lucy stood to remove the empty plates from the table that he glanced out of the windows, conscious of the blackness outside. The elevated roadside streetlamp cast an amber glow across a portion of the dense front garden but was limited in its reach by the foliage. The pair of semi-detached houses were positioned centrally in the plot and the caravan nestled close to the detached garage. It stood on a section of curved tarmac which would have allowed the previous owners a decent turning circle when accessing the garage. The vegetation just beyond the pitted and crumbling tarmac's boundary obscured the moonlight and much of the artificial light emanating from the surrounding houses. Shrouded in darkness and overshadowed by the plants, the caravan felt very isolated. Although sociable, Turner could see a certain appeal to this secluded setup but as Lucy looked up from the kitchen worktop and out into the relative darkness, he could discern her soft features contort into a frown. Apparently lost in thought, she nibbled at her lower lip.

"Lucy, now how are you feeling about your first night in the caravan?"

Lucy sighed in response. "I confess I'm nervous about it. Up to this point, living in a caravan sounded novel and a little bit thrilling. Now it's dark though, I'm feeling some apprehension about being here alone. I'm sure I'll settle into it. It's probably just that the initial excitement and adrenaline of completing on the purchase, setting up the caravan and making a start on the house is ebbing."

Conscious he was witnessing one of Lucy's rare admissions of vulnerability, Turner feebly reassured her, "You'll be fine." And, more light-heartedly said, "So, what's your setup going to look like? Where exactly are you going to be sleeping while this is your base?"

He followed Lucy with his eyes as she indicated towards the two sofas at the front of the caravan. "I think I will in due course pull out the slats from that central chest of drawers and convert the sofas into a large double bed. That would then give me a decent sleeping quarter at the front end, this kitchen and dinette area in the middle and to the rear I of course have access to the shower room and toilet plus the triple bunk, which I'll use for storing plans, paperwork, clothing etc."

Turner's gaze followed the direction that Lucy had indicated. Along the one wall, to the left of the main entrance door, when looking at it from the door, stood the kitchen and to the right of it a set of three bunk beds. Each level had a wooden side guard, presumably to prevent children falling out, but that would serve to restrain anything Lucy were to choose to store within them. Furthermore, each level was shrouded by its own individual curtain so that anything Lucy were to put on the bunks could be conveniently hidden from view. As he cast his eye around the wider space, he espied all manner of clever storage solutions and had to acknowledge that a wall dedicated to bunk beds for makeshift storage was an ingenious way of exponentially increasing Lucy's office space without encroaching on her living area.

"I'm hoping not to really need to use the shower and instead try to wash at the gym until such time as I have a bathroom up and running in the main house. As you know, I don't really have any friends locally so can't readily pop round to someone's house for dinner and a wash."

Hoping to reassure her by focussing on the positives, he said, "We'll just have to get your master suite completed as quickly as possible then. Also, I'd like to think you would consider me a friend."

Lucy blushed. "Thanks, Turner, I'm conscious I have a hard time trusting people after everything that happened with Mark but I value whatever this is that we have." Then, hastily, in an overly jovial tone she said, "You know what they say though, a friend in need…is a pain in the arse." Her feminine giggle mingled with his more masculine guffaw.

"Surely that's something you heard on site. It sounds exactly like something Andy would say."

"Possibly although I don't want you to feel I'm just tapping you for your superior building knowledge."

"Ha, finally she acknowledges my superiority!" he laughed. "Besides, a girl like you can tap me anytime you like."

He looked into her eyes and pasted a smile on his face to reassure her he was teasing, whilst secretly acknowledging to himself that many a true word was said in jest.

"Can I help you get organised for your first night here before I make a move? I mean, before I head off."

With that, Lucy hopped up and retrieved a deep purple sleeping bag, white pillow and checked blue cotton blanket from her bunk bed storage and laid it across the front left-hand sofa. The sleeping bag looked like a throwback to her childhood. Rather than being a shiny nylon type sheath that's warmth would be coded with a tog rating, it was a more traditional almost duvet-like cotton material. It was folded down its length, like a two layered rectangle and had a large zip across its base and up the full length of one side. As Lucy surveyed where she would be sleeping, Turner looked at the pitiful setup and couldn't help but feel a bit deflated for her as her first night solo in the caravan loomed. Lucy temporarily appeared sombre. Before he had a chance to check himself, he uttered,

"You know, I'd be happy to crash here for your first night so that it doesn't feel quite so daunting." Not wanting her to question his motives, he hastily continued, "I mean, it's already late and we've both been hard at it this afternoon and no doubt you'll want to start promptly again tomorrow." He finished by clarifying: "I'm offering to stay just as your friend; nothing more."

Unable to easily read Lucy's expression, he explained further, "I can sleep on the other sofa. You take the sleeping bag and, if you can spare it, I'll use the blanket."

As Lucy hovered, uncertain, Turner got to his feet, inched past her, removed the back rest cushions from the sofa and heaped them on the chest of drawers. Despite having little experience of caravans, he also knew the two large sofas could function either as single beds or be made into a double by pulling out slats from beneath the chest of drawers between them. The back sofa cushions could then be laid out along them. Conscious, however, of jeopardising this softening in her approach to him, he made no further reference to this alternative configuration. Instead, he proceeded to stretch out on one of the sofas to demonstrate what he had in mind and help reassure her that he would be comfortable and not encroach on her space.

Hesitantly she said, "Turner you must have somewhere better to be. Besides, you haven't got anything to sleep in."

"I'm a guy. I'd go on holiday with a toothbrush and a spare t-shirt. I can manage an impromptu night in a caravan."

To demonstrate this, Turner met her gaze. Tentatively but confidently, he began to remove his layers, scanning her face for any sort of reaction that would suggest his actions were misplaced. Very aware that she was watching him closely, he undressed just to his boxers. With a mix of pride and pleasure, he revelled in the intensity of her gaze. He reclined on the sofa, trying to appear casual and unaware of her stare, pulled the blanket up to his waist, contriving to leave his torso and upper body exposed for Lucy to continue to absorb.

Appearing to suddenly wake from her reverie, in response, Lucy simply turned on the dimmed under-cabinet lights at the front of the caravan and turned off the brighter ones in the kitchen. She busied herself with what he assumed was her night-time routine and disappeared into the cramped bathroom cubicle. For a few moments he lay there, arms folded behind his head and staring up at the pale ceiling and rooflight above him, unsure how he had managed to occasion a reality in which he was about to find himself sleeping within arms' reach of Lucy.

The flimsy bathroom door reopened with a quiet squeak of its hinges and Lucy reappeared in a figure-hugging white vest top and matching pyjama shorts. As she self-consciously approached him, she fluttered her hand over her right hip. It struck him that she had made the same movement previously when arguing with Mark. The cotton shorts that only just covered the curve of her pert behind promptly drew his attention and he studied her approach with barely concealed delight. He held his breath so as not to audibly groan with appreciation at the sight of her understated sensuality; girl next-door fantasy indeed. Lucy somewhat awkwardly shimmied her way into the traditional sleeping bag and attempted to zip herself in. The zip caught at her waist where the teeth were a little damaged and, promptly accepting defeat, she just pulled the two sides together over herself.

She turned onto her side to face him, resting her head on her arm, unruly ringlets of her ponytail framing her face. The ends of the tendrils hung in such a way as to caress her perfectly silhouetted breasts. The weight of the sleeping bag meant he could also easily discern the rising curve of her hip and the dip down to her waist. He mentally saluted the damaged zip as it prompted the sleeping bag to flop away from her body at her midriff. Mind in overdrive, he realised that, barely a metre from him, she would be sleeping braless. Her nipples were pressing against her vest. Fuck. *How am I going to sleep with that image seared into my eyelids. I don't know how she doesn't see her own beauty, but fuck that's hot.*

Seemingly unaware, Lucy arched her back to stretch and get comfortable, inadvertently revealing the curved line of her breasts yet more clearly to him through her top, hard nipples poking at the fabric as she nestled into her bed. With a final tantalising movement, she said, "Night, Turner. Thank you for this." Then, reaching up to the little under cabinet pull cord for the lights, she gave it a tug and, with a click, the caravan was put into darkness. *If only swallowing ibuprofen would prevent me from waking up stiff,* Turner again lamented ruefully as he too tried to settle.

CHAPTER 7

Lucy stirred, shivering and cold. In stark contrast to how she'd felt when she had drifted off to sleep hazy and warm, the caravan now seemed damp and unwelcoming, almost hostile. She had peacefully descended into sleep, enveloped in the comforting familiarity of her sleeping bag and to the reassuring backdrop of Turner's muffled but steady breathing. She must have been genuinely exhausted after their effort stripping wallpaper because, for a welcome change, rather than lying there listlessly into the early hours dissecting the errors of her previous personal and professional endeavours, she felt like she had fallen unconscious within minutes of her head hitting her pillow.

With reluctance, she opened a sleep-filled eye to check the time on the caravan's miniature wall-mounted clock face. She trained her heavy eyes on it affectionately. The circular glass dial was vaguely reminiscent of her late grandfather's naval barometer. The little gold hands signalled it was five o'clock. Although the caravan was largely still shrouded in darkness, a cursory glance towards the windows revealed the pale grey light of dawn highlighting the gaps between the window frames and the blackout blinds stretched over them. As had been the case with the few caravan holidays she had been on as a child, she noted the peculiar way caravan blinds could be both pulled taut and yet somehow simultaneously creased.

She realised, with resigned disappointment, that the sleeping bag's faulty zip had failed her in the night as her upper half was now lying exposed with the comforting weight of the sleeping bag ceasing abruptly at her waist. Still on her side, her bare left shoulder felt frigid to the touch and despite the blanket and sleeping bag still covering her lower half, the cold had permeated bone-deep down to her now icy toes. Her breath juddered as she exhaled. She fought the urge to allow her teeth to chatter.

Apparently blissfully impervious to the cold, Turner's chiselled form was visible in the pale dawn light. With drowsy interest, she watched him slumbering on the opposite sofa. He looked peaceful and yet like a marble hewn sculpture of masculinity incongruously reposed on the caravan's dated upholstery. Almost guiltily, she studied every exposed inch of his perfectly toned and proportioned body; the defined abs, muscled arms, slightly protruding Adam's apple and sleek neck sweeping up to his stubbled and chiselled jawline. Although Mark had been a gym frequenter, his sedentary role had also taken its toll on his physique. In contrast, Turner's muscles and frame were the product of performing physical work coupled with an understated care for himself and his wellbeing. She realised she found this natural masculinity more alluring. With mild amusement, it occurred to her that, if she were to have to define him in one word for Rachel, it would be 'strapping'. A term she had never thought to refer to anyone or anything else as being. For once, she felt reasonably confident her outspoken friend would second the one-word summation. She shivered again – a combination of the crisp air numbing the skin unprotected by her impotent vest and the lusty sight of a virile Turner she voyeuristically drank in before her.

He stirred and, without opening his eyes and yet somehow aware she was staring at him, grasped the corner of the blanket in his fist. In a languid motion, he lifted his toned arm to create a shrouded gap along the length of his body into which he casually invited her.

Lucy's mind started spinning through various different scenarios. Turner, with arm still steadfastly held aloft and in a husky morning voice said, "Frozen Features, you're eyeing up my blanket like you're about to rip it from my limbs. Either you morph at dawn into some kind of ravenous man-eating vampire with an insatiable thirst for blood which, to be fair, doesn't sound all that bad to me or you're developing hypothermia. Either way, you might as well sidle over here, snuggle into this Lucy-sized cavity I've created and share my warmth."

As Lucy still faltered, he continued with a teasing tone, "Or you can fight me to the death for the blanket but I'm no gentleman in bed and, seeing as you've spent the last few minutes staring at my physique, I'm pretty sure we both have an inkling who'd win that contest."

Not entirely convinced as to whether it was the desire for his warmth or an attraction to Turner himself that first compelled her to move, Lucy scooted over to him and, with her back to his front, moulded her body along his sculpted length. Her skimpy vest and cotton pyjama shorts only slightly dissipated the furnace like heat that radiated from his bare skin to hers. The contours of her body fit perfectly into his and the contrast was rousing between lying alone bitterly cold one moment and now warmed as little spoon from head to toe nestled into him. Contrary to his assertion that he was no gentleman in bed, Turner kept his frame respectfully still, presumably to reassure her that the decision to cuddle into him was hers and that his intentions were, for the most part, honourable. After a few moments' pause, he tentatively lowered his blanketed arm, enveloping her fully in his succouring embrace.

Lucy relaxed into it, resting the side of her head on Turner's bent left arm and pulling his comforting right one in towards her, securing herself in place. She couldn't remember the last time she'd felt so protected, so safe. She revelled in the moment, savouring the alien tenderness in his gesture.

Ensconced in the warmth of his embrace, she lay still so as not to break the moment. She must subsequently have drifted back off to sleep as, what felt like only seconds later, she realised that the light beyond her closed eyelids was now far brighter than it had been when she'd allowed them to flutter shut. With a pervading pleasure, she found herself to still be cocooned by Turner. His peaceful slow breathing suggested he too had drifted back to sleep and, each time he exhaled, an almost imperceptible draft caressed the side of her face. The warm eddies of air around her ear both tickled and teased.

Suddenly aware that the onset of pins and needles in her arm had caused her to stir, she shifted her weight back, angling herself further toward Turner's firm torso and releasing the arm she had inadvertently been lying on. Freeing her tingling arm brought almost immediate relief but, as she arched her back and hips, her bum ground into Turner and, with a disquieting satisfaction, she found he was hard. *Eek. I should pull away.* Whilst considering her immediate instinct to do so, she found herself wrestling with the desire to subtly adjust her hips further to explore his size and the exquisite sensation of his firm arousal against the curve of her buttocks and lower back. Self-consciously, she recognised the patulous heat between her legs as it sent arousing pleasure spiralling across her flushing skin. It had been so long; every inch of her being felt alive, her senses alert and suffused with anticipation.

With her faculties so delectably intoxicated, coherent thought evaded her. Despite this, she understood her traitorous body craved Turner's. Incapable of resisting the impulse to do so, she arched her back and seductively rolled her hips against him. Turner's steady breathing was interrupted by a deep groan escaping his lips.

He tilted his mouth towards her ear and, with a hoarse, strained moan, whispered, "Fuck, woman. I'm trying to be on my best behaviour. I thought you wanted me to play the role of knight in shining armour and, despite your barely there PJs and your phenomenal body pressed temptingly against mine, I've so far been able to preserve your honour."

He paused, sending a heady, close breath towards her ear. Even that comparatively insignificant action aroused her, making her body thrum with freshly awakened desire. The contours of his washboard abs and the hair of his happy trail were discernible through the thin fabric of her nightwear. Her abdomen thrummed delectably as she pressed her backside against his arousal. Turner practically growled in response.

"Your perfect little ass circling my morning wood risks overpowering my attempts at self-restraint."

Turner released Lucy, hastily nudged her away and shifted onto his back. Apparently perceiving her confusion and disappointment in the wake of his rejection, he then angled his head towards her. Lascivious smile on his face, he looked like an errant teenager contemplating his first sexual encounter. He grasped her hand in his and guided it down over the tent in his boxers. With a charged moan, he let it linger there for a moment and then resolutely replaced it at her side. Teasing, he continued, "Rest assured, this knight in shining armour's sword is painfully hard for you."

Lucy giggled at his reference to her wanting a knight to help with the build.

Turner looked smug in response and then, in a low voice, continued, "Ha, sorry. To be serious for a moment though, I want this… I mean, really want this but I want it when you're sure all of you is ready for it rather than because we've been swept up in the moment."

Somewhat mollified, Lucy couldn't resist perpetuating the analogy. It somehow felt less uncomfortable than more formally acknowledging the reality of his rebuttal when she would readily have given herself to him had he allowed her.

"I take it then, Good Sir," she teased, "that you're offering to keep your eager sword sheathed for me but ready to serve when called upon? If I understand correctly, you're doing so because you aren't in fact looking for a conquest but something more meaningful. Is that fair?"

"Yes," he laughed. "Sounds like the twenty-first century twist on a traditional fairy tale."

With that, he shifted. Reluctant to lose the comforting warmth of his body, Lucy continued to lie in place, making no move to help him extricate himself. Righting himself in spite of her resistance, he stood and began to pull his crumpled jeans back on. Likely failing to conceal her disappointment, Lucy tried to subtly watch him, internally bemoaning the travesty that was witnessing his body being re-hidden beneath his clothing as she did so. She knew she would never be able to casually look at his fully clothed self again without picturing the Adonis disguised beneath.

Reluctant for Turner to see the effect he was having on her, she hopped up and turned away, opened the fridge and poured herself an orange juice into one of the caravan's plastic travel-friendly tumblers. She tilted her head back, took a couple of cool, thirst-quenching gulps and savoured the sensation of the fluid swirling around in her mouth after the dryness of sleep, before swallowing the concentrated citrusy taste down.

"Ahh, I cast the temptress from my bed – if you can call it that – only to find myself watching her enthusiastically gulp down fluid instead. To some, you may just be having an innocent drink but I'm so wired after our sleeping setup that my mind is picturing something else entirely… Let's have a slug too please and then we absolutely need to leave the confines of the caravan. It's not yet 8 a.m. but, if we remain in this enclosed space together for much longer, I can't be held accountable for what happens next."

By way of acknowledgement and in the absence of conceiving a witty response, Lucy passed the beaker to him. She observed coyly as he emptied it in one swallow, deposited it back in her waiting hand then quickly ducked his way out of the caravan and into the morning light.

As Lucy went to reach for her own clothes and dress in relative privacy, Turner popped his head back through the door frame.

"Right, much as it pains me, I'll leave the lady to dress without an audience. When I pulled up yesterday, I'm sure I saw a greasy spoon type café a few doors down the road. I'll go get us bacon sandwiches or similar while you get set up with the stripper." He paused. "Ha," he uttered awkwardly, "you'll think I have a one-track mind. Genuinely, this time, no pun intended."

Smiling to herself, Lucy returned to the main bedroom to prepare for another day's hard labour. Turning the wallpaper stripper on, she considered how much more progress they had made the day before than she would have accomplished by herself. Just as the wallpaper stripper finally began to hiss, Turner walked in. They each sat down, backs to the wall and ate in amiable silence. Lucy was cross legged and noted that even the way Turner chose to sit, legs casually extended out in front of him, conveyed an aura of unaffected masculinity. With each additional mouthful, she expected him to announce his imminent departure. They had spent sufficient time on site together at Oakland Walk for her to come to know his routine and he would need to be departing for work shortly. Although he seemed relaxed and unhurried as he ate, she could already keenly feel the disappointment and the void he would leave. In the twelve or so hours since he'd arrived at Sunnyside, she realised it already felt quite natural to have him there. Their sexually charged camaraderie was a welcome backdrop to the overwhelming task at hand. Keen not to appear needy or indeed to demonstrate any vulnerability by virtue of acknowledging how much she had enjoyed his presence, she decided to send him on his way. If she suggested he depart before he broached the subject then she could reassure herself that her swelling emotions remained in check and her defences intact.

"Thanks for the breakfast, Turner, and for the help yesterday. You should head off now, though, so that I can crack on with this and you can go open up at Oakland Walk."

She screwed the sandwich wrapper into a ball before tucking it into the bin liner of discarded wallpaper trimmings. Feigning decisiveness, she picked up the wallpaper stripper and scraper and pointedly began scratching away at the wall. She felt uncomfortable at dismissing him so unceremoniously but tried to draw some consolation from convincing herself that her emotional walls remained firmly in place, shielding her damaged heart from further harm.

In her experience, men always chose the path of least resistance and so she fully expected Turner to follow suit and elect to just leave. To her surprise, he instead proceeded to finish his sandwich at his own pace. He then pulled himself to his feet and laid a hand on Lucy's arm to encourage her to turn toward him.

As she rotated, he sought out her eye contact, met and held her gaze and gently but firmly said, "Lucy, I can see what you're doing. You're already trying to put your barriers back up. I know you've been hurt but I'm not Mark. I know we kept it jokey and light-hearted earlier but I meant what I said. I can't tell you exactly what we have or where it's going but I want to explore it together and I promise I'll always be honest with you."

He went to retreat from the room, smiling goofily over his shoulder to lighten the tone. "After I finish at Oakland Walk, I'm all yours…"

Before Lucy could decide what he'd meant, she found herself blurting out, "I'm meeting with a property finance company to effectively pitch for some funding in relation to the new builds either side of the existing houses at Sunnyside. I'm prepared, I have my pitch sorted and my numbers. Would you consider coming along as moral support, though, please?"

To her surprise, Turner nodded his head enthusiastically. "Yes, absolutely, I'd be delighted to," he uttered without hesitation.

"Yay, that's great! Thank you! The meeting's going to be held here so the financiers can better see what I'm hoping they'll lend against. If I can walk them round the houses, they'll see what an opportunity they represent. It might work in my favour."

They swapped details as to when the meeting would take place and agreed to reconvene back at her house at the end of the day. Formalities concluded and conscious Turner really needed to get to work, Lucy waved him off reluctantly.

"Okay, I know I've gotta go," he said in acknowledgement. "Thanks again for last night and looking forward to seeing you later," he proceeded to call as he withdrew from the bedroom.

Standing still in the centre of the otherwise now empty master bedroom, she listened as his footsteps receded. The intermittent hissing of the wallpaper stripper demanded her attention but, before stoically returning to the task at hand, she looked out of the window to watch him stride out to his van. He folded himself into it, performed a neat little manoeuvre and, with what appeared to be a broad smile on his face, proceeded to drive away. She immediately felt his absence. His presence had seemed to fill the space and, without it, the house felt emptier. Nonetheless, she resolved to put him out of her mind for the time being and focus her attention on her bedroom whilst continuing to mentally prepare for the crucial meeting. She wanted the safety net of knowing third party finance would be there to fall back on should she require it.

She toiled away for the next few hours. Despite the water hissing and bubbling, the monotony of stripping the walls of wallpaper was quite mesmerising and meditative. It was only as she set to scrubbing any remaining fragments of paper from the walls with sugar soap and a sponge that her mind was able to wander. Turner's comment of 'I'm all yours' kept replaying in her mind. Had he been insinuating he would then be free to assist her refurbing the house or that he would be hers in a more meaningful sense. She cautiously acknowledged to herself that she suspected she wanted both from him. Painful experience however had taught her that, first and foremost, she had to be able to rely on herself.

Bafflingly, Turner seemed to be attracted to the strength he could apparently identify in her even though she herself felt it had been lost somewhere along the way. Absentmindedly, she brushed her fingers over her right hip and the Latin words tattooed there. For the first time in months and in no small part due to Turner, she thought that perhaps she too could detect a hint of her previous emotional strength returning. Moreover, given her contract at Oakland Walk would soon conclude, maybe labouring together in private at Sunnyside would give her the opportunity to fully explore her feelings for him. *However it pans out, I hope he feels the same way.*

CHAPTER 8

As Turner drove away, he couldn't remember ever having felt so elated. Catching a glimpse of himself in his van's visor mirror, he realised he was grinning from ear to ear. As he turned into site, Andy was standing at its heras fence gates. It brought him some satisfaction to find even someone as large as Andy had to grapple with the chains and padlock.

Turner pulled up to the gates, catching Andy's attention with a rev of the engine as he did so.

"Aw, mate," Andy piped up, "I thought this was going to be the first day since we've worked together that you'd be late. Another few moments and I'd have managed to get the site open and you'd technically have been tardy."

Andy stared at Turner through the open window and continued, "She must be one special lady for you to delegate locking up last night to me and to almost miss opening up too. Tell all!"

Turner smiled and shrugged his shoulders. "Sorry, Andy, I'm not going to risk it by kissing and telling even if to my best mate. I concede, though, that my good mood may involve a woman."

Andy guffawed, "It's written all over your face. We both know you can't lie; I can read you like a book."

"Yeah, I'm a lucky man!"

Andy smirked. "A lucky man who got lucky by the looks of it. Boom," he continued as his huge hand fist pumped the air.

Turner interjected with a good-natured, "Let's not get carried away. Just to be clear and for the record, the former yes, the latter no. I am lucky but I didn't get lucky. I tried to be the perfect gentleman and, successful or not, I've got the worst case of blue balls to show for it. I was so hard this morning that having all the blood down there keeping me at attention was giving me a headache. I down-played it as morning wood but, fuck, I felt like a human tripod."

Andy doubled over laughing in response. Tears streaming down his face he said, "Sounds real smooth, mate." Andy pushed the gate open.

Turner rolled his van forward and called through its open window, "Aw, kick a man while he's down why don't you."

"That's what friends are for. No one I know, I assume?" Andy asked, raising an enquiring eyebrow. Turner, feeling uncomfortably transparent under the scrutiny of his friend's pointed gaze, thought Andy looked as if he had his suspicions.

Rather than suffer the consequence of his honesty betraying him, Turner let his foot off the brake, allowing his van to gather momentum. Continuing to roll it forward, he resolved that simply not answering was better than either breaking Lucy's confidence or attempting to fib, which both he and Andy knew he would fail at abysmally.

Driving on into site, Turner resolved to practice what he preached and to focus his attentions on Oakland Walk even though he was sure the day would painstakingly tick by as his mind entertained thoughts of Lucy. For the first time ever, he could relate to the lads' inability to fully separate their work and personal lives. It finally resonated with him why they paid lip service to his requests that they leave their personal lives at the site entrance when they came to work even though they'd often talk amongst themselves about girlfriend problems, family issues etc.

With the show home nearing completion, though, now was no time to be distracted. He would have to stay focussed and approach all the tasks, subcontractor issues and snagging queries that arose that day with his usual attention to detail.

As the end of the day approached, however, an alien sensation – nervous anticipation perhaps – built within him. He'd been excited at the prospect of seeing Lucy again from the very moment he had pulled away from Sunnyside Road. Offering his moral support at the late afternoon meeting provided a convenient reason for being back in her company. Being an inherently practical and hands-on person, he had never felt much enthusiasm for meetings but accepted they were a necessary aspect of his role. With amusement, he noted, however, that he was uncharacteristically eager to be present at this one even though he would most likely just be required to sit patiently outside. Perhaps that helped account for the appeal. He would have the benefit of seeing her and wasn't required to participate at the meeting.

Rather than try to justify another hasty departure to Andy and, to avoid facing the inevitable ribbing that would come with this, Turner made himself scarce as the other lads packed up their tools at the end of the day. He always marvelled at how they could apparently be working hard at 4:25p.m. and yet have downed tools, cleaned off their equipment, packed away and be ready in their vans, engines idling, by 4:29p.m. so as to eagerly depart site in a haphazard convoy come finishing time one minute later.

After everyone had gone, he conducted a quick end-of-day tour of the progress in the show home. He admired the tones of the carpets, paintwork, flooring, skirting, doors and windows as he walked around. Lucy had vision. There was a welcoming, understated continuity to the space. The transition from room to room flowed. It felt light, airy and welcoming.

Lucy had also insisted on implementing certain exacting details. She, for instance, wanted no visible joints in the carpet. Whilst this stipulation meant there was more wastage, with large rolls of off-cuts heaped in every room upstairs, and the cost had been marginally higher than would otherwise have been the case, the sense of high-end sophistication created by such meticulous design more than compensated for this. Increasingly aware of construction's environmental impact and that Lucy herself had chosen the colour scheme for the show home, it occurred to Turner that he could give the skip-bound off-cuts to Lucy in case she may be able to use them at hers.

He manhandled the packaged rolls down to the front hall and, inspired, also made sure to locate his own festoon lights and transformer. Indispensable on site at certain times of year, they made it possible for the lads to continue working as dusk fell. Now the second fix electrics in the show home were complete, Turner's reel of yellow light fittings and cable, bulbs strung along its length, was stacked to one side and redundant. He carefully loaded them into the van.

As he crossed the site, he also admired the show home's exterior. The band of Staffordshire blue bricks, the canopy porch and anthracite grey windows all contributed to the cohesive high-end design-led feel. He even admired the bird and bat boxes Lucy had gone to great pains to ensure would be incorporated. She had even researched which elevation they should be mounted on to be of most appeal to their prospective winged inhabitants. Turner had come to appreciate and understand that Lucy had considered everyone and everything in her recommendations for Oakland Walk.

He stood for a moment to appreciate her touches, including the sight of the saplings planted at intervals along the garden fences. Next, he entered the welfare unit for an ungainly wash and freshen up to make himself more presentable. He told himself he was doing so to add more credibility to Lucy's pitch by being dressed smartly, consciously superseding the thought that putting effort into his appearance might really be for her benefit. Either way, better to be smart than to be dressed looking like the reality: a foreman who had spent an arduous day on site compounded by couch surfing the previous night in his love interest's caravan.

Moreover, he had to concede he hoped he might find Lucy inclined to pick up where they had left off that morning. It seemed so surreal. He had fallen completely under the spell of this woman so full of contradictions. Just a few short weeks after meeting her, he was wholly enthralled by her. She held his attention, captivated him even, in a way no one else ever had. Just idly pondering this unexpected and foreign reality meant he had to contend with a semi-erect dick as he soaped himself, washed, towelled dry and re-dressed. He was conscious his hard-on continued to linger inconveniently as he tackled his twice daily battle with the site's padlock, chain and gates. This being one of the few tasks on site he derived no enjoyment from performing.

En route to Lucy's, he took a planned detour via a Tesco Express and purchased a variety of antipasti and mezze items along with a crisp bottle of Sancerre. The chilled wine stood in the same aisle of refrigerated shelving as the juices and, recalling how Lucy had downed juice that morning, he impulsively added a large carton of orange juice to his basket. Hastily throwing these onto the blanketed seat next to him, he drove on. Aiming to be discreet rather than announce his arrival, he pulled up and surreptitiously parked his van out of sight. He pulled the reel of festoon lights over his shoulder and, loaded with the transformer – an innocuous but always surprisingly heavy item – in the other hand, dodged the front of the house and scurried round to the rear.

The mature apple tree in the rear garden was his destination. Up close, it was even more verdant than he had recalled. Vibrant green foliage and twisted low hanging branches radiated outwards from its trunk to create a natural canopy that partly shrouded the grassed area beneath. The tree was situated in a secluded section of garden behind the existing detached garage. Hovering in its shade, he carefully unravelled the reel of lights, wove the armoured plastic yellow cable in a uniform diagonal pattern around the tree's gnarled trunk and then stretched the cable from branch to branch. He placed the transformer at the base of the trunk with the festoon's plug positioned neatly alongside, before pausing to admire his handiwork.

He discerned the tinkle of feminine laughter emanating from the interior of the property. The familiar and enticing timbre of Lucy's giggles struck him as incongruous as it floated down to him from the upstairs bedroom's decrepit window and bounced off the building's neglected exterior. Hoping to catch a glimpse of her, he cast his eyes up towards the window, now free of mildewed curtain. His eyes followed a crack that snaked up the side of the building. Given it originated at the base of a drainpipe, where the roof water would disappear off underground, he assumed the building had suffered from a collapsed drain at some stage in its sorry past. The crack looked stable and hence historical but he resolved to address this on Lucy's behalf in due course.

The priority now was to help with any outstanding preparations for the finance meeting and then implement his master plan to woo Lucy. Satisfied with his efforts to adorn the apple tree, he made for the front door, calling out a greeting as he approached.

On entering the house, he was again met by the scarred carpet. His eyes followed its dated pattern from its source behind the door to the threshold of the kitchen. Head inclined towards the meandering design, he momentarily registered a shadow flit across the thready patina. As he glanced up an immaculately dressed woman was teetering towards him. Only just avoiding colliding with each other, she halted gracefully inches short of him. She possessed the bright red hair of Ariel but was dressed more like a dominatrix than a mermaid from a children's story. Extending a perfectly manicured hand towards him, she purred an introduction,

"Hi, I'm Rachel. I'm Lucy's best friend. I've popped up from London for a housewarming visit to this glorious monstrosity of hers." She looked him up and down appraisingly. "You must be Turner. I've heard a lot about you and, although I'd love to stay, I've got to dash for my train. Obviously, I'd be keen to help too but tools and I have a long-standing agreement. We resolutely stay away from each other. Besides, the finance meeting is imminent and I want to make myself scarce beforehand. I don't want to be distracting to the attendees." She winked conspiratorially. Then, as she continued towards the door she called out, "Lucy, I love you. This place will be great. In the meantime, I agree… strapping."

"Oh, do you need assistance with some kind of strapping?" Turner asked. "If so, I can help bring it in for you."

"Ha, no, Turner. Thanks for offering, though." She sauntered past him, calling, "Bye." Rachel elegantly tottered a high-heeled route back down the drive, precariously dodging the cracks in the corroded tarmacked surface as she went. Once she was obscured by the creeping vegetation, he sought out Lucy, finding her in a makeshift office space she had established in the centre of the antiquated living room. An imposing brick-clad feature fireplace that must have been in vogue some fifty years prior served as the centrepiece of the room and the backdrop to the meeting venue.

"Hey, you ready?" he asked.

Lucy sighed. "As I'll ever be," she said, sounding nervous. "In case I forget to say it later, thanks for coming. I'm not really sure what prompted me to ask you to but I appreciate that you have and hopefully having someone with your expertise here and with whom I've worked at Oakland Walk will add some gravitas and endorsement to my proposal. I need the safety net of having their funds behind me."

"To be honest, it's good work that you've managed to persuade them to come for a visit to site and indeed almost outside conventional office hours," Turner replied. "That's an achievement in itself! I'll be sure to introduce myself when they arrive, look like I'm doing something meaningful and then make myself scarce upstairs. I can measure up the timber for the stud walls between your master, walk-in wardrobe and ensuite. You know what they say…"

"Measure twice, cut once," they both said in smiling unison.

Any further opportunity for conversation passed, though, with an intrusive chorus of male voices alerting them to the financiers' arrival. They crossed the threshold in suited unison, triggering a splintering reverberation as the front door swung and hit the internal wall of the porch. Aiming to appear polite and mild-mannered despite their entrance, Turner welcomed them as agreed, noting they were all, at first glance, arrogant power-dressing suited men. He hoped Lucy wouldn't be charmed by their ingratiating manner. If this were to prove to be the type of man she was attracted to, Turner realised with acute disappointment that he may not meet her criteria as convincingly as he considered her to meet his.

He strode up the stairs to measure the timber studs as they filed into the sorry lounge, now a makeshift meeting room for the occasion. The door was closed behind them. Although he strained to listen as he worked, he couldn't discern much of what was being said in the room below. He felt frustrated at just hearing the rumbling of voices rather than the specifics of what each was saying. He silently willed for Lucy's pitch to be well received, and was relieved, sometime later, when he heard a creak of the living room door as it complained at being reopened and the sound of voices filtered up the stairs.

The voice of the smarmiest dresser carried clearly up to him as he asked, "So, Lucy, last question and just out of curiosity, what's the relationship between you and the site manager?"

There was an expectant pause, during which Turner could picture Lucy mentally composing her answer. She giggled, sounding nervous, under what he imagined was Smarmy Suit Man's unwavering and condescending stare.

"He's called Turner. And, as we've both already explained we worked collaboratively together, as colleagues, on the new development at Oakland Walk. My brief was to make it more desirable and hence to help it sell."

"Well, you're certainly doing a convincing job of selling yourself to us. It makes you a desirable proposition," Smarmy Suit Man said, emphasising the last couple of words. "I wasn't, however, asking for your CV and working history. I meant, what's the deal with you both…personally?" he probed.

"Oh, I see. I'm not sure how it has any bearing or how it is any of your concern". Lucy's voice sounded clipped, each word enunciated in a very deliberate manner, one that Turner had come to view as the forebear of a put-down. He hoped Lucy's retort to Smarmy Suit Man's asinine queries would be unusually scathing. A small part of him, however, waited expectantly, curious to hear how Lucy would describe their relationship if she were to choose to do so.

Turner assumed the man must have continued to stare at her expectantly because, after another pregnant pause, she uttered, "This project is mine alone and I'm asking you to consider it on its own merits. At a push, my professional relationships with tradespeople and subcontractors may be of some relevance to you but my personal relationships certainly aren't. Yes, I will engage third party trades. Whether Turner is one of them and what my personal relationship with him is or indeed what my personal relationship with anyone else is, is exclusively our business, i.e. his and my business not yours and mine."

After an audible intake of breath and a further pause, she continued, "If that's all, I'd like to take this opportunity to thank you all very much for your time and look forward to receiving further details from you as to what assistance you may be able to offer me in due course."

A muffled shuffling of feet could be heard in response before the booming voice of the same loathsome suited individual cut in at greater volume, "Thanks, Lucy, I was just trying to garner a clearer picture of the softer details around the proposition. Of course, if we're to control the purse strings on this project, it would make sense if I were to come to site from time to time and we were to foster our own mutually beneficial working relationship. The more closely we can work together, the smoother your project will run. Rest assured, we'll be in touch. I plan to make you an offer you can't refuse!"

Turner, frustrated at being unable to see Lucy's expression in response, wasn't sure whether the cock womble was referring to the financing, to Lucy or both.

He fumed. No wonder Lucy's faith in men and, by association, in herself floundered. She had perfectly innocently sought financial backing and the broker who attended had used it as an opportunity to insinuate that her project would be more successful if she aligned herself with him and presumably offered him some form of relationship on the side. At this embryonic stage in their own relationship, Turner acknowledged the only viable course of action would be to let Lucy make her own decisions. He wouldn't railroad her as these other individuals seemed to have chosen to do but instead would allow her the space to use her own judgement.

He resolved to bite his tongue and, finding her standing somewhat shell-shocked at the bottom of the stairs, encouraged her outside. She stood catching her breath for a moment as he retrieved the blanket and nibbles from the van.

"Hey, it's okay," he said, laying what he hoped felt like a reassuring hand on her arm. "We can talk through how it went if you'd like to but, if not, nothing will be achieved by immediately dissecting it." He paused to scan her face and, lightening his tone, continued, "I have a surprise for you."

He set off down the side of the garage with Lucy following behind.

"Wait here for a moment please," he said. "No peeking."

Lucy smiled in response but dutifully remained where he'd indicated.

Turner quickly laid out the trusty blanket he always kept in his van beneath the tree. He arranged the various items of antipasti and mezze dishes in the centre of the blanket and around the uneven mounds of the tufted grass beneath. He pulled the plastic film lids from the various containers and poured the Sancerre into a plastic tumbler that he had spotted discarded on the side, hastily rinsed out and sloshed wine into, before surreptitiously carrying it outside to incorporate it into their picnic dinner. After some rearranging, he called to Lucy from the rear garden.

He stood nervously at the ends of the reach of the sprawling tree's limbs and observed with relief as she took in the sight of her beloved apple tree adorned in lights that twinkled as its green leaves swayed gently in the breeze of the dusky sky. The stunned smile that spread across her face filled him with warmth.

"Given you made dinner last night, I thought I'd reciprocate. I wasn't sure exactly what you like so got a bit of everything."

"Turner, it's perfect, thank you!"

Delighted, Turner gazed at her face as she blushed, sat down legs crossed next to him on the blanket and daintily selected a random array of finger food laid out before them.

"Hey, thought for the day," he said, "as I'm feeling inspired by our surroundings. Actually, it's Albert Einstein's thought but he said: 'there are two ways to live your life. One is as though nothing is a miracle. The other is as though everything is a miracle.' It feels fitting."

Absorbing his words, she enthusiastically agreed, "Yes, take the chorus of birds chattering and singing in the background. The wildlife is serenading us. As the native species I've chosen for Oakland Walk mature, I hope wildlife will return there too. It has to be a significant improvement on the car park that was there beforehand!"

Appearing to listen intently to the sounds of their surroundings, she continued, "Ooh, I'm not brilliant with birdsong but I recognise that distinctive two-syllabled song."

"I've no idea!" responded Turner.

With a mischievous smile, Lucy continued, "They're green and yellow with a striking glossy black head and white cheeks."

She paused expectantly before continuing with another clue for him, "They're a woodland bird that has adapted to more manmade habitats. Exactly the sort of bird we'd hope to encourage here."

Turner continued to look blankly back at her so she continued, "They're a familiar sight in gardens."

Turner desperately cast his eyes around the rear garden searching for a bird that might meet Lucy's description, albeit not convinced he'd be able to name it even if he happened to see one.

Putting him out of his misery, she exclaimed, "They're great tits!" Lucy beamed, despite feigning exasperation at his lack of avian knowledge.

Turner's roving eyes met Lucy's gaze and inadvertently swept downwards over her cleavage.

"Yes, indeed they are!" He winked.

Turner watched on, amused, as Lucy blushed and then quickly proceeded to act as if he'd said nothing at all, instead returning to chatting easily about the plants around them and reiterating her desire to ensure the garden would in time only contain native species. They nibbled and picked at the plastic containers of mixed food as they did so. Pausing to take turns drinking from their shared beaker of wine.

Although relieved that he'd seemingly distracted Lucy from the meeting, in the moments of amiable silence, Turner's thoughts kept returning to the questions raised about the nature of his relationship with her.

Tentatively, he broached the subject. "I'm not sure whether this is the time or place or indeed if there is an appropriate time or place but I heard that twat probing you about your personal relationships or, more specifically, your relationship with me."

"Ugh, I know," she replied, throwing her hands up in indignation. "I hope I put him back in his place. He had no right to ask and I found it patronising and insulting that he implied he'd be keener on this project if I were to somehow align myself with him. It should be considered on its own merits!"

"I agree entirely. It's none of their business," he said and then paused to regroup as he considered how to segue to the question he actually wanted to ask. "I'd like to think, though, that whatever this thing is between us is our business, yours and mine that is," he said, softly repeating the words he'd heard her use. "Even if you hadn't given it much thought until now, had you answered the twat's questions, what would you have said?"

"You mean how would I describe the dynamic between us?" Lucy enquired, her demeanour giving nothing away.

Turner nodded, hoping it would encourage her to elaborate.

"Well, I guess I would have said that we have a certain professional commitment to each other from working together on the build at Oakland Walk. Hmm, sorry, I'm thinking out loud." She paused, apparently not entirely happy with her wording. "Actually, given I'm shortly finishing on your site, perhaps I'd have said we *had* a commitment there and that we've developed a mutually respectful working relationship. I think I'd then explain that I'd hope to see that relationship continue at Sunnyside. I'd likely also have said you're supportive of me, my plans for my site and that you have a working understanding of my finances."

Lucy paused again. Turner scanned her face as she still hadn't yet covered off what he was angling for. She continued, "I'd have said that constitutes a relationship of sorts but a friendly one. If I had had to label us, I'd have said we're in a committed platonic relationship with each other." She broke eye contact to scan the garden. Apparently contriving not to meet his gaze, softly, she uttered, "I guess that makes us friends with benefits."

Turner almost choked on hearing the words. Shocked, he asked, "Sorry…it makes us what?"

Lucy coyly returned her gaze to meet his. "Friends with benefits. We've worked at Oakland Walk together and I'm hoping you'll continue working on Sunnyside with me. That's a reasonably long-term commitment. You know my plans, you have an idea of my financial position and, on a personal level, you're slowly building a picture of my strengths and weaknesses, my insecurities, my history and so on. I'm garnering the same backstory about you. All these things imply a commitment, a relationship of sorts which, in our case, means our friendship comes with additional benefits."

"Oh," Turner said, lost for words. "Lucy, I like the explanation but…erm…friends with benefits enjoy *sexual* benefits. Friends with benefits is normally a synonym for fuck buddies. They gloss over all the meaningful stuff, swapping that for rampant sex instead." An awkward sounding chuckle escaped his mouth with his held breath.

"Ah, how embarrassing," Lucy replied, face flushing discernibly in the fading light, hands shooting up to cover her eyes. "I'm so naïve."

"No," Turner reassured her, chuckling, "it's endearing…"

Lucy looked unconvinced. In the ensuing silence, Turner realised she had begun to shiver as dusk had since descended properly and the temperature had fallen. Although she made no move to draw their evening to a close, night-time was slowly enveloping them.

"Your teeth are going to start chattering next… I've had a lovely evening but it's probably time to call it a night." Conscious of not wanting to spoil the ambience between them nor to pressure her in any way and still unsure how to follow up on her analysis of their dynamic, he began to return the empty containers to the carrier bag. He shook out and folded his blanket and unplugged the lights. His senses were immediately heightened by having been plunged into darkness after extinguishing the warm glow of the festoon lights. Cautiously, he followed her back to the caravan in a heavy silence. She made no move to discourage him from trailing behind her.

Trying to alleviate any apprehension Lucy may feel at having him back in the confines of the caravan, and indeed her anxiety at facing what would likely be her first night alone, he said, "You must be exhausted again this evening. I've had a lovely time and the choice as to what happens next is entirely yours. I can head off now or we could share some more wine but, if we do, I would then need to stay over again. I'd never drink and drive but do need the van for work tomorrow morning. Obviously, if you're okay with it,

I'm happy to adopt the same sleeping arrangements as last night."

He waited nervously, studying her face to gauge her reaction. To his satisfaction, Lucy laid her fingers over his on the wine bottle and encouraged him to pour the remaining pale fluid into the tumbler.

"I've really enjoyed this evening," she said. "Thank you. The finance meeting felt like such a big deal beforehand and it's hardly crossed my mind since. Erm, to be sure we're on the same page, though, I need you to know I'm not planning on offering you any extra benefits if you stay over again this evening."

Gently clutching her hand in his and resting the other on the side of her face to softly encourage her to meet his gaze, Turner replied, "Don't worry. I'm not asking or expecting you to. I'm offering to stay over on whatever terms you'd like."

They consumed the tumbler's contents in relative silence, both seated on their respective sofas on either side of the caravan. Lucy then retreated to the bathroom cubicle and began to perform the same bedtime routine as the night prior. With barely concealed glee, he relished the sight of her return in the same skimpy sleeping apparel as he had enjoyed just 24 hours beforehand. He had idly fantasised about it multiple times in the hours since. Lucy drowsily settled onto her sofa-cum-bed, and Turner obediently stripped down to his boxers and unfurled himself along his own, lying rigidly atop the unyielding, textured upholstery.

"Night, Turner," she murmured. "Thank you."

"Goodnight, Lucy, sleep well," he replied in a whisper.

Supine, arms folded behind his head, he listened to her delicate breathing as she drifted off to sleep. She seemed to settle quickly, presumably tired from toiling at the walls, the meeting and, he hoped, as a result of drawing some comfort from his presence. In the vestiges of light cast by the glowing clockface and pilot lights of the caravan's various appliances, he fancied he could make out the feminine curves of her silhouette. The thought of her scantily clad form lying so close to his made him rock hard again. *Traitorous dick!* He knew the likelihood of having a good night's sleep would be slim as he tossed and turned and tried to occupy his mind with anything that would mitigate the distraction of the enchanting woman next to him.

At some stage, he must have slept fitfully because he subsequently woke with testosterone coursing through his veins and his dick still agonisingly hard. Although the exact content of his fast-receding dream eluded him, he sensed he'd been enjoying it. He concluded Lucy must have played a central role in his somnambulant mind's fantasy as his persistent erection stood at attention ready to revel in performing its role in his fading dream's next scene.

The minutes proceeded to tick by uncomfortably, gradually morphing into hours, as he ineffectually willed his throbbing erection to subside. To his consternation, it brought into sharp focus for him that his previous sexual encounters had been lacking. Even just having Lucy's slumbering form *almost* within touching distance was confoundingly becoming the most potent aphrodisiac he had ever experienced. Alarmed, he concluded he would have to address the situation before she awoke as it would be too humiliating to have her come to in the morning and be greeted by him still awake and bleary eyed with upright shaft pointing conspicuously up towards the ceiling, vying to escape his boxers.

Ill at ease and, as the blue dawn light began to creep into the confines of the caravan, he tried to angle himself away from her, tilting himself slightly towards the caravan's external wall that ran down the length of his bed. Awkwardly, he reached down with his left hand to push the waistband of his boxers below the base of his shaft, which pulsated agonisingly as it sprang free. An involuntary groan escaped his lips before he could clamp them together so as to seek his release as quietly as possible. He circled his girth with clasped fingers and pumped up and down his length. After hours spent painfully erect, he had been convinced he would blow almost immediately but the muffled rustling of his blanket as he palmed his dick, the unhelpful angle at which he was propped and the thought of Lucy waking to find him masturbating in her caravan were distracting him from the urgent task at hand.

Lucy shifted in her sleep. He froze as he waited for her to resettle. Like a statue, he hesitated and then cast a wary glance over his shoulder. Satisfied that she was still out for the count, he furtively picked up momentum as he rhythmically stroked himself. *Fuck. Please finish, please finish,* replayed like a mantra in his mind. Of course, as is invariably the way, his desire for a hasty release served to have the opposite effect.

Absorbed with his own frustration and in order to manoeuvre himself into a better position, he shifted onto his back and adjusted his exasperated grip on himself.

"Turner," Lucy whispered, "are you okay?"

Shit! Even in the pale light, she could surely see he had his hand firmly clasped around his exposed throbbing shaft. The pale veined skin would be highlighted against his dark boxers like an unwelcome beacon proclaiming his desire.

Numbed by the thought of the sight that Lucy must be able to discern in the gloom, words failed him. He waited for her reprimand, voice heavy with betrayal or disgust but, as the seconds passed, no such admonishment escaped her lips.

Again breaking the silence, she whispered huskily, "Don't let me distract you."

Turner couldn't believe his ears. Rolling over and turning her back to him, it appeared she was simply going to go back to sleep. *What the hell?* For the second time that evening, she'd shocked him.

"Fuck, woman," he groaned. "You are the distraction."

Mercifully though, the distress at having been busted hard dick in hand, prompted his erection to subside. It shrivelled away exactly as he wanted the rest of him to be able to do. Mortified, he lay there straining to detect any indication as to whether she was in fact going back to sleep. More likely, she too would remain uncomfortably awake, head reeling at having witnessed such a graphic display of his unrestrained horniness. Whilst Turner tossed and turned self-consciously, Lucy lay motionless.

Just as he finally surmised she must have nodded off again, her voice pierced the cloying silence, "I can't get that image out of my head. Even though it's dark, I got a pretty good look at you."

Oh fuck, she's gearing up to chuck me out in the middle of the night.

"Am I really the cause of…that?" she enquired cautiously.

"Yes, of course you are," he replied, hoping he didn't sound exasperated at how obvious he thought it was and how sexually pent-up he felt. "Surely that's not so hard to believe. You seem to be blissfully unaware of how sexy you are and the effect you have on me." He paused and clarified, "Well, you *were* blissfully unaware until a few minutes ago that is. Ugh, I'm sorry. Throbbing dick in hand isn't exactly how I'd imagined telling you I like you," he said ruefully. "At some point over the last few weeks, I've realised I find you insanely attractive and, for the second night in a row, I'm lying in a confined space with said dynamite in reach and semi-naked. The pre-bedtime mention of friends with benefits hasn't helped either in so far as it's given, at least one part of me, all sorts of inappropriate content to get hard over."

"I'm so embarrassed about that," Lucy muttered in the gloom.

"You're embarrassed…?" Turner asked incredulous. "Let's put that in context. At this moment, you're embarrassed that your understanding of friends with benefits wasn't entirely accurate. I, on the other hand, got so carried away thinking about what the reality of being friends with benefits might entail that I've been lying here in your caravan, while you slept no less, with Pam and her five sisters desperately trying to sort me out."

"Pam and her five sisters…?" Lucy replied, voice rising in question. "Oh, oh, I get it," she stuttered after a pause. Turner laughed looking down at himself and surveying the compromising scene that Lucy must also have been able to make out from her sofa. "In the grand scheme of embarrassing moments, I think I have you beat," he continued. "On the plus side, the mortification seems to have finally seen off my raging hard-on. Pam's no longer needed."

"Sorry to kick you whilst you're down," Lucy giggled in the semi-darkness. "But good thing Pam was on hand to help, literally and figuratively." She chuckled louder, clearly amused at her own joke. "I'm not sure *this friend* is ready to offer you that kind of benefit yet." With that, she fluffed her pillow, readjusted her sleeping bag and rolled over, again with every semblance of planning to return to sleep.

Turner continued to lie there stunned in uncomfortable silence. Although his erection had subsided, sleep still wouldn't come easily. His subsequent rest was fitful at best. He wasn't sure whether he had actually even managed to drift off before Lucy began to stir again as the morning light filtered through the gaps between the blinds.

"How did you sleep?" she whispered as if their exchange of only an hour or two prior had already slipped from her mind.

"Erm, if I'm honest, I'm not sure I did sleep. I think I've just laid here cringing."

Lucy shifted on her bed. "I'm not convinced I slept all that much either since we…spoke. I haven't been able to erase the image of you from my mind."

"I'm sorry," Turner interrupted.

"No, no it's not that," Lucy clarified. "I found it…arousing," she elaborated, in a husky voice.

Fuck, what do I say to that? Turner thought. After what felt like an eternity, time frozen still, Lucy moved herself into a sitting position. Turner had no idea what to expect next. Her actions gave nothing away as to whether she was about to ask him to leave or something else. Enraptured, he watched as she reclined on the corner of her sofa, diagonally across the space from him. Still just out of reach.

"Unless you object," she murmured, eyes scanning his face, as she lifted her left foot onto the top of the chest of drawers that separated their two beds and settled the right foot's sole down on the sofa beside her, "I thought I might reconsider my position in relation to the benefits."

Turner nodded vigorously, relief tinged with anticipation flooding through him. Maintaining his fascinated gaze, she deliberately hitched her knees and tilted her pelvis towards him. Although still separated by the gap between their respective sofas, he was mesmerised as she sensuously brought her fingers to her mouth, parted her pouting lips and very deliberately sucked on her middle three fingers in turn. She then walked her glistening, saliva-coated fingers down her body, pushed her skimpy shorts to one side and began to caress herself in an exquisite circling swirl. With the fabric of her sleepwear clinging to her, he lost all coherent thought as her probing fingers bewitchingly sank inside her. Her hips rocked as she caressed her body with her other hand. *Fuck.*

Her hands morphed into his in his mind, his dick instantly hardening again in his palm. He daren't move or extend his own arms to touch her for fear of the erotic vision ebbing away before his eyes. With each shaky breath that escaped her lips, her body arched, enabling him to trace the profile of her erect nipples against her cotton vest. He longed to peel it from her body as the raw chemistry flowing between them intensified his desire for her. Her yielding body stiffened subtly with the increasing pressure of her dainty, probing fingers. She remained like this for some time, fingers tracing a spiralling pattern across her damp skin and gasping softly as she pleasured herself. The muscles tightened in his jaw as her eyes dilated and began to glaze. His cock twitched involuntarily as she caught her lower lip between her teeth, seemingly teetering on the edge. Her fingers grazed her entrance as she whimpered appreciatively.

Now painfully hard again, Turner began to rub himself in unison with her. The speed and pressure of the sweeping motion of her fingers over her entrance increased further. Her body bucked and arched, her breath catching with each wave. He pumped himself as her ragged breaths became interspersed with increasingly frequent moans.

Her head rolled back, exposing her pale neck and sending hair cascading behind her. "Come with me, Turner," she commanded, eyes closed in pleasure, as she plunged her fingers into her slick opening and climaxed with the most erotic mewl.

Before his stunned self and overawed body could register the scene and commit every detail to memory, she seemed to be up and standing beside him, still panting softly as her orgasm subsided. Grasping his right hand and, fingers interlocked with his, she pulled it between her legs. *Holy shit. This is intense.*

She cupped their interlaced hands over her wetness, accentuating the most delectable, subtle pulsing as her core repeatedly clenched in ecstatic response to her orgasm. His mind grappled to process the sensations. Her body trembled and, raising his eyes to her face, his gaze faltered at her red and swollen lips where she'd bitten down on them in her release. He relished the sight as he played with himself. There was a sheen to her skin. She glowed, breathing shaky as her body continued to experience sensual tremors of satisfaction. It left him powerless to resist. He upped the tempo of his own movements at the hottest, most intense vision before him.

A trail of fire pulsed to his crotch. With his chest also now constricting with the pleasure, he intensified the erratic rhythm of his strokes. The friction of his frantic hand rubbing his throbbing length was delicious, even more so given Lucy's proximity as he was able to substitute his hand for hers in his mind. She stood over him, watching him pleasure himself but not participating save for her nails digging into his fingers, which she still held flush to her body. She was anchoring his hand in place and, despite his consuming desire for her, preventing him from probing her wetness. It sent him crashing over the edge too, cock appreciatively firing its load with all-consuming spasms. His body convulsed and quivered all the way down to his toes, which cramped satisfyingly at his powerful release. Turner lay there in stunned rapture.

In what he was sure must be a pitiful attempt to disguise how overawed he felt, he wiped himself with his boxers and shifted onto his side, grasped the blanket in his right arm and again invited Lucy to spoon with him. Words failed him. As she lay down beside him and pressed herself into the nook of his body, Turner was sure they both knew that he was utterly powerless to resist her and that, despite their contrasting sizes, she was in fact entirely in control.

CHAPTER 9

Lucy was scandalised at what had come over her. Despite Turner being her physical dominant, she felt wholly empowered with him. He hadn't pressured or ingratiated himself on her. She didn't detect even a trace of manipulation. Instead, she had chosen to bring him into the caravan, she had encouraged him to stay and she had willingly and vocally participated in what had ensued. Nonetheless, the vortex of contrasting emotions now whirling within meant she felt relieved that they had settled into what was fast becoming their customary spooning position. It enabled her to retreat into her own thoughts, evaluate the wonderful rawness she felt and bask in it before again acknowledging Turner's presence and needs. For his part, she inferred from his relaxed grasp that, convincingly satiated, he was finally able to doze.

Her mind seemed to be in overdrive; on the one hand, reduced to its basest emotions and sensations and intoxicated accordingly and, on the other, analysing. She contemplated the irony that so much in life was about sex, perhaps apart from sex itself. Had the preceding few minutes simply been the culmination of the last few weeks' interactions between them or was there more to come?

She needed to be reassured that the differences she perceived between Turner and Mark were indeed present rather than a figment of her imagination. Eschewing the inherent vulnerability in articulating her thoughts, she felt compelled to voice this to Turner. Not entirely sure whether he was awake or in any state to coherently respond, she whispered, "That was intense."

Turner nodded. "I was just thinking exactly the same," he mumbled.

"Erm, Oscar Wilde is credited with having said that 'Everything in the world is about sex except sex'." She paused as she continued to consider the writer's words. "He considered sex itself to 'be about power'."

"Erm, are you okay?" Turner whispered back, his tone sounding like he genuinely cared about how she was feeling.

"Yes, I guess I just feel a bit exposed and wanted some reassurance." She braced herself, fully expecting to discern his body tensing behind her as a result of broaching a potentially difficult topic.

He languidly pulled her closer to him and replied, "I'm no Oscar Wilde but I'm pretty sure you controlled what we just shared. So, I guess you have all that sexy power he spoke of.

"You're so petite and perfectly formed. Outwardly, I'm bigger and stronger, and you'd expect, by association, that I'd naturally be in control and yet you rendered me powerless to resist. I find it humbling that you, and I guess women more generally, have the courage to share your bodies and beds with men as we're often physically stronger. Know your strength, Lucy. I don't think many men would display such bravery if the roles were reversed."

"I guess my previous relationship conditioned me to think that men only really want sex. With the benefit of hindsight and, hurtful though it is to acknowledge it, I'm not sure how much more I was to Mark than a convenient regular lay."

Flustered and not wanting him to think ill of her, she continued, "Obviously, he was far more to me than that but, by the end, it was apparent we'd viewed our relationship from diametrically opposing perspectives. I thought it was meaningful. I don't think the same could be said of him. Sorry to mention him after what we've just done. I'm feeling a little raw, ecstatically so but raw nonetheless and I don't want to blindly stumble into making the same mistake again."

Nuzzling his face into her neck and ear, he replied, "It's okay. I'm sufficiently confident in who and what I am, and comfortable in my own sexuality that I'm not that easily threatened. To be fair, it's early days. It's understandable that you have some reservations and are drawing comparisons. I think everyone does, although not that I have an obvious past candidate who'd compare to you. Besides—" He chuckled. "We've already spoken at length about my relationship with my mum, which is also something of a faux-pas, so I'm in no position to judge you for airing perfectly legitimate emotions even if that involves mentioning an ex." The smile was audible in his voice. "Also, anything you say to the detriment of my rivals can only be a good thing from my perspective," he teased.

He continued, "Just to reassure you, though, sex isn't just a bodily release for most men either. Don't get me wrong, you just made my release phenomenal but, in all seriousness, it's about an emotional connection for us too." Poking fun he added, "Given you've brought up Mark, I feel I can commit another post-coital no no and again reference my mum. She'd argue that, for men too, sex embodies love and care and offers support and comfort. It satisfies our need, like yours, to feel desired, and, incidentally, that was fucking hot."

He paused then continued, "I don't want to speak out of turn, Lucy, but, from what little I witnessed of Mark that day in the cabin, beyond being a complete cock womble, I'd say he's also a narcissist. You can't judge yourself by the standards he expected of you."

Lucy tried to process the meaning of his words, stifling an inadvertent giggle at his use of cock womble. It sounded so amusingly incongruous coming from Turner.

"He tried to manipulate you to his own ends and compromised your self-esteem in the process. I have it on good authority, though, from she who shall not be named again while we're lying in flagrante," he reassured burrowing his face into her neck, breath sending warm currents of air across her neck and cheek, "that, perhaps counterintuitively, narcissists are often attracted to strong, confident and self-assured women. The raving feminist disguised as my grey-haired mother would argue he more likely pursued you because he recognised that you were strong-willed and talented."

Scanning her face, he continued, "You'd know better than me whether he indeed had narcissistic traits but, if so, I'd bet a key part of your appeal would ultimately have been that you'd reflect well on him."

Turner pulled her closer. "And that he cheated or lost interest or whatever it is that happened between you isn't a reflection on you either."

Lucy nestled into him, drawing comfort from his contact.

"Incidentally, I'm grateful that whatever happened happened because we wouldn't be here together now if it hadn't. For what it's worth, any faults he perceived you to have were more likely a reflection of his own deep-rooted insecurities and really nothing specific to you.

Caressing her side, he continued, "That day in the cabin, I would have intervened sooner if I'd thought you needed me to. It took every ounce of my self-restraint not to."

His fingers flexed against her skin. Lucy couldn't imagine Turner hitting anyone but the way his hand clenched seemed reminiscent of making a fist.

He returned to softly running his fingers over her skin. "As I recall, he said you were overreacting and that it was your fault your relationship broke down. I don't believe that for a second. Everything I've seen of you so far says otherwise. I think he wanted to blame you because the alternative would necessitate some self-reflection. That would challenge his perception of himself.

"I'm sure he also said something along the lines that you'd never find anyone as good as him. Firstly, I disagree and—" Teasingly, in her ear, whispered, "Here I am."

Lucy smiled at his attempt to lighten the tone, softening towards him with every additional word that escaped his beautiful lips.

"Deep down, he knows you're a good person and so tried to appeal to your better nature by saying you did this to yourself. As I've already said, he's a cock womble."

Lucy sobbed quietly as she absorbed the weight of Turner's words. "I feel so stupid. I dedicated three years to him and couldn't see him for what he was. You saw right through him in moments."

"Lucy, don't be so hard on yourself. I've had a lifetime of listening to a matriarchal feminist-cum-farmer's wife. Like you, mum's a catalogue of wonderfully endearing contradictions. Besides, how agitated Mark was in the cabin showed he feels strongly for you. The downside for him is that he also seemed to possess a complete lack of empathy."

"Ugh," she sighed. "I can see what you're saying makes sense. Just now, I finger fucked myself in front of you and felt like an absolute goddess as you watched on—"

A LABOUR OF LOVE

"Ha, I think that's the first time I've heard you swear," Turner cut in. "Anyway, I'd echo that sentiment. You looked like an absolute goddess too."

Lucy, glowing at his compliment, pressed her hips back towards him. His body responded, muscles stiffening at the contact.

"Anyway, it felt amazing and freeing to lose my composure completely and to feel elation not shame in that. I'm conscious it's a big no no to draw comparisons but, with Mark, afterwards I'd sometimes struggle to shake this uncomfortable sensation of having been used.

"I'm embarrassed to admit it but, the first time we had sex, it was actually in a side office at an art gallery during a corporate event. At the time, I was naively flattered at how commandeering he was with me. I guess I don't have any objections to it being a bit rough per se but somehow it felt degrading too. Afterwards, in the cold light of day, I felt more sullied than sensuous, dirty rather than desired.

"I saw that as a reflection of my prudishness and inexperience, though." She cringed. "I can't believe that even until yesterday I thought friends with benefits was friends plus knowledge of finance or shared work commitments or something. That's naïve!"

244

"So what if it is," Turner interjected. "I found it endearing," he continued, sounding amused. "Maybe you were just looking into the future, staring into a magic eight ball, as I'm pretty sure we definitely now qualify as being friends with benefits at the very least, more even."

"Ha," Lucy replied, feigning indignation. "I think we might have passed that base already. Seriously, though, the whole relationship left me confused, not knowing my left from my right, questioning my own judgement, and I'm not sure how I grow to trust myself and my own judgement again let alone have confidence in someone else."

Softly, Turner said, "I'm not sure whether it helps or makes it worse but I doubt his behaviour was specific to you."

Lucy's muffled reply escaped the pillow into which she'd shielded her grimacing face. "Oh God, I feel like we're exorcising my demons as we rake over the ashes of my past failed relationships. It does make sense, though. He always wanted his own needs satisfied first and, if I'm completely honest, didn't seem concerned as to whether mine were met. I just took that to be representative of all men. My own climax often proved elusive. At the time, I put that down to my own sexual shortcomings."

"Fuck, Lucy," Turner uttered on a hot breath into her ear as he ground his pelvis into her backside and rolled his hips against her. "You've just bestowed upon me the most intense sexual encounter of my entire life and that was *without* having sex. Don't question your sensuality; own it! You're beautiful, feminine and insanely attractive."

Lucy softened a little and allowed the positive glow from their encounter to wash back over her. Turner gave her a reassuring little squeeze. She then watched as Turner slowly pulled himself back from her, his hand trailing her side as he did so, like he too wanted to preserve the contact. He righted himself into a seated position, limbs still resting against hers and fumbled around amongst his discarded personal effects with no obvious purpose. As he extricated himself from amongst the bundled blanket, she was left cold along the skin he had exposed. He pulled his boxers up over his defined quads, readjusting himself as he did so. Fascinated, she watched, as he shuffled over to the caravan worktop, noticing with satisfaction that he was already uncomfortably hard again, his desire clearly not having been affected by the talk of ex-boyfriends, mothers and emotions.

He swilled the largely evaporated dregs of the previous night's wine from their shared tumbler down the sink, then rinsed and filled it with juice. Lucy didn't recognise the carton and was sure she had finished the one she'd bought the day before, so concluded he must have brought it with him.

Aware she was watching and by way of explanation, he said, "I picked up some juice. I noticed you drank some yesterday and thought maybe you'd prefer it to tea or something."

This small act alone brought the difference between Turner and Mark starkly into focus. Mark had always wanted her to drink tea because that was what he thought people expected. Turner, on the other hand, had observed Lucy's preference for juice and had thoughtfully purchased some more for her. He hadn't been prompted or asked. Instead, he had made a note of this little detail and picked some up for her with no expectation of receiving anything in return. She inwardly laughed. *Rachel will be delighted! She always bloody said the guy for me would notice my love of juice!*

She gratefully took a sip before sidling past him in the aisle, as sensuously as she could muster, on route to the toilet cubicle at the rear to wash and dress. She admired his confidence in dressing in front of her but didn't yet feel that same ease robing and disrobing under his gaze. Ridiculous really, given what they had just done. Furthermore, everything he had said and made her feel prompted her to surmise his gaze would be wholeheartedly appreciative if she were to let him watch her dress.

The faint reverberation of her mobile phone vibrating on the kitchen worktop alerted her to a text. Disappointed at being brought back to the mundanity of reality rather than the glorious bubble they'd occupied for the preceding few hours, she continued to dress in the cubicle. Once satisfied that she looked presentable, she opened the cubicle door to find Turner scooping up his keys, phone and wallet. With some disappointment at his apparent haste to get to work, she stood, face upturned, as he inclined his head towards her. He pressed a fleeting whisper of a kiss to her cheek before pulling open the flimsy caravan door, waving his goodbye and departing.

Lucy dolefully watched his receding form darting through the vegetation and down the drive before her phone's follow-up vibration reminded her she'd received a message and brought her focus back to the caravan. She glanced at the illuminated screen, face lighting up to see a message from Rachel.

Hey Juicy, Bet you smashed it at the meeting! That's my girl! I hope having the site manager present helped.

Take full advantage of him! Can't wait to see you again. Miss you! Xx

Lucy smiled inwardly at Rachel's support. It still surprised her how the pair of them had become so close, her perfectly styled, manicured and coiffured friend. She giggled at the sight of Rachel tottering across the cracked front drive in her customary killer heels the day before. She had looked more like a power-dressing dominatrix than someone who had come to tour a friend's new home and refurb project. She chuckled too at Rachel having agreed that Turner was strapping only for Turner to completely misread her and offer to retrieve the mystical straps for her from wherever she had stashed them.

Lucy recalled the conversation she and Rachel had had when she'd visited. They had discussed her reservations with getting involved with someone again. On the one hand, keen to explore what she could have with Turner, on the other, apprehensive about the impact on her fragile ego if things were to go wrong between them. She had voiced to Rachel how at ease and confident in himself Turner appeared, the attention he had paid in the cabin to her interaction with Mark and his emotional intelligence. In stark contrast to Rachel's demeanour when discussing Mark, she had brimmed with praise for Turner despite only really being able to judge him based on Lucy's manner when talking about him.

"You're so animated, so enthusiastic…so alive when you speak about him," Rachel commented.

The voice of reason in her own inimitable way, she also challenged Lucy's reservations, "I would only ever want to be with someone I could hurt and indeed who would be capable of hurting me. I know that sounds counter-intuitive but if I feel strongly enough for someone and sufficiently connected to them, then that exposes both of us to the possibility of being hurt. Like with Ant, for example, I know I try to avoid speaking about him but, when we were together during and after uni, it was amazing! We both threw ourselves into our relationship and were completely immersed in it and each other. I guess we were too young for it to work out, though, and, when we broke up, that pain, that sense of loss was almost unbearable. Still now, some years down the line, no other relationship I've had could compare to that intensity, that vulnerability of placing your heart in someone else's hands and hoping they'll be careful with it."

Rachel continued, "I would rather have that strength of feeling and accept the potential implications of that passion than settle for mediocrity. It would be cynical and unfulfilling to seek out someone to whom I'm indifferent simply to shield my heart from possible pain. I want to choose to experience life's highs and lows in glorious technicolour."

Rachel's words struck a chord with Lucy.

She continued, "Even if the worst were to happen and you were to go your separate ways, you're strong. Have faith and confidence in who and what you are. Believe your tattooed reminder to yourself; you're capable, you're resilient and Turner would be privileged to have you."

"But, Ray, what if I fail?"

Rachel responded reassuringly, "That's a possibility but, look at it from another perspective. What if, as per your tattoo, you fly?"

Lucy smiled at the recollection. The conversation between the two of them had taken place whilst they'd surveyed Sunnyside's sorry kitchen and the beautiful, mature garden beyond. Discerning birdsong in the background, Rachel had insisted Lucy also scan the garden for the avian source.

"Can you see the bird that's making the call we can both hear?" she asked, hand indicating where she thought the song was originating from.

"Yes," Lucy had replied uncertainly, pointing out a feathered flash of green and yellow, not sure what Rachel was getting at. "It's one of my resident great tits perched on a branch of the apple tree."

"Well, clearly it has impeccable taste in trees," Rachel replied, eyes roving over the tree's branches. "As that one is spectacular. More importantly, though, look at it sitting in the tree as it sings confidently. It can do so because it isn't

afraid that the branch might break. Do you know why that is?"

Just as Lucy went to reply, it became clear Rachel meant it as a rhetorical question continuing, "Because it doesn't need to trust the branch. It trusts its own wings instead."

"Aw, that's a lovely, fitting sentiment but, I guess to continue the analogy, I feel like my wings have been clipped after my bad experience with Mark."

Sympathetically, Rachel replied, "That may be so but now put your faith back in Jesse Quinn Thornton's words, Juicy."

Heeding Rachel, Lucy returned to her phone and, smiling naughtily, typed a quick reply.

He was great during the meeting and...after! I think he genuinely likes me. I'm just trying to get my head around liking him too.

Last night had magnified just how masculine Turner was; the archetypal hot-blooded male. She hadn't really focussed on it previously but, realising he was wrestling with his lust and testosterone-induced impulses around her, had made it clear that he must previously have been forcibly downplaying these desires so as not to scare her off. Perhaps, with Turner's help, she could move forward with confidence. She had shown him her faults, her insecurities, even spoken of her past boyfriend and their sex life and he had taken it all in his stride. She couldn't resist also sending Turner a message too.

Thanks again for an amazing night! Have a good day at work and maybe stop by later if you want to? x

Lucy felt like a nervous teenager. It had been so long since she had flirted or bantered that she couldn't remember the etiquette. In the past, she would have waited for the guy to message first but surely she and Turner were adult enough to know what they wanted and hence beyond playing games with each other. Rather than sit, staring eagerly at her phone, she resolved to set back to work on the master bedroom walls and finalise the layout of the ensuite bathroom, the type of tiles she wanted etc.

Hours later and, as she knew Turner's working day would be drawing to a close, she couldn't help but feel disappointed that he hadn't been in touch. She resolved to work as late into the evening as possible in the main bedroom to distract herself. If she could get the walls finished, ready for painting or wallpapering, she could then just flop exhausted into bed in the hope that sleep would quickly overcome her as a result.

CHAPTER 10

Turner awoke feeling groggy, torn from sleep by the shrill ringing of his alarm. It was the first time in weeks that he'd still been out cold when it had gone off. He supposed it wasn't surprising given the effort required and pressures of the colossal task to get the show home at Oakland Walk complete. His tiredness was compounded by the couple of pleasurable but disturbed nights couch surfing at Lucy's. Now back in his own bed, he tried to convince himself that finishing the show home was of such priority that he couldn't allow himself to indulge in revisiting flashbacks of the time with Lucy. He had felt superhuman the morning he'd left hers and ecstatic that, as he'd slowly coaxed Lucy out of her shell, she had laid herself bare for him.

But, as he'd been packing up to leave, she had received a text and he hadn't been able to resist reading it as it had flashed up on her screen. Although uncomfortable about the inadvertent breach of her privacy, this was outweighed by seeing the sender was saved in her phone as Ray. Much as he racked his brain, he couldn't remember her having mentioned a Ray and didn't appreciate his suggestion that Lucy use him to her advantage. He had willingly given his help but would he have done so had he considered that there might be an ulterior motive beyond her enthusiasm for his assistance?

The sensory bombardment he felt in her presence was dissipating with some physical distance between them. He needed to be able to take stock and required some separation to do so. The text Lucy sent him moments after he had left her very much made it sound like the feelings he had for her were reciprocated but he nevertheless found himself faltering when it came to responding in kind. Nonetheless, he felt a conflicted desire and responsibility to help her expedite her master bedroom and ensuite so that she at least wouldn't be obliged to remain in the caravan indefinitely.

As he'd elected to return to his place last night, Lucy would have had her first night alone in the caravan. He wondered whether she had suffered his absence as acutely as he had felt hers. He knew that once he was on site and, despite the frantic pace to get the show home complete, she'd keep returning to the forefront of his mind. She had after all chosen the colour scheme and finishing touches for the show home. It was coming together beautifully and her influence was inescapable.

Although the commute to work wasn't long, it was a journey he knew so well that Lucy was able to keep filtering into his thoughts as he drove. Keen for a reprieve from her clouding his mind and aware he needed to focus on making the transformation of the show home as apparent as possible, Turner sought out Andy as soon as he arrived at Oakland Walk. He asked Andy to work his way round the house removing discarded packaging, excess paint and any carpet off-cuts Turner hadn't yet stacked in the hall. They surveyed the task together, walking from room to room.

"I know I say it on every project but I can never get over how much a new house can absorb. We always end up drowning in mountains of packaging. Every bathroom fixture and fitting, every kitchen unit, door, all the light fittings and so on – surely they don't need this much wrapping. I know they've all got to be protected in transit but it seems unnecessary."

"Nah, Gaff, you've got it all wrong," Andy corrected jokingly. "I like to think of it as Christmas coming early. I tell myself I'm unwrapping presents and so love every minute."

Turner smiled at his friend's infectious positivity.

"I like your style. Once you've cleared the house of wrapping paper then, can you amass all of the excess materials – carpet off-cuts, underlay, paint, skirting, whatever you find that's still usable – and load it into your van please."

"Happy to." Andy shrugged in acknowledgement. "But you got something or indeed someone on your mind, Gaff? You remember I'm not your cheapest labour?" he asked as he bent, spreading his arms wide to haul a large roll of carpet onto his shoulder.

"No, I'm perfectly aware. No distractions here. You can carry twice what the other lads can so you'll do it in half the time. It's all part of my grand master plan." He winked, tapping his temple.

They both looked at the heavy roll of carpet, resting limply over his shoulders and sagging at each end. Andy carefully rotated ready to navigate his way out through the door opening en route to his battered red van. Unlike Turner's grey run around, Andy's red long wheelbase was a packhorse, much like Andy himself. Its cavernous interior would readily accommodate the superfluous materials.

As ever, Andy was seeking opportunities for extra work. Hopeless with money for as long as he and Turner had been friends, Andy tried to squeeze in some bathroom tiling in an evening or perhaps rebuilding a damaged garden wall at the weekend to help supplement the income from his site work. In Turner's opinion, he needed to manoeuvre himself into a position where he could buy a small property of his own, leverage his skills to revamp it and, thereby, slowly begin to claw his way up the property ladder. That, of course, first necessitated managing to accumulate sufficient funds to get on the first rung.

As Andy returned for a second load, Turner filled him in, explaining, "Lucy chose all these finishes. Given she has a tight budget for doing up her own place and this would all be skip fodder otherwise – we all know they don't want it back in store – I thought you might like some extra work dropping it to hers."

"Sure, Gaff," Andy replied affably. "Everyone's a winner."

It had already occurred to Turner that by arranging for Andy to assist Lucy, he would be helping them both. It also enabled him to take a step back to allow himself the headspace to interrogate his intentions with Lucy a bit further. Acutely aware of her fragility after Mark, he wanted to be sure he wouldn't hurt her and equally didn't want to leave himself exposed to getting hurt either.

He looked back at Andy, who was making light work of his load. Part of the reason why Turner's projects were so successful was because he had learnt to play to the various lads' strengths and, in Andy's case, this involved acknowledging that he was not only physically strong but also far better suited to the heavier duty roles than the titivating.

"Andy, the cleaners are beginning to descend on the show home. We both know you're better at taking things apart than putting them back together, Billie Jean, so maybe now's the time please to drive the stuff over to Lucy's."

"Enough said. Suits me!" Andy replied, already rummaging in his pocket for his keys in order to make a prompt exist.

Turner smiled to himself. Having Andy off-site for the afternoon would be far more constructive than having him remain on site. "I think she's going to be delighted with it all," he muttered quietly to himself.

"Let's hope so, Gaff," Andy called back. "With any luck, she'll give you a special thank you." He winked mischievously over his shoulder, insinuating with a wave of his hands what sort of gratitude he was envisaging her bestowing on Turner.

Thank fuck he wasn't a fly on the wall in the caravan. We'd never hear the end of it!

With Andy out of the way, Turner could dedicate his attention to the others at Oakland Walk rather than trying to plan for damage limitation. Watching Andy stride away with his head held high like he couldn't wait to escape, Turner began to laugh. He brought his hands up to clasp either side of his head as his mind conjured an image from their previous site. Not in the least bit funny at the time, it perfectly captured how Andy's clumsy enthusiasm for helping with the finishing touches often had the reverse effect.

The show home was finished and, together, the pair of them were performing a walk round, traipsing from room to room, checking they were satisfied all snagging was complete. Working as a tag team, they examined light sockets for flecks of paint, skirting for scuffs, windowsills for accumulated dust and more. For whatever reason, checking the kitchen was last on the list. Their eyes were drawn simultaneously to a slight inconsistency in the finish of the white emulsion on the ceiling. The rest of the lads were working on the landscaping just beyond the kitchen bi-folds, which were open to air the show home ready for the series of viewings booked for its imminent open house. Andy bounded outside like an over-sized, enthusiastic puppy, grabbed a hop-up and positioned it on the tiled floor beneath the minor blemish in the paint's surface. Armed with a pot of white paint in one hand and a brush in the other, he jumped up onto the hop-up in an easy leapfrog.

At that moment, Michael Jackson's 'Billie Jean' began to blare out from a radio somewhere.

"Watch this," Andy cried, face alight with excitement. He proceeded to attempt a dance pose vaguely reminiscent of one of Michael Jackson's trademark moves. Bending his knees and leaning backwards, he made to rise onto his tiptoes. Apparently forgetting to take into account physics and gravity, shifting his weight onto his toes at the front of the hop-up, unbalanced it. Turner watched on horrified as Andy's expression instantly changed from one of mischievous glee to dread. The hop-up tipped forward with the instability caused by Andy putting his weight onto his toes. Andy, equally destabilized, fell backwards off the hop-up, sending cascades of white paint across the immaculate, new kitchen.

Although Turner could laugh about it now, he had been decidedly unimpressed at the time, as were all the other lads who had all had to stay on site late into the evening. Everyone had been on hands and knees, soaking up the paint with any cloths or rags they could lay their hands on, sponging it off the surfaces and painstakingly wiping it from between the tiles where it had pooled in the grout lines. Needless to say, he was confident everyone would be breathing a collective sigh of relief to see Andy pulling out of site early today, tasked with a separate errand.

Before Turner knew it, lunchtime had rolled around and he was just about to steal away for a moment of solitude in the cabin when, amongst all the commercial vehicles coming and going, Lucy's Yaris pulled into site. Almost before the car had come to a stop, she had hopped out, spotted him and was cutting a determinedly straight path towards him. Rather than engage in front of the lads, he waved to indicate he was heading towards the cabin, hoping that would encourage her to change course and do the same.

"Hey, I'm just going to grab some food. Do you want to join me in the cabin?" he asked lightly.

In acknowledgement, Lucy kept pace, silently striding along at his side and following him up into the cabin. Before he had managed to close the door, she gushed, "Thanks so much for all the stuff you had Andy drop round. I left him unloading. Yay! I'm so excited to be able to use it all," she bubbled. Then, pointedly, and with a hint of hurt in her voice she said, "Is there a reason you didn't bring it yourself, though? Are you avoiding me?"

"Erm, it's not that. I'm busy on site trying to get the show home finished and, until I'm done here, I really need not to get distracted."

"So, now I'm a distraction *again*?" she challenged, a mixture of unease and indignance flashing across her face, tone entirely different from their previous conversation about her being such.

"No, well, yes, maybe. Hopefully a welcome distraction," he said sheepishly. "I just need some time to get my head around it." Turner changed tack, unable to resist airing the queries playing on his mind. "Have you had any other visitors to yours?" he asked, giving Lucy the opportunity to confess and hopefully therefore allay his fears.

"No, just you, Rachel, the finance guys and now Andy with the goodies, for which I'm very grateful. Why?"

Turner raked his fingers through his hair, stalling for what to say next.

"I want to believe you but, in the caravan, when you were changing, you got a text and I just happened to look at it. I'm sorry. I know I shouldn't have but it flashed up on the screen and I'd automatically glanced at it before I thought to stop myself. I'm sorry to ask and I'm conscious I have no real right to but who's Ray, Lucy? When did he visit and, although it's really none of my business, why does he call you Juicy? And, also, I'm not keen on the thought that I'm being taken advantage of or, worse, that some third party is encouraging you to take advantage of me."

He observed Lucy's expression as he spoke, watching the indignance slowly fade and, it appeared, morph into amusement as she raised her hands to encourage him to pause and draw breath.

She took a small step in his direction and began ticking his questions off on her fingers as she spoke. "You should have said something. I haven't snuck some guy over to visit me and hidden him from you. Ray isn't a guy. Rachel is Ray because she is my most treasured, positive and supportive friend. She's my Ray of Sunshine."

Apparently pondering the message, she continued with a slightly embarrassed smile.

"And, yes, I suppose her message did encourage me to take advantage of you but not by simply tapping you for construction help and knowledge. She's so much more comfortable with her sexuality than I am. I'm her prudish friend, albeit apparently aside from when I'm with you. Regardless, she knows I like you and she wants me to take advantage of you…you know, that way instead," she said uncomfortably before brightening. "Huh, she actually wants me to tap you or have you tap me." She giggled. "It's a happy coincidence that you're a skilled builder too."

"Why Juicy then?" Turner asked tentatively, "Or don't I want to know?" He winced humorously awaiting a response.

"You already know the answer to that," she said, a mixture of mirth and frustration playing across her face. "Think back to the other night...and try to work it out."

Turner fidgeted under her stare as his mind raced. Surely she wasn't asking him to voice the only reason he could surmise. He squirmed as she gesticulated with her hands that he speak.

"This is uncomfortable," he groaned. "Erm...when you touched yourself, as you got turned on...you were moist," he stuttered uncomfortably, shrugging his shoulders.

Turner registered that Lucy looked equally horrified. "No, you twit," she exclaimed, clearly utterly mortified, hands flying up to cover her eyes and mouth.

The seconds dragged on before Turner realised her shoulders were beginning to shake and, when she pulled her hands from her face with a grimace, she began to laugh.

"I like juice! It's as innocent as that. You even got juice for me because you'd clocked I drink juice. Rachel noticed the same early in our friendship too and, probably largely to annoy Mark who always seemed to want me to conform in meetings and drink tea or coffee like everyone else, she went out of her way to call me Juicy, which I'd let slip was my childhood nickname.

"Also," she continued, looking pained, "please never use the word moist again. I don't know any woman who likes the term."

Becoming underwhelmingly familiar with the sensation in her presence, relief again washed over him. Turner clarified, "So I'm not simply a handy friend with benefits whilst you're pursuing someone else—"

"Handy, yes, and in more ways than one." Lucy giggled suggestively with a wink. "But no, to be clear, there isn't anyone else. I like you."

"In that case, I'd be delighted to give you a hand anytime," he teased before squarely meeting her gaze. Raking his fingers through his hair and feeling sheepish, he continued "I'm sorry. I jumped to completely the wrong conclusion. In my defence, it's because I like you too and I'm in unfamiliar territory here. I shouldn't have read your message and, once I'd done so, I should have spoken up straightaway rather than withdraw a little."

"Ha," Lucy exclaimed. "I knew there was something up and that it wasn't the case that you were suddenly too busy. Good thing I found some of that courage you keep telling me I possess and manned up enough to come here to speak with you about it."

Turner reached out and pulled Lucy into an embrace. "I'm truly sorry," he whispered.

Her muffled response sent a pleasurable current of warm air across his chest.

"It's okay. I'm implementing a three strikes and you're out policy though!" she giggled. "Our talk about Mark reminded me of the importance of implementing boundaries so I'm afraid you're now going to be subject to the advice you gave me. That being said, you clearly do have a lot going on here and I've left Andy back at Sunnyside so I'd probably better leave you to it. Come join me later if you'd like to, though. Not the most exciting Friday night for you but I'm going bed shopping, as there's bound to be a lead time for one, and then I'll just be cracking on at home."

Appeased, Turner agreed to do so, bent to deposit a chastened kiss on her upturned cheek and, feeling taller with the weight lifted from his shoulders, headed out into the chaos, as yet untouched lunch in hand. He glanced back over his shoulder to watch Lucy safely navigate her way across the forecourt to her car. With a wink he hoped was sufficiently subtle that only she would detect it, he continued to watch as she pulled away and then he ducked back into the show home.

He didn't have much opportunity to ponder the implication of their first proper outing together being bed-shopping before the end of the day rolled round again. The days where he was in constant demand always seemed to pass in a blur. Andy had remained at Lucy's or, at least, hadn't returned to site so Turner surmised he had elected to continue at hers. In his capacity as a subcontractor, Andy had greater independence and autonomy than an actual employee might have. Turner couldn't oblige him to be on site or dictate the hours he worked. Nonetheless, he suspected it suited everyone that Andy remain occupied elsewhere that afternoon.

Silver lining, with Andy absent, there won't be anyone to clock my departure and mock me mercilessly.

After locking up, Turner set off for the out-of-town shopping centre Lucy had mooted. Divine Beds was a large, utilitarian industrial unit on a trading estate of similarly sized and equally non-descript retail outlets selling electronics, clothing and pet-related products. He wondered at how the car parks of such soulless large-scale shopping precincts always seemed to be heaving with shoppers even on a Friday evening. He hated shopping! It only served to highlight how exceptional Lucy must be that he was here. *I've got it bad,* he bemoaned to himself. *It was baffling enough to hear myself jump at being present for a finance meeting. Worse, now I'm brimming with nervous excitement at the prospect of accompanying her bed shopping.*

Striding towards the shop, he couldn't believe this would be the venue for their first date! With anyone else, he would have found even the suggestion disconcerting. Pace quickening with anticipation and awed by her magnetic appeal, he eagerly walked through the sliding doors into the cavernous store. The beds, mattresses and associated furniture were packed in neat rows across the ground floor and, it appeared, on a mezzanine above. He spied Lucy, with her back to him, ambling along the aisle of bed frames. Reluctant to draw attention to himself, he paused beyond the threshold, taking a moment to admire her silhouette. He observed her unseen as she casually strolled from bed to bed looking intently at the labels of each. Her effect on him was undeniable as he admired her sleek figure. His eyes followed the graceful but subtle sashay of her hips as she sauntered down the aisle. His reaction to her was visceral, instantaneously prompting a rush of warmth to his groin.

She innocently but nonetheless delectably bent forwards to examine the board next to a grey bed base. Even in side profile, the movement accentuated the contours of her feminine figure. *Oh, to have her bend over a bed for me like that!* Shaking himself from his reverie and conscious of not wanting her to believe he was late to their rendezvous, he set off towards her, silently applauding and savouring the view as he approached.

Lucy's face lit up on spotting him, a reaction Turner relished. The discomfort of their earlier exchange forgotten, superseded by the pleasure on her face mirroring his own.

"I think I've chosen a bed base already," she announced happily, bouncing with excitement. Lucy stepped aside with a feline flourish of arms, enthusiastically indicating the one by which she stood. "And it's exactly as I envisaged it being too. Look, it's upholstered in a soft-to-the-touch, matt-grey linen-style fabric," she uttered as she reverentially trailed her palm across the tall, cushioned headboard, its material punctuated by a buttoned design.

"It's perfect!" she exclaimed, still visibly hopping with glee. "If I were a bed, this is the bed I'd aspire to be. It's beautiful in an understated way, elegant without being ostentatious and is also practical because it's technically an ottoman too. She demonstrated the latter assertion by raising the mattress at the foot end to reveal an empty divan base. "I can already picture the neatly stacked towels and bedlinen I'll store in there," she exclaimed with a level of excitement that seemed entirely disproportionate but was also both infectious and endearing.

Turner couldn't however resist capitalising on her analogy and, lowering his voice so only she could hear him, murmured, "I think it's very you, Lucy. Incidentally…" He paused. "If you were *this* bed, I'd want to be in you all day."

A muffled squeal escaped Lucy's lips as she blushed. "Turner!" she admonished playfully. "Seriously, what do you think?" she asked as she lowered the hydraulically raised mattress and then stretched out along one side of it, indicating that Turner lay beside her. Once sprawled on it too, he inclined his face towards hers and, just inches away, winked cheekily.

"We'd have to try it out properly for me to be able to give an informed opinion either way. Seems good though."

Amused, he observed her pale skin flush further. "You're incorrigible!" she retorted in mock horror, giggling. "The mattress is comfortable too." She rolled away from him to study the board and continued, "Ooh, I can buy the frame and mattress together today and benefit from some kind of saving. And, although there's a lead time on the bed, we could take the mattress away with us."

Clapping her hands delightedly as she bounced on the mattress, she continued, "Turner, I'd love to have a proper mattress at home!"

Finding the entire experience arousing, amplified by now lying on an actual bed next to Lucy, her wriggling and writhing beside him, Turner's mind was clouded by lust and singularly focussed on conjuring unhelpful double entendres and innuendos. Before he could stop himself, he laughed out another, "If you're going to bounce and bob on it this enthusiastically back at yours for me, I'll do whatever you want or need to help get it home."

Beaming ear to ear but clearly not wanting to be excluded from the pun game, Lucy uttered her own decidedly unsexual but on topic reply, "Spring into action then please. I'll pay whilst you call Andy to see if he can nip over in his van to ferry the mattress back to Sunnyside. I could then meet you and Andy back at home to unload. Eee, I'm so excited! Thank you, Turner." She squeezed him in apparent delight before hopping off the bed and onto her feet.

"Joking aside for a moment, it's genuinely my pleasure." Throwing his hands up in amused consternation, he clarified, "I mean, it *is* my pleasure but my pleasure to be able to help rather than my pleasure in the other sense. Although, to be fair, it'd be my pleasure that way too."

"Ha, come on you. Let's go get down to business." She beamed at him, the joke clearly deliberate judging from her amused expression, before spinning on her heels and making towards the checkout by the exit.

Smirking, Turner slotted in behind her to enjoy the view. The woman's enthusiasm and positive attitude were contagious. He was already buzzing from being in her company when she cast a chaste glance back at him, met his eyes in open challenge and said, "Maybe I can come up with a way to thank you properly later."

Keen to keep up his side of the deal, Turner dutifully placed a call to Andy who, mercifully without questioning him, agreed to hop in the van and head over. Once Lucy had paid and left, and Turner had hung up from Andy, he ambled aimlessly around the soulless shop. He knew that Andy refraining from asking questions over the phone was a temporary reprieve in the interests of efficiency. He'd be subjected to a veritable inquisition as soon as his friend arrived.

Andy often masked his intelligence by making jokes and clowning around but, beneath that, he was sharp. Turner was sure Andy already had his suspicions about them as he'd previously noticed Andy observing him interacting with Lucy. Running his hands through his hair, Turner prepared himself for the inevitable interrogation. *If by some miracle he hasn't yet connected the dots, there's no way I'm going to*

*get away with bed shopping and roping him in to transport
her mattress home.*

Keen to distract himself, Turner made for the mezzanine
and stumbled upon a section dedicated to soft furnishings.
Bed linen, throws, pillows and cushions stretched before
him. Inspired and suddenly imbued with purpose, he set to
locating the items he wanted and retrieving them from the
shelves. He sighed. If Andy still had any lingering doubts
about whether Lucy was his love interest, that he was going
to find Turner laden with soft furnishings destined for Lucy's
home would confirm it. Above all, though, he hoped he
accurately recalled her description of the bedroom she
desired at Sunnyside.

By the time Andy pulled up outside, Turner had paid for his
own purchases and had persuaded a lanky shop assistant to
help him manhandle Lucy's new mattress to the pavement
out front. Wrapped in plastic and determined to bend at
unusual angles and fold in the middle, it had proven difficult
to get it out of the shop in tandem with the young, gangly
assistant.

"Don't ask, mate!" said Turner smiling ruefully as Andy
approached them, stationed one at each end of the mattress.

Presented with Andy's looming presence, the assistant
hastily scuttled off, returning with the bedlinen, pillows,

cushion and throw Turner had purchased. Andy assumed his position at the mattress and, effortlessly, he and Turner lifted the unwieldy item in practised unison. Between them, they scooped up the other items too. Turner loaded them carefully into the cab of Andy's van whilst Andy, still chortling to himself, focussed his attention on strapping the mattress upright to the van's interior with ratchets.

Andy immediately piped up as Turner reappeared, "So, am I not asking about why you're bed shopping with Lucy or am I not asking about why I'm helping her out at your request or am I just not asking about Lucy more generally? Because I've got to say, I have a lot of questions."

"Can I just say I'm helping a friend?" Turner asked awkwardly.

"Of course you can." Andy smirked. "But it's obvious neither of us believe that. To be fair, I had my suspicions and, walking around Sunnyside today, I could tell from the quality of the stud walling that you've been going to Lucy's. There's no doubt she's got great vision and she may be a good DIYer but no way she did the timber work herself. Seeing you laden with stuff for her combined with the goofy smile and spring in your step confirm it, though. Please don't try to pretend otherwise. We both know you won't fool anybody, least of all me!"

Turner threw up his hands in a teasing gesture of resignation. "Yeah, it's early days but I think she's pretty awesome. I've already come close to messing it up though. She's previously had a bad experience, you know, with that dick who came to Oakland Walk, and doesn't want to fall into the same trap again. I reassured her about what she should be able to expect from a normal, decent guy and then promptly screwed up. I've apparently already had one of my three strikes." Turner grimaced as Andy studied his face, amusement dancing in his friend's eyes.

He continued, "I've never really been all that fussed before but Lucy's this intriguing, intelligent, feminine individual packaged in a body I find irresistible. I mean, look at me, having only ever been interested in the superstructure of a building, literally the bricks and mortar, here I am eagerly buying soft furnishings for someone who, only a few weeks ago, I thought I disliked."

Andy interjected, "Mate, I know I banter but I also pay attention. I've watched how you've responded to Lucy ever since she first appeared on site. Your body was physically attracted to her from the outset. I could see you'd be into her from that very first dressing down she gave me. It's just that it seemed to take the rest of you a little longer to realise. Now, you just need to get comfortable with it although, judging by your purchases, you seem to be getting there." Andy looked smug, apparently pleased with his foresight in having identified the relationship potential before Turner had, and equally amused at now standing outside a bed shop loading cushions into his van.

"I hope so. I've always admired the relationship my parents have and, being around Lucy has made me realise that I aspire to the same thing. The transactional sexual encounters I've had to date suddenly feel like they'd be less satisfying now I've seen an alternative that appeals. I'm realising I'd like something more fulfilling and maybe that could be with Lucy. I don't know. It's still so new but I'm keen to give it an opportunity to become something."

"Mate, don't overthink it," Andy replied. "Take it a step at a time." With a cheeky grin spreading across his face, Andy continued, "By helping her get a bed, you've already taken the first step towards either transactional sex or long-term relationship. Not having a bed is conducive to neither! It'll be what it will be and, with a bed on the scene, you can together enjoy sussing out which of the two."

Turner smiled at the reassuring predictability of his friend's teasing and sometimes crude encouragement. "Let's get back to Sunnyside then."

Andy agreed, muttering good-naturedly, "Fancy spending my Friday evening trying to help you get laid. When did I become your wing man?"

When they arrived back at Sunnyside in convoy, Turner fully expected Lucy to be hopping about with impatient glee on the drive. She wasn't. Casting his eyes up to sweep the building, movement from the master bedroom caught his eye, where he spied her waving enthusiastically down to them. She called down to explain she was bursting with excitement but also wanted to be productive so figured wallpapering by the window was the best compromise. Turner admired her motivation as he and Andy set to unloading the mattress, picking it up between them and marching it into the house. Negotiating the front door, hall and stairs was easy with Andy at the lower end, taking the weight, and Turner guiding the mattress over the nosings of the stair treads. Together, they effortlessly manoeuvred it into the master bedroom and, tweaking its plastic sheathing to ensure it remained protected, leant it up against the wall adjacent to the door.

Turner scanned the room to study progress. He was impressed at what he saw, the old wallpaper fully stripped and the walls sugar soaped clean and smooth. Any little nicks, scuffs and imperfections had been painstakingly addressed with filler and sanded flush to the walls' surface.

In the centre of the room, Lucy had setup a trestle table and, although she'd paused to eagerly oversee the mattress' arrival, had her earthy toned wallpaper, complete with subtle golden hue, spread out before her.

Turner buzzed with nervous anticipation. The room was beginning to take shape exactly as he recalled Lucy having described. He resolved to keep the gifts to himself at least until Andy had departed. Mercifully, almost immediately upon setting the mattress down, Andy announced, "Unless you need anything else, Lucy, I'll leave you guys to it. It's sad enough that I have nothing better to do with my Friday evening than deliver a mattress but don't think my ego will shoulder sitting here in your master bedroom like a third wheel."

Andy smiled broadly and openly as Lucy thanked him for all his help and then swivelled round to give Turner a sly wink as he made his hasty exit. Once alone again, Lucy smiled shyly at Turner before grabbing a piece of paper from the nearest windowsill and holding it out for him to study.

"Another exciting development," she announced. "This is the master ensuite layout and, amazingly, Andy had time this afternoon to collect the tiles, fixtures and fittings I had chosen and reserved from the supplier. He's stashed them in the bedroom across the hall. With a bed now on order too, my master suite is coming together far faster than I'd dared to hope. Take a look."

Turner obediently went to examine the various items with a view to making a start on the bathroom itself. Finding everything to still be boxed up, he returned to the main bedroom with the intention of reviewing the bathroom design. Eyes drawn to Lucy instead, he stood in the doorway for a moment and observed her at the trestle table. She was unfurling wallpaper from the roll along the length of the tabletop. Holding it in place with one hand as its ends curled up, she identified the length she required and efficiently sliced it across its width. As she measured and cut, Turner admired her lithe limbs and physique bending, stretching and reaching. Watching her wallpapering felt like a strange time to have the desire to kiss her but he found observing her feline movements erotic.

The lace outline of her bra was discernible beneath her vest top and her nipples pressed against the material. She also nibbled her lower lip as she concentrated on the task in hand. Her long lashes were directed down at the wallpaper and table in front of her and her naturally sculpted eyebrows furrowed in focussed concentration. As darkness was descending outside, her pale skin almost glowed under the warm light emanating from the ceiling pendant.

Turner's dick stirred as he observed her from the doorway. With an ache between his legs and an inward groan, he feigned an interest in more closely inspecting progress and walked over to the wall behind her, running his hands over its now smooth surface. He positioned himself between it and Lucy, observing her from behind as she bent away from him over the trestle table. She was innocently leaning over it with her backside towards him in much the same arousing stance as she'd unwittingly adopted in the bed shop.

Hardening dick starting to strain against the crotch of his jeans, he copied her stance and cautiously leant forward over her. In a slow yet confident movement, he grasped her hands to pull her upright, her back still to him and primed for her to cast his hands off or ask him to stop. She did neither so Turner gently pulled Lucy into an embrace, hands caressing her waist as he passed his arms around her front. Her pliant body made no indication she would resist so, with her back pressed to his front, he traced the curve of her breasts, waist and hips, teasing them both as he did so.

He roamed his hands over the swell of her breasts, bent to gently scrape his teeth across her shoulder, grazed his lips along her neck and nibbled at her earlobe. He was mesmerised, simultaneously watching and feeling her chest rise and fall with quiet laboured breaths as she melted into him. With his breath shaky too, he pressed his unshaven face into the nape of her neck. As he nuzzled her silken skin, smooth and flawless beneath his lips, a deep groan escaped him. Lucy reacted with a sensuous whimper and rocking hips. Hesitantly, he reached his hand down to the waistband of her yoga pants. Lucy arched her back and angled her hips to guide his tentative hand downward.

In tender exploration, he slipped his fingers beneath her leggings and then traced his way beneath the top of her knickers. Her body yielded to his fingers as they slid between her legs and explored her opening. Turner craved more from her, stifling a moan of his own as she sucked in sharp seductive breaths. With his need intensifying, he teased her with urgent fingers, revelling in her slick wetness and coaxing little involuntary mewls of pleasure from her as his thumb grazed and circled her clitoris. Cock throbbing and twitching, he whispered hoarsely, voice strained with the effort of trying to control his hungry desire, "Lucy, you know that rough and degrading sex you indicated you'd potentially be up for having if it were on your own terms, can I tempt you to have it with me…here…now?"

Her body stiffened but, instead of declining, to his intense pleasure, she writhed against his tented jeans as his erect dick throbbed in anticipation.

She uttered a strangled, "Yes," voice sounding heavy with the same yearning he felt.

Unable to restrain himself a moment longer, he flexed his fingers at her entrance, before plunging into her soaking heat. Her hips bucked salaciously in unison with his rhythmic movements. Their breath coming in jagged gasps. Reluctantly, he pulled his probing fingers from her to roll her yoga pants and lace knickers down below her knees. With a broad firm hand pressed into the small of her back, he encouraged her to bend forwards over the trestle table. With his other hand, he unbuttoned his jeans, pulled down the zipper and tugged down his jeans and boxers, eager dick springing free.

He paused, concern permeating him. "Shit, Lucy, I'm so sorry. We can't do this. I haven't got a condom on me."

Lucy reached her hands back towards him and clenched one round his girth. "It's okay, I'm on the pill," she responded urgently. "I'm happy to promise this is out of character for me and that we're safe if you're able to do the same."

Turner nodded sincerely behind her, his chin brushing the top of her spine with each enthusiastic bob of his head. In a lusty rush, Lucy continued, "I'm also pretty sure you told me never to apologise for what I want and right here, now, I want you and…I want it rough and degrading."

Still bent forward at the hips, movements constrained by her leggings at her knees, she pressed her backside towards him.

"Tell me again that you want this!" he urged on a choked breath.

Lucy almost giggled in frustration. "Do you *really* need to be told twice?" she teased.

"Okay, hell no," he uttered, voice strained and muscles flexing with intense need.

Pushing her down over the trestle, so her chest was resting on its surface, he then lifted and angled her peachy behind, spread her wet opening with his fingers and growling one profane syllable, carefully guided his veined erection inside her. He eased himself in, not wanting to hurt her, and to give her the opportunity to control what happened next. Clearly taking it as her cue to set the pace, she snaked one graceful arm back behind herself and, nails digging into his buttock, guided him deeper. Her muscles clenched and then moulded around him as she drew in his full length.

Her body stiffened beneath his grasp and she let out an impassioned whimper as her core sensuously yielded to him and absorbed him to his base. It took every ounce of his self-control not to come straightaway. He paused, relishing the sensation of his length inside her consuming wetness.

She ground against him. Taunting, he withdrew until the tip of his dick sat at her opening and then tentatively re-entered her.

In response, she let out a lusty strangled cry, the most erotic sound Turner had ever heard. Rocking her hips, she guided his movements, setting an increasingly frenzied tempo. Her thighs quivered under his hands from the exertion of the contorted position. Although bent forward, she rose up on her tiptoes to angle him deeper and writhed up along the length of his hard shaft. Her scent surrounded him, the exposed pale skin of her perfect bum flushed beneath his firm grip. Her vest top had ridden halfway up her back enabling him to admire her physique, the slight bumps of her spine and, either side thereof, her muscles pulled tight with the delicious, frenzied slapping of her backside against him. She moaned salacious words of encouragement through hot shaky breaths. "Deeper, Turner," she instructed him. Pulling him into her, "Yes, right there," she moaned, showing him what she wanted from him to maximise her pleasure.

Matching her pace, he thrust forward as she arched back towards him, keen to ensure he remained *right there* where she wanted him. The heady desire to please her also served to heighten his own exquisite enjoyment. His arousal elevated in synchronicity with hers.

"I want to feel every inch of you inside me," she commanded as she quivered around him.

He focussed all remaining coherent thought on fulfilling her demands. The powerful chemistry between them was all consuming. His tendons pulled taut in his arms, the muscles of his quads tight and burning as he held onto her waist to keep their movements in unison. She moulded around him, melted into him, pressing against his arousal as his cock twitched and throbbed. Both with sweat-slicked skin from their frenzied exertion, he marvelled at her stamina as she clasped her dainty fingers around the rim of the tabletop to grab an upright strut and continued to rock herself backwards and forwards on his erection with trembling jagged movements.

Increasingly frenzied, she drew her other hand back from his buttock, clawing at his skin as she did so. He delighted in the sharp sensation of her nails grazing his skin. He teetered on the edge, almost coming undone, as she reached her freed hand down to her slick wetness, pleasuring herself with rough circles of her fingers. His base and balls, aching and heavy with desire, brushed against her fingers as he passionately thrust into her whilst she rubbed herself in small swirling motions. Over his own ragged breathing, her breath was catching, interspersed with the hottest moans of pleasure. Her slippery interior began to clench beautifully around him.

"Harder," she commanded on the exhale, guiding his movements as the exquisite trembling spread outward from her thighs and core. Her fingers still desperately rolled over her soaking heat. Turner relished the consuming intensity of their bodies grinding against each other. His rock-hard dick throbbed gloriously inside her. Frantic now, Lucy let out a baleful mewl through gritted teeth and pouting swollen lips, grinding herself against him. As she teetered and clenched around him, absorbing him fully, he revelled in the rhythmic sensation of his dick stroking her interior. Releasing herself and the table strut, she reached back and clawed at his buttocks, pulling him into her in increasingly rapid bursts. Then, with the same sexy gasping mewl he'd heard that night in the caravan, she climaxed hard. Her pelvic floor muscles clamped around him, pulsing and throbbing along his length, abdominal muscles beneath his hands convulsing in ecstasy as the rest of her body trembled. She drenched his shaft with her intoxicating wetness radiating from between her legs. Seeing and feeling her come undone was the hottest experience of his life. Mind-blown, every sinuous fibre in his body taut with lust and the all-consuming need to have her, he pushed his aching hard dick into her with one final thrust to its base. It throbbed and jerked in gratifying release as he spilled into her. Her core responded by deliciously and almost painfully constricting and contracting around him, sucking him into her deeply and delightfully holding him in place as it drew his full load.

They stayed like that, bent over, bodies flush to one another, sweat-slicked skin, legs trembling and chests rising and falling with shaky breaths as their near simultaneous orgasms subsided. Although overwhelmed after such an amazing mind and body altering experience, Turner tenderly circled his arms around her waist to embrace and reassure her. In soft, affectionate movements, he kissed her neck and cheek as he held her close. Slowly, he returned to his senses. Regaining coherent thought, he focussed back on their surroundings. "Fuck, when did it get pitch black outside." He let out a muffled giggle and uttered, "Like me, I bet the neighbours have just had the show of a lifetime!"

CHAPTER 11

Feeling unexpectedly empowered despite the acute embarrassment at what the neighbours might have witnessed, Lucy ducked beneath the height of the window ledge and scurried from the bedroom with Turner hot on her heels. Surprised at herself for having been so forward with him and so vocal about her desires, Lucy basked in her post-coital glow. She immediately thought of Rachel, now better equipped to understand Rachel's buzz from her own past sexual antics, her desire not to settle for just someone and how that played into her zest for life and thirst for adventure. Rachel would no doubt be proud of her and her scandalous behaviour. She was after all now even more pro Turner given he'd labelled Mark a narcissist. To Lucy's amusement, Rachel had immediately resolved to supersede the nickname she had previously given Mark, 'Dick', with 'Mark the Narc'. She had sounded quite smug at the new moniker.

Brought back to the present as she approached the caravan in the gloom, Lucy yanked open its flimsy door and leapt inside giggling, chest heaving with the sprint from the master bedroom. Turner bounded in behind her, spinning her round for an enthusiastic embrace and to plant a teasing, conspiratorial kiss on her upturned, grinning mouth.

"Wow, that was amazing!" he exclaimed. "The most fun and the best sex I've had in forever!"

"Me too." Lucy beamed. "I think I could get used to the idea of asking for what I want if that's the outcome."

Turner laughed mischievously. "If that's the sort of thing you want, rest assured, you're never going to have to ask me more than once!"

Together, limbs intertwined, they flopped down on his length of sofa.

"Well, in that case, you're going to have to man up and get over your fear of fitting curtain poles. I don't want to put on another display for the neighbours."

"Ha," he guffawed. "With an incentive like that, I promise I'll be straight on it tomorrow morning."

"Oh, so you're staying?" she asked coyly.

"Absolutely, if that's okay with you." He continued, "I can't imagine sharing something so intimate with you and then just leaving you here alone. I'd very much like to stay please."

Glowing from the inside out, Lucy happily set to performing her bedtime routine as Turner equally contentedly muttered that he was spent after the frenzied day on site and, subsequently, the evening's sex.

After Lucy finished in the confined space of the combined toilet and shower cubicle, Turner wedged himself inside, crashing and bashing to Lucy's amusement as he tried to wash within the cramped room. Lucy gawped at his physique as he again returned to the front of the caravan. Lying back down, he invited Lucy to spoon with him. She nestled into his angular, muscled body. She felt small in his presence, protected by his embrace. Lucy melted into him as Turner wrapped his blanketed arm around her and his fingers sleepily caressed the curves of her hips, thighs and waist.

Lucy, cosy alongside Turner, quickly fell into a contented slumber. At some point in the night, she was vaguely aware of him having crept from the bed but felt so comfortably nestled in the alcove he'd left, she hadn't fully woken. In the morning, with her dream ebbing away as it faded back into her subconscious, she tried to reconjure its content and Turner's presence therein. Once sentient again, though, she realised Turner was back in position snug behind her. His right arm was draped over her front in a close embrace and his left in the crook of her neck like a muscular bolster pillow.

She was delectably encouraged back to wakefulness by the subtle eddies of air from his quiet exhalations tickling her neck as he snoozed. His chest soothingly rising and falling along her back, stubble on his chiselled jawline softly grazing her face and, as she moved, forming gentle resistance as it caught wayward strands of her hair. With light streaming in around the caravan's taut blinds, she savoured the pleasurable tranquillity, feeling rested but eager to continue with the master bedroom. With the weekend stretching before them, significant progress could be made, particularly if she could persuade Turner to stay to assist.

He exhaled a sleepy sigh as Lucy began to stretch.

"Morning, sleepyhead," she whispered, turning to gaze at Turner's serene slumberous face.

Turner blinked, disorientated, so she continued, "Rise and shine. It's another beautiful day at Sunnyside."

"You have no respect for the weekend," he grumbled good-naturedly in a husky morning voice.

"I'm excited to set to work," she replied as she gazed at him. "I'm taking Rachel's advice. I have two whole weekend days to take advantage of you every way I can and I plan to make the most of the opportunity."

Her suggestive words in his ear seemed to have the desired effect. Prising his eyes open, he clawed his way back from his somnambulant reverie, blinking away sleep and stretching as he did so. He leant into her to murmur, "I'll work to the bone for you if you're offering a repeat performance of last night. It's the first time I've offered such payment terms but, for you, I'll readily and enthusiastically work for sexual favours."

Lucy giggled. "How poetic. Let me guess, what you're insinuating is that you're prepared to work to the bone for me in order to get to actually bone me."

"Yes," Turner chuckled, now fully alert. "A succinct and accurate summation of my offer."

"Come on then. Hop to it. The early bird catches the worm and all that."

"Ack, Lucy, I confess I've never been the earliest of risers, perhaps with the exception of Mini Me down below who seems eager to stand to attention day and night when you're around. Incidentally, Bird, it's the second mouse that gets the cheese."

"Bird?" Lucy questioned grinning quizzically.

"Yes, I'm not sure I'm onboard with calling you Juicy. Bird came to me in the night as a potential nickname for you."

With his right palm resting on her side, he teasingly ticked the points off on his fingers by gently pressing them onto her skin, "You're clearly an early riser and…you have great tits." He paused mischievously before finishing with, "Plus, in your garden, you're keen on wildlife and you're female and hence technically a bird. I've chosen Bird with the utmost respect and affection for you."

Lucy was unconvinced but too keen to set to work on the house to challenge him further. Instead, taking a different tack, she opined, "You know, it's just occurred to me that the late bird doesn't necessarily even get to catch the late worm as I guess the early bird eats that worm too. I'm sure there's a subtle message in there about the importance of seizing opportunities when they're presented to you."

In response, Turner teasingly made to grasp at her. Lucy giggled, prizing his fingers away and rising from the sofa. Feigning reluctance, Turner also rose from their sofa lair and began to pull on his faded jeans and a clean white t-shirt that tantalisingly constrained his muscular arms. Once dressed, he gulped down some juice then announced, "I'm starving. I'll pick us up breakfast baps from the café again." With that, he hopped out of the caravan and strode through the overgrown garden towards the road.

Lucy was just making her way back into the house when Turner returned with the salty scent of bacon sandwich preceding him. With man-sized bites he consumed his on the walk back to the house. As they entered the master bedroom together, Lucy's eyes were drawn to the window where a grooved recess had been carefully hewn into the plaster of the ceiling. Incredulous, she spun round to look at Turner who was studying her face for her reaction.

Stunned, she looked from him back to the ceiling in disbelief only for him to shrug nonchalantly.

"I really wanted you to get a proper night's rest but I was so wired lying next to you in your semi-naked slumber that I was struggling to keep my hands to myself. I consequently snuck out in the night to work on a surprise for you."

Profoundly moved by the thoughtful gesture and suddenly better understanding Turner's reluctance to get up, given he'd been toiling away in the night whilst she'd slept, she stretched up onto her tiptoes to kiss him deeply and passionately.

"Turner, this is the best gift ever, thank you," she murmured with a hot breath into his ear.

"I've actually got something else for you too," he replied, grinning at her and perpetuating her full-body embrace. "But we first need to finish the wallpapering and lay the carpet."

Having clearly attempted to carve out the ceiling plaster along the joint of the wall with a multitool and a pad saw in the night, Turner retrieved his router and set to finishing the channel into which the shallow profile wave curtain rail would be installed. To the whine of power tools, Lucy consumed her sandwich, intent gaze following Turner around the room as she did so. She found herself ogling his muscles shifting beneath his t-shirt where it was pulled tight by his movements across his defined back and over his sinuous arms.

Once he'd patched the lip of the plasterboard, he joined Lucy to apply the final couple of lengths of wallpaper to the feature wall before swiftly tidying the room and clearing the tools, rubble sacks of discarded wallpaper and other miscellaneous scattered items of building detritus. As Lucy swept the floor, Turner ferried everything out, either downstairs for disposal or across the landing where he stacked it neatly ready for further use.

"Obviously, it would be better to do the underlay and carpet once you've finished painting the walls but I'm conscious you might struggle to do this in the week if I'm not here. You can always cover the area with a dust sheet if needs be when you're decorating. It wouldn't be the first time I've laid carpets before we've finished decorating! Just don't let Andy anywhere near it."

Turner then singlehandedly carried through and unfurled the underlay. Lucy fully intended to start the cutting in on the remaining three walls with her paintbrush but was entranced, lauding the practised efficiency with which he approached each task and, more enticingly, the way his actions drew her attention to his underlying physique. When he bent down, weight supported by his quads, the tautness of his jeans stretching over his thighs and backside drew her appreciative gaze. As he worked to unfurl, cut and glue the underlay and then the carpet, she watched on. Her eyes focussed on his shoulders as his muscles bunched with the effort, her heart rate and breathing syncopated with the barely perceptible rising and falling of his broad chest and her senses alert and tingling as the muscles twitched in his jaw with concentration.

Before long, Turner had installed the carpet and, with an amused smile on his face, instructed, "Lucy, stop showing the walls your paintbrush for a minute please. Can you instead hoover the lint from the new carpet?"

Somewhat embarrassed at having been so intent on watching him, she realised she'd achieved little more than threatening to paint the wall, brush held absentmindedly in her hand. Spurred back into action by Turner's teasing, Lucy worked her way around the room, crawling around on her knees pulling the small vacuum attachment in painstaking strokes across the carpet. Meanwhile, Turner manhandled the new mattress into position. Once happy, he sliced the plastic sheathing from it with the penknife that perennially lived in his pocket.

Delighted at the sight of her brand new, albeit bare, mattress positioned against the wall, she stood in quiet appreciation. She had wondered whether she would rue the decision to leave her ornate four-poster bed and gaudy gilded mirror in the rental when she'd left but the lone, unadorned mattress, sat neatly on her new carpet, looked so much more inviting than the ostentatious items she'd left behind. She rejoiced in casting off the vestiges of her failed relationship with Mark and ringing the changes with her new-look bedroom.

Whilst she paused in the centre of the room, Turner reached his arms around her, clasped her hands and drew them up to her face to cover her eyes.

"Keep them shut for me please until I say otherwise," he murmured seductively into her ear.

Curious and impatient, she nonetheless left her hands over her eyes as he pulled his own fingers away and withdrew. She heard him dash out of the room. When he returned, she could discern an intriguing rustle of plastic packaging and fabric accompanying his movements. The seconds ticked by with her rooted to the spot, nervous anticipation building to a crescendo within.

After what felt like an interminable wait but was in fact probably just a couple of minutes, Turner instructed her to open her eyes. With an over-the-top theatrical flurry of his hands, he bowed to perform a sweeping display of the vision before her. Turner had covered her mattress in the soft furnishings of her mind's eye. Awestruck, she marvelled at his ability to have pictured and recalled her image for her bedroom so accurately. Only a few days prior, the bedroom had been a dissonant, tired space and, now, despite the absence of furniture and curtains, and even though the walls still needed painting, the sparse room felt warm and inviting like the romantic boudoir she desired. Lucy was overwhelmed as she surveyed the crisp white duvet and pillows, two on each side exactly as she had pictured, and the various textured grey and toffee-coloured cushions staged in front of them with the sumptuous large faux fur throw spread at the end of the bed, its tones pulling the other colours together in a harmonious montage.

Without warning, Lucy leapt into Turner's outstretched arms, wrapping her own tightly around his neck and pinning his waist with her legs in an ecstatic and emotional embrace. Although caught off guard, he held her aloft with ease. He shuffled towards the mattress at his feet and bent his knees to bring them to rest on the soft throw, which bunched beneath them. Whilst Lucy still clung to him, overwrought at the thoughtfulness of his gesture, he bent forwards at the hips. She only registered the understated movement when her back and head came to rest on the luxurious pillows and mattress. With her lying supine on the bed, legs clamped around his waist, Turner - entirely unfazed - rested his elbows either side of her shoulders, holding his weight above her. Although Lucy felt as if she were the one holding him in place, in one fluid and sedate movement, Turner had laid her on her back in the centre of the mattress with his body casually positioned over hers. Lucy settled her head back between the pillows to lock her gaze with Turner's.

"Thank you, Turner, truly, from the bottom of my heart," she mouthed almost silently, eyes misted as she tightened her arms around his neck, forcibly pulling him into a deep kiss.

Whilst still propped on his elbows, leaving an intoxicating gap between their bodies, Turner obligingly dipped his head, eyes fixed on her pouting mouth to meet her lips. Lucy purposefully caught his lower lip between her teeth, again reminding him that she could control the pace even though he was her physical master. Turner complied, gaze locked with hers, hovering above her expectantly and sucking in a sharp breath as she tugged softly on his lip. Appreciating that he was voluntarily submitting to her, she released his lip and dragged her tongue across his parted lips, leaving a sheen on his mouth. She revelled in observing the primal effect she had on him, lifting her hips to meet his and seeing his eyes cloud with desire as she did so. From the taut sinews in his neck and shoulders and the bunched muscles holding him in place, she sensed the testosterone coursing through his veins, his potent physical impulses clearly vying with his mind as he made a concerted effort to restrain himself.

Imbuing her actions with a sultry challenge, to test his resolve and tantalise him further, she rolled her hips, arching them towards his pelvis and grinding against his crotch. She delighted in his carnal reaction, noting the denim of his jeans tenting with his arousal. Each time she pressed her hips to his, his well-endowed dick strained yet more against the crotch of his trousers. To prolong the expectant pleasure, she altered the pace, lowering her hips back to rest on the mattress again and lifting her mouth to the side of his face, sending a hot caressing breath down his neck as she sucked his earlobe. She gently tugged and nibbled in turn, carefully but firmly teasing it between her lips. Turner's muscles tensed in response, his body perceptibly stiffening with the erotic stimulation. With their clothed bodies brushing together, Lucy's nipples hardened.

Much as Lucy delighted in Turner's visceral response to her, she relished seeing him avidly watching her body's every reaction, his green eyes blazing. His eyes never left her. She followed his gaze as it wandered appreciatively across her skin. Her body reacted to him. When his eyes settled on her chest, her nipples grazed the fabric of her vest top in response as it clung to her glowing skin. His broad, manly chest rose and fell in synchrony with hers. She revelled in the tingling heat radiating from between her legs and sending gratifying pulses of electricity around her hips and into her lower back.

Lucy craved the sensation of his bare skin against her own, his broad muscular angles against her softer pliant frame, his sinuous arms enveloping her and his powerful hands grasping her smooth skin.

"Take off my yoga pants," she instructed in a voice she barely recognised as her own.

Turner immediately obeyed, rocking back onto his knees to grip the waistband of her lycra leggings at both hips. He peeled them down her legs and off in one fluid motion. His casual prowess, the practised and accomplished ease with which he heeded her desires, fuelled her excitement further. She watched his face intently as his eyes roamed lustily over her legs and abdomen.

"What's this?" he uttered with a stifled groan, eyes catching on the small, inked section on her right hip, fingers tracing it in awed fascination.

"It's a tattoo," Lucy giggled as she twisted beneath him to display her right hip.

"I can see that, but you didn't say you had a tattoo. It's hot. You're a woman of intriguing contradictions. I want to discover them all. Everything you do is so considered, though. It must mean something to you."

"Yes," she murmured, eyes locked with his, "it's a private reminder to believe in myself, a mantra by which I aspire to live my life. *Alis volat propriis.* It's Latin. Loosely translated, it means she flies by her own wings."

"Fuck, that's even hotter," he growled. Maintaining her eye contact, he sought her permission to remove her vest top. "May I?" he enquired in a hoarse voice, gravelly with need.

Lucy nodded, running her tongue over her swollen parted lips as she did so. In captivated silence, punctuated only by their ragged breathing, Turner tugged the top over her head and, whilst she held her arms aloft, he traced the edge of her bra round to the centre of her back. In an expert movement, he released the clasp, his eyes drawn to the curve of her breasts as they were freed from the sheer fabric of her bra. Unable to wait for her instruction, he pulled the bra over her arms and discarded it behind him. Turner paused above her, eyes roving longingly over her naked body. Lucy revelled in the sensation of being so scrutinised. She tried to see herself through his eyes and, perhaps for the first time, feeling beautiful as she too studied the swell of her small breasts, the deep pink of her swollen nipples and the flawless skin of her hips and thighs. His eyes bore into her skin, making Lucy ache between her legs as she lay naked beneath his impassioned gaze. His appreciative eyes wandered over every inch of her exposed skin and she felt revered and empowered

In one graceful movement, he pulled his t-shirt over his head, the fabric tussling his brown hair as he did so. Then, he bent towards her inked hip and dragged his tongue over it. A choked groan, charged with desire, escaped his mouth as he did so. It sent a delectable current of warm air over the sheen of saliva left by his tongue, in turn heating and cooling her skin and heightening her feeling in the process.

In that moment, Lucy felt fully seen. She had revealed herself to Turner and was experiencing myriad new sensations as a result – worshipped, revered, like a goddess in her own skin. There, in her spartan bedroom in her decrepit house, she lay resplendent on her new mattress with Turner poised above her. Seeing her own yearning and awe reflected back at her in his face, her axis shifted. It dawned on her that this was living life in glorious technicolour, the full spectrum of emotions, the scintillating kaleidoscope of sensations. Lucy wanted to experience it all and, casting aside her inhibitions and self-doubt, reached her delicate fingers up to the button of Turner's jeans. Her fumbling fingers released it easily, helped by the tension on the denim as his erection pressed against it eager to spring free and delight in fulfilling its purpose. She fervently pushed the uncooperative fabric down over his tensed buttocks and revealed his balls hanging heavy with expectant need. She struggled to push the jeans further down his athletic legs. Turner shimmied his way out of them, practically clawing them off over his feet in his haste.

He then paused, hovering over her. Although easily able to dominate her, he tenderly awaited her next cue. She pulled him down towards her, his weight delectably pressing her into the mattress and constricting the space in her lungs. With the delightful reminder of his strength and stature, she revelled in taking gasping breaths to fill her chest. His cock twitched provocatively against her abdomen, causing her internal muscles to contract in appreciation. With his brawny but lean body flush to hers, she continued to suck in ragged breaths. She wrapped her hand around his shaft, delighting in the pre-ejaculate beading at the tip as a visible indication of the effect she was having on him.

She reached over with her other hand to clutch at Turner's. He shifted his weight onto one elbow, releasing his right hand and obligingly interlacing his fingers with her own. She guided his hand downwards to cover her wetness, pleasure spreading from the pressure of his fingertips to where his thumb pressed against her clitoris. His probing fingers sank into her slick opening, stroking her inside and sending a trail of fire spiralling from her core. Mirroring his urgency, she tugged on his veined length. Her hips bucked, body writhing erratically as she reacted to his every assertive stroke, his accomplished fingers slipping into her. Her core tightened around them. Wholly in tune with her pleasure, Turner withdrew his hand and with shaky breath, sweat-slick skin and muscles heaving, buried his head between her thighs. Lucy lost all coherent thought, nails digging into his shoulders and hands clutching at his hair to help guide his movements. She whimpered, thighs quivering as his tongue caressed her. Increasingly frenzied, she savoured the sensation as he bobbed his mouth against her opening, tongue swirling and darting into her soaking heat between his own shaky breaths. Her hunger to have him inside her intensified.

To save herself from coming completely undone, she reluctantly pulled away from his mouth's reach and, snaking her leg around his waist, pulled them both over. Once they had rotated sufficiently, she palmed his broad tanned chest, pushing him back into the mattress. With Turner now supine on the bed and amongst the dishevelled bedlinen, she straddled him. She had command of his mouth, red and swollen like her own, and bent forward to kiss him hungrily. Whilst their lips were locked, her trembling fingers trailed down his arms to clutch both of his wrists. She guided his hands to her hips and then closed hers over his to encourage him to grasp her pelvis with the span of his large palm, his fingers splayed across her lower back. She pressed herself against his arousal, prompting him to groan into her mouth. She rubbed her wetness along his length, delighting in feeling his dick throbbing at her entrance as she did so. His body stiffened involuntarily as he clung to his resolve to allow Lucy to set the tempo.

As she released his lips, a tortured animalistic sound escaped him as he obviously battled his intensifying need. She felt like a sultry temptress, gazing down at his muscled body straining instinctively beneath her, tendons pulled taut and chiselled jawline ticking with the effort of restraining himself. Succumbing to her own desire, she aligned her entrance with his twitching tip and tantalisingly lowered herself onto his length. His hands dug into her hips as if he were clamping them there in an attempt at self-discipline to try to quell the urge to hasten her delectable descent. She rotated her hips slowly, feeling her core yielding to his size as she gradually absorbed his cock to its base. She paused, body stilled and with eyes fixed on his, caressed her body with her own hands as he watched on reverentially.

She began to ride him roughly, grinding up and down with wanton abandon, pressing herself against his solid erection on every descent and savouring the aching tingling that radiated from her core with the pressure of meeting his body hard. She dug her nails into his chest to gain better purchase, intrigued by the angry red marks she left on his skin. He seemed immune to the discomfort, intent only on where their fervent bodies met with increasing ardour. Together, they found a perfect rhythm of pleasure, his engorged cock pushing into her with each thrust and prompting strangled whimpers to slip from her parted lips. They panted with the pleasurable exertion. She writhed atop him, relishing the sensation of his cock inside her.

Lucy surveyed his masculine torso and straining arms, revelled in the singularly focussed expression on his face and delighted in his hands clawing urgently at her pelvis in his quest for their mutual release. She was conscious her movements were becoming more erratic, and her breathing laboured as she began to tire from her body being kept tantalisingly on the edge of climaxing. Every inch of her thrummed with exhausting pleasure. Apparently detecting this, Turner reached round to cup her buttocks, his contoured forearms lifting her with ease. Effortlessly taking her weight, he began to move her rhythmically up and down his length, enabling her to simply savour the intense sparks of pleasure building inside her as she melted into him. The tingling heat made her gasp in ecstatic agony. Her pelvic muscles throbbed as they constricted round his shaft, drawing him into her. Every pulse seemed to be reflected in Turner's own reactions, his body instinctively responding to the same alternating pressure on his cock that she was delighting in. Her thighs quivered where his hands grasped her. Turner's movements became more frenzied. With his eyes burning into her soul, she let him tip her forwards and, whilst he kissed her deeply, he rocked her hips backwards and forwards, grinding her soaking heat against his flexed muscles. His cock throbbed inside her as it pinned her writhing body in place; the depth of the position the perfect balance between pain and pleasure. Lucy saw stars, her hips bucked, thighs trembled and body stiffened as the tingling heat coursed up her back, round her hips and radiated from her core.

"Fly for me, Bird!" Turner uttered hoarsely before clamping his lips back to hers.

Where she'd been teetering, his final instruction sent her over the edge. With a gasping breath and strangled moan into his mouth, she climaxed, her pelvic muscles blissfully clenching, relaxing and clenching again around his girth. Whilst she savoured the throbbing in her centre, his entire body stiffened beneath her with the visceral release as he came, his dick pulsating within as he spilled spasmodically into her. She delighted in the resulting dampness.

Lucy collapsed onto his heaving torso, the beats of her racing heart mirrored by his own hammering against her chest where her body lay flush to his. She moulded herself along him, her body melting into his sweat-slicked skin. He enveloped her in his arms, fingertips caressing her bare skin as she nuzzled into him. Save for their shaky breaths, they lay in spent silence as their orgasms subsided, bodies intertwined, her senses intoxicated and mind overwhelmed by the hot barrage of intense emotions.

Eventually, Lucy broke the rapt silence with an amused murmur into his chest, "Fly for me, Bird?" she teased.

Feigning indignation, Turner murmured, "I was in the midst of the hottest most intense experience of my life. I think my mind was already blown by that point so it was all I could come up with."

Kissing her softly on the shoulder, he smiled mischievously as he continued, "To be fair, it seemed to do the trick. The name is staying. You even have a tattoo about wings and flying and, if nothing else, I'd definitely like you to be my Bird please, if you'd like the same of course."

Lucy giggled in response. "Yes, I'd like that too and, incidentally, every inch of me feels exquisitely sated. I guess you could argue I feel like I'm floating on air, which I suppose is birdlike. Granted, it's tenuous, but I also get that you clearly aren't fully onboard with Juicy."

Turner placed his fingers gently under her chin and, tilting her head so he could hold her gaze, tenderly continued, "Lucy, I *am* fully onboard with all of this though—" He waved his arms expansively, and she had a feeling he was talking about everything – her, her home, and indeed the broader project at Sunnyside.

"Thank you, Turner," she purred, eyes misting at the touching reassurance of having him voluntarily voice his commitment to her and to her build. Resting her head back on his chest, almost inaudibly she whispered, "You make my heart soar." Then, beaming, suddenly continued, "I guess that seals it then. Bird it is."

Turner gave her a squeeze, no doubt processing her words, as he looked around the room. "You know, I think everything about this room is perfect as it is. Who needs furniture when we have a mattress and our bodies to share. We are, however, going to need a functioning bathroom and kitchen pretty soon if we're to be spending more time together here."

Lucy sighed. "We've already established I haven't got the money to do it quickly."

Turner smirked as he animatedly announced, "Wow, I've just realised Sunnyside is the exception that proves the rule... You *can* have the build cheap, fast and good. I'll readily accept sexual favours as payment."

Lucy blushed, both touched and turned on at the prospect. Turner pulled her into his chest. Her entire body reacted to his touch with newly awakened desire. As the warmth spread from her flushed face and danced over her skin, he hoarsely whispered, "It'll be a labour of love, Bird."

ACKNOWLEDGEMENTS

Conscious that the acknowledgements only ever resonate with the author and people they specifically reference, I'd just like to say a blanket thank you to the friends and family who've either actively supported me in this endeavour or tolerated my enthusiasm for it with good-natured resignation. As this is an erotic romance, I'm not sure how you'd feel about finding your names individually documented in black and white for all to see. Regardless, you know who you are and I thank you.

One specific shout out though... Sarah Smeaton, I am eternally grateful to you for having so meticulously edited this book. It's been an absolute pleasure to share this journey with you. You've not only significantly enhanced the content but also my experience of writing and publishing my debut novel. My heartfelt thanks! I'm already excited at the prospect of collaborating on book two!

Printed in Great Britain
by Amazon